Fade to Black

By
Jeffrey Wilson

JournalStone
San Francisco

JOURNALSTONE
YOUR LINK TO ARTISTIC TALENT

JournalStone books may be ordered through booksellers or by contacting:

JournalStone
www.journalstone.com
www.journal-store.com

ISBN: 978-1-936564-85-9   (sc)
ISBN: 978-1-936564-92-7   (ebook)

Library of Congress Control Number: 2013935629

Printed in the United States of America
JournalStone rev. date: June 14, 2013

Cover Design: Denise Daniel
Cover Art: M. Wayne Miller

Edited by: Elizabeth Reuter

Dedication

For Wendy, Connor, Jack and Emma
As Always

Acknowledgements

When you first start to write, you have no idea how much work other people will have to put into your work for you to succeed. These last few years have shown me that more than anything. Chris Payne and his staff at JournalStone Publishing are an amazing group of professionals who are totally committed to their side of the craft. Chris is more than a publisher and editor—he is a true friend that Wendy and I will always cherish.

Thanks to the team at JournalStone for again taking my roughly edited words and polishing my story into a novel. Special thanks to Elizabeth Reuter for the incredible patience and perseverance it takes to edit my work and to M. Wayne Miller for capturing my words as art.

For this book especially, I want to thank all of the men and women of our armed forces and the families who wait patiently at home. Thank you for your service and sacrifice. I pray for you all a safe return.

Endorsements

"A brilliant combination of war novel and supernatural thriller. This book could only have been written by an author who knows firsthand the blood, sweat, dust, and terror of combat." - Tom Young, author of *The Mullah's Storm, Silent Enemy,* and *The Renegades*

"Wilson just keeps getting better and better. *Fade to Black* is a death-limbo drama that plays masterfully with melancholy notes of heartbreak backed by the roaring horrors of modern warfare. In the last fifty pages, you'll bite off every fingernail waiting to see the final outcome!" - Benjamin Kane Ethridge, Bram Stoker Award winning author of *Black & Orange* and *Nightmare Ballad.*

"Wilson weaves terror and tenderness into this harrowing, supernatural tale of one man's perfect life turned upside-down by the horrors and sacrifices of military combat." - Brian Andrews — Author of *The Calypso Directive,* 2012 USA BEST BOOK Awards Finalist

Lisa,

Thank you for

your Service!

V/R

Chapter
1

Casey didn't hear the bullet until it whistled through what was left of the wall and chunks of rock rained down on his helmet. He unconsciously pulled his head down and raised his shoulders as if that would keep the high-velocity round from the enemy AK-47 from spattering his brains all over the ground. Casey's heart pounded in his chest, but he embraced the feeling of terror and let the power of it energize him. Over the last few weeks the jacked up feeling had become like a drug to Casey and his friends. He had learned quickly to embrace and channel it into energy and sharpness—especially in the last few hours. Casey took a few slow breaths to dampen his tremors, but felt the fear clear his mind and sharpen his focus.

Good.

He knew the younger boys hunkered down beside him needed their sergeant—an old man at twenty-six—to stay iced.

Casey leaned his regulation Kevlar helmet back against the sandy wall as more chunks of brown cement broke loose and joined the dust and sweat in the collar of his body armor. He barely noticed. His mind focused instead on the frequent sharp pops of rifle fire from the dusty street on the other side of their fragile barrier.

We're in the goddamn O.K. Corral.

He squeezed his eyes shut to clear away the sweat that burned behind his Marine Corps issued Wiley-X ballistic sunglasses. For all their expensive, high-tech gear, they were sure as shit taking a pounding from the robed, and mostly barefoot, men shooting at them from the blown out doorways and rooftops on the other side of the wall.

The fine, blowing dust burned his throat, and he continually spit to clear the grit from his mouth and teeth. Casey gripped his rifle firmly in his gloved right hand as he listened to more pops of small arms fire around him. A whistle of rounds passed over the short wall, and he turned and looked at the men beside him, all pressed awkwardly against the sand and stone barricade that kept them from view. Some were shaking, but all were ready. They were Marines.

Casey knew they were not the same men who had stormed into the Jolan neighborhood of Fallujah thirty-six hours ago. The grab-assing teenagers were now blooded Marines. They were more than warriors—they were his other family.

He ducked as another high-velocity round exploded the top of the wall just inches from his head.

Fuck.

The insurgents on the other side of the wall were holding true to their vow to fight to the last breath of the last man. The fighting had been bloody and continuous, and he and his men were tired. Maybe too tired. The ambush had separated the six of them from the rest of the platoon, and one of his boys, Kindrich, from somewhere in Tennessee, lay in the street on the other side of the wall. He was badly hit, probably dead. Casey had seen him take a round in the head, and he had grabbed for him before machine gun fire had forced him to hurl himself over the wall screaming to his men.

"Take cover! Take cover!"

Now they were pinned down, enemy fire eating away at the wall above their heads, sending more sand and dust down on them. This was the real shit, and Casey shifted his limited options through his mind. He knew the only real plan available. Time to move out.

Casey forced the flashing images of little baby Claire from his mind. He missed her more than he could ever have imagined, and for the first time in his career in the Corps, he considered that he might not see her or Pam again. But right now he had work to do, and his best chance of getting home to them was to push them from his mind and concentrate on the job.

He looked at his men and pointed with one finger to himself and two other Marines—Simmons from Albany and McIver from Northern Virginia. He then made a walking stick figure gesture and pointed to the end of the wall, fifteen feet away. He pointed the same two fingers to his own eyes. In silence he told his men, *the three of us will move to the end of the wall and take a look.* Then he swept his hand over the other two and raised a closed fist. *You guys stay here.*

Casey and his two young colleagues crawled on their bellies, tight against the wall, rifles cradled in their arms, as they had trained to do a thousand times. They reached the end of the wall in seconds and Casey raised a closed fist. The three stopped and readied their rifles. Then he waved his hand and looked over his shoulder to get the attention of his other two men. Once sure he had their eyes, he made another signal.

Covering fire.

The boys behind him rose up simultaneously, each on one knee, and swung their rifles over the wall, firing blindly into the street. As they did, Casey peered around the corner, dropping his helmet in the dirt, and looked out into the kill zone.

Holy shit!

Muzzle flashes lit up from almost every window he could see on the right side of the dirty road, and several from the rooftop. A piercing scream from behind him ran up his spine like someone had thrown a toaster in his tub, and he pulled his head back, hollering as he turned.

"Cease fire! Cease fire!"

Behind him one of his waiting two men slumped on his side against the wall, motionless. Dark blood poured out from his head and face onto the dirt. Bennet from San Antonio. Fancied himself a guitar player and sucked at basketball.

Fuck! Fuck! Fuck!

The other Marine hunched over his buddy and packed a field dressing onto his face. Then he looked up and shook his head.

Son of a bitch!

Casey's mind reeled. The rest of their platoon had taken cover around the left side of the block and should have been working their way around to the far left corner. Casey decided they would have to make it from their wall to the far right corner. Then they would try and make contact with the rest of the platoon to converge from two corners, attacking the right side positions.

They sure as shit couldn't stay where they were.

Kill the enemy.

He looked again at Bennet's crumpled body and the black blood pool that grew rapidly in the sand, encircling his head like a strange cloud.

Especially now.

Casey hand gestured for his remaining men to join them at the corner of the wall. They would make a dash across the intersection, down the right cross street. He had seen no fire from the left, so hopefully they would not be in a cross fire. As they moved across the intersection they should progressively lose a line of fire from the farther positions as the angles changed. They had no other choice. No rescue party was coming—the big, armored LAVs weren't close enough to get to them in time, and he couldn't wait for air support from the Cobra helicopter gunships that orbited just outside the city. The enemy had a bead on them and soon the rocket-propelled grenades would come, and their flimsy wall would be gone.

Once his men crunched in beside him, they huddled together, helmets touching like a football team, and Casey whispered out his plan. They would sprint one at a time, under covering fire, and then each would try to set up a new covering fire position as they arrived at the corner. As he finished an explosion from behind drove them down onto their faces. When Casey looked again a huge hole gaped in the wall at their previous position and Bennet's body had disappeared beneath a heap of rubble.

Time to go.

Casey looked at his young men. Simmons shook badly.

"You with me, Simmons?"

The boy looked up at him. His lip quivered, but he nodded. Casey pulled the young man's helmet against his own, his hand firm on the back of his friend's sweaty neck, and looked into his wet eyes. "We're gonna be ok, Simmons. Just stay with me and stay tough. Hoorah, Marine?"

The boy squeezed his eyes tight and leaned into his sergeant, then opened them and set his jaw.

"I'm good, Sar'n," he said, then nodded his head and added "Hoorah!"

Casey spun a finger over his head twice and then pointed his hand to the corner that was their objective.

Move out.

Casey leapt to his feet, fired his rifle from a raised and aimed position at the nearest window, and kicked off his sprint. Immediately the air around him came alive with whistling rounds and bright tracers. As his second boot hit the sand, a tremendous impact in the center of his chest knocked him backwards off his feet. His helmeted head smacked the corner of the wall hard enough to set off white explosions of light in his eyes. Then he thumped hard on his back in the dirt.

Dazed and deaf to the gunfire around him, Casey lifted his head and looked down in horror at the center of his chest, where a charred hole smoked eerily in the brown canvas of his body armor. He probed the hole with a shaking left index finger and felt a hot piece of metal burn his fingertip. The round had not penetrated! Hands grabbed at him from behind the wall, and dirt kicked up in his face as the enemy adjusted fire. With a burst of strength from some unknown source he pushed away the hands clawing at his load-bearing vest. He pushed himself up to a squat, intent on restarting his sprint. When he made it to a low crouch he felt a violent, burning pain explode low in his throat and again he was driven backwards into the dirt.

Casey could hear nothing, but felt hands again on his vest and arms. He was dragged roughly back behind the wall, his eyes staring up, terrified, at a hazy blue sky. He became aware that the rough hands on his throat were his own, and that they were hot and wet. His view of the sky was suddenly blocked by dark shapes that slowly took on the images of his friends' faces. What were their names?

"Sergeant Stillman! Sergeant Stillman!"

"Casey—dude, can you hear me?"

The voices were like an old recording playing way too slow in another room. He tried to speak, but instead coughed and felt warm stickiness flow down both his cheeks. Then the faces were gone for a moment and a tremendously large shadow blocked out the low sun. A helicopter? The world was getting dark and he closed his eyes. He saw his wife's face, smiling at him, and Claire, little feet kicking as she smiled up from her crib at Daddy.

My girls. I have to get to my girls.

He should be going home. Where was the dusty tornado to bring him home? He didn't know what that thought meant, but it somehow made sense to him.

Then everything went black.

Chapter
2

He sat up screaming, his hands clutching his throat and his body drenched in sweat.

"Help me! Oh, God, I'm shot! Oh! Oh, fuck!"

A light clicked on and soft, warm hands grabbed his shoulders. He pushed backwards with his feet reflexively at the strange but gentle touch, and then the soft ground disappeared from beneath him and he felt himself fall. He landed with a sharp pain on his left hip and then pitched backwards, the back of his head striking hard on the corner of a wooden box. Stars again. Then he lay there gasping and confused.

"Jack? Omigod! Jack, baby, what is it?" A beautiful angel, ringed from behind by light, peered down at him from—a bed?

No, not an angel, though just as beautiful.

"Pam?" he croaked.

"Baby, it's me. What is it? What's wrong?" His angel slid off their bed onto the floor beside him, her legs across his, her hands cupping his face. Her brown eyes had tears in them, her face full of fear and concern. "Jack, what is it? What happened?" Her soft fingers went through his thick, black hair. At the back of his head they brought a burst of pain. He watched her pull her hand away and she looked at two fingers, wet with blood.

"Jack! Holy shit, baby you're bleeding! Are you all right? Honey, what is it?" She looked pleadingly into his eyes.

Pam…right? Who the fuck was Jack? Wait—just wait a goddamn minute.

Jack pushed himself up on unsteady arms. He swallowed the burning bile down hard.

I just need a minute.

He instinctively wrapped his arms around his crying wife.

Right?

He held her tightly and the images of the wall in Fallujah faded away, but slowly. He rocked his wife in his arms and his eyes swept the now more familiar room. His bedroom. Their bedroom.

A nightmare?

But the most vicious, realistic nightmare he had ever had. The feel of sand and the smell of dust and gunpowder still clung to him. Jack's breath stuck for a moment in his throat when he saw a darkening sky. But the hazy dusk faded rapidly away, replaced by a swirled stucco ceiling and a slowly turning ceiling fan. In the distance he thought he heard the fading sounds of a helicopter and gunfire; then they were gone. He breathed again.

"It's ok, baby. I'm all right." He rocked his wife. "I'm ok, Pam, just an unbelievably horrible nightmare."

I'm home. I'm home with my girls.

"Baby, your head." Pam held up two fingers, still wet with fresh blood—his blood, but at least not from a seven-six-two round tearing out his throat. Jack dragged fingertips across his perfectly intact throat and then felt the back of his head. A small gash bled lightly under his fingers. He steadied himself against the box on the floor, which turned out to be a nightstand when he looked at it.

"I'm ok, honey. Just hit my head on the nightstand. My God, what a horrible dream."

Pam looked at him tentatively and touched his face. Her eyes softened, and she took a deep breath.

Jack closed his eyes tightly and forced the lingering images from his mind as his breathing slowed. His body ached, and he felt a chill as the last of the sweat dried on his skin. Then he slowly pulled himself to his feet and helped Pam up off the floor. Far away he heard a soft sobbing voice.

"Mama!"

The sound of his baby girl's voice filled Jack with warmth, and a calm flooded over him. He was ok. He was home.

Pam wiped the tears from her eyes. "We woke Claire," she said, and then, "I'll go." She kissed Jack on the cheek. "Get some ice from the kitchen for your head. I'll meet you there."

Jack headed down the weirdly unfamiliar stairs, but as he reached the bottom, things started to feel more recognizable. He reached his hand out and touched a large, framed picture—the one of Pam with her head on his shoulder and Claire in her arms. The picture comforted him, but at the same time its image of him, his thick dark hair a bit longer than now, felt out of place. Jack shook his head, the motion causing a slight wave of recurrent nausea, and entered the kitchen.

Fifteen minutes later, Jack sat at the kitchen table, an ice pack held gingerly on his head, a glass of milk in his other hand. The confusion was clearing, but there remained a lingering sense that something wasn't right. His hand trembled as he raised his glass to his lips and drank. He was so goddamn thirsty. His throat was on fire, and he was sure he could smell the persistent and distinctive odor of fine powdery sand on his skin—a familiar smell. Jack coughed gently and felt a burning low in his throat. He tasted the coppery taste of blood. Pam came in, wrapped in a blue terry robe, and kissed his cheek again.

"You ok, baby?" She sat beside him at the table and caressed his arm.

"I think so," he replied.

"Jack, my God! I mean what in the hell was that all about?" Pam leaned her head softly on his arm. "Jesus, Jack, you scared the hell out of me."

Jack squeezed his wife's arm and thought a moment.

"I don't know, baby. I've never dreamed anything like that before. God, it was so real."

Pam gazed lovingly at him and her look made him feel real.

"You want to tell me about it?"

"Well," Jack began slowly, "I was in the war. In Iraq, you know? I guess I was like a Marine, but I wasn't me. I was, sort of like someone else..." Slowly Jack recounted the details of his dream to Pam as best he could. When he got to the end, the part where he, or Casey or whoever, was shot, he felt a lump in his throat and was surprised when his eyes filled with tears. He looked up at his wife, comforted again by the beautiful gaze which looked deeply into his.

"I just wanted to get home to my girls," he said and his voice cracked.

Pam held his gaze a moment and then stood up. She took the ice pack gently away from his head and examined his wound. Jack could picture her wrinkled brow and pursed lips in his mind and smiled.

"No more bleeding," she announced.

Then she took both of his hands in hers and pulled him to his feet. She wrapped her arms around him and hugged him tightly, her face soft and warm on his chest. Her hair tickled his chin.

"Come on, my war hero. Let's get back to bed."

Pam turned and led him by the hand to the stairs. "God, Jack. No more CNN headline news for you for a while, ok?"

Jack chuckled, squeezed his wife's hand, and then slipped back under the covers of their bed. "Yeah, I guess so."

Pam curled up beside him under the sheets, her head on his shoulder. Her long hair lay across his chest, which she stroked gently and soothingly. Her touch was like magic.

"Teaching biology too boring for you, Jack?"

Jack hugged his wife and said nothing. As Pam drifted off to sleep, he lay thinking over and over about the images that remained. He was also haunted by a surreal feeling. In the dark he tried to imagine the rest of the room—what color the curtains were, where the closet was. He was dismayed to find the answers that came to him were hesitant and unsure. Unreal was the right word, he thought. He reached out his hand and fumbled for a light on the nightstand. It felt unfamiliar, but he finally found a switch on the base. He clicked it on.

The curtains across the room were blue and yellow, just as he'd guessed—or known, of course. And the closet door, though still uneasily unfamiliar, was right where he had thought it would be.

Pam squeezed her eyes tight and mumbled, "Y'ok?" sleepily.

Jack clicked the light back off and rubbed his wife's arm.

"Sorry."

As he drifted off to sleep, Jack was haunted by two things. First was the names of his dead Marine buddies, which ran through his brain again and again, almost like a ringing— Kindrich from Tennessee and Bennet from Texas. The other was the disturbing realization that had Pam not said he was a teacher, which now of course felt right in an unsettled way, he wasn't sure he could have come up with his job on his own.

Other than leader of Marines.

Hoorah.

Then he drifted away to nowhere, away from his bed, away from Fallujah, to a deep and dark sleep.

A dreamless sleep.

* * *

The unreal feeling quieted but never really left. Jack woke to Pam's gentle prodding, but he didn't feel at all rested. He showered and dressed absently, his mind drifting back to his dream over and over again. Though it lacked the intense reality of last night, it still had a quality to it, a rightness that was disturbing. The dream itself and the terror it brought seemed much less intense, but it bothered him how real and vivid his memory of his Marines had been—his friends, as if he really knew them. Jack wondered if he had somehow incorporated real people into his dream, like Dorothy had in *The Wizard of Oz*. It all seemed so real. Not only could he picture them as they had been in battle together, but he found he could picture them in other settings as well. He had a vivid picture of Simmons laughing, eating brown rice out of a brown plastic bag, and leaning against a sand berm. He had what felt like a memory of dragging a shit-faced Chuck Bennet, out of a bar near Twentynine Palms Marine Corps Base in California. He had fallen down beside Kindrich's Mustang and then started laughing uncontrollably. The clarity of these "memories" bothered Jack even more than the images from his nightmare. Where in the hell had those pictures come from? He knew Simmons had a girlfriend, but he couldn't remember her name.

Jack realized the water running down on him from the shower head had turned lukewarm. He pushed the thoughts from his mind again and escaped the now chilly water. As he toweled himself off, he forced his mind instead to his girls. That was the only reality he needed. The thought of them and his life with them made any attachment to the characters from some crazy dream seem ludicrous.

Pam and Claire are my reality.

Jack looked at himself in the foggy mirror, squinting to somehow see behind his own eyes. He saw nothing but his own face. Why did these "memories" seem so goddamn real?

In contrast, as he walked around his house, kissed his wife, and sipped his coffee, he felt unnatural. Or staged, maybe. Yeah, that was more it. He felt like he was role-playing, almost. The undertone really bothered him and he couldn't shake it. The only thing that felt completely real and natural about the whole morning was Claire. He picked her up from her high chair to kiss her good-bye, and she grabbed his nose, burped, and then smiled a giggly smile at him.

"Daaa-dy," she cooed.

Jack felt overwhelmed for a moment by his love for his little girl—by her look, and touch, and smell. The feeling seemed to push his uneasiness into the background. By the time he slid into the driver's seat of his green Volvo, the feeling was just noise, barely available to his senses, and easily drowned out by Toby Keith singing about his "Whiskey Girl" on the radio.

The school day passed by smoothly at first. As Jack got into his role of teacher, the dreamlike quality dissipated. He taught his third-period class a review of the cell cycle, and answered his students' questions without thinking. That was good, because on the few occasions when he did think about the questions, he would feel a momentary panic, as if he didn't know what he was talking about. Then the answers would just pour out as soon as he opened his mouth. A few times he felt the nagging sensation of getting away with a charade. The ten minute breaks between classes, when the room was quiet and he had nothing to focus on, brought the anxiety back and the dream images came to him. He could almost smell the distinctive odor of Iraqi dust. Then the next class would begin and the images would fade away again. By lunch period the dreamlike feeling again seemed only background noise, and he headed out of his classroom to get something to eat.

"Hey, Jack!"

Jack turned around and saw a man about his age looking at him with curiosity. He was dressed in chinos and a black T-shirt under a blazer. Jack felt his heart quicken, but he didn't know why.

"Yeah?" he answered uneasily.

"You may have the others fooled, but I know what's really going on here," the man said in a thick Chicago accent, his hands on his hips.

"What do you mean?" Jack shifted uneasily and felt his mouth go dry. What was this guy's name? Chad?

"Lunch room is this way, pal." He looked stern. Jack stood still, unsure what to do. Then the man laughed and strode over, wrapping an arm around Jack's shoulder. "I thought you quit smokin', dude!"

Jack relaxed and let out his breath.

"Yeah, I did. Just habit I guess." Jack didn't remember ever smoking. He turned and walked in the other direction with his friend.

"You bring lunch or are we scoring burgers?"

"No…uh…I didn't bring anything," Jack answered.

"Sweet!" his friend replied, rubbing his palms together. "Finally took a stand against Pam's healthy life plan, huh?"

"Yeah," Jack laughed. That felt right somehow. Salad and dressing in separate Tupperware. He relaxed again.

"Shapin' the young minds, pal?" his friend asked as they walked through the double doors into the noisy lunch room. Young teens laughed and talked loudly at the round institutional tables spread out around the room. Jack scanned the colorful homemade posters scattered randomly on the walls, telling of upcoming club meetings and a dance next Friday.

"Doing my part, Chad," Jack replied easily. They grabbed trays and slid them down the twin metal bars, past prepackaged salad and little bowls of Jell-O. Chad stopped in front of the grill. A middle-aged woman stared back at them with a wry smile from under her blue, net-covered grey hair.

"Two cheeseburgers, Sheila, but you can put 'em both on one bun," Chad ordered.

"You know I'm not supposed to do that," Sheila said with an insider's smile.

"Yeah, yeah. Come on, sweetie. And extra fries with that, ok?"

Sheila sighed and turned to Jack.

He smiled. "Same," he said.

Jack followed Chad out of the line with his tray, and the two wound their way through the scattered tables to the exit. Several yards down the hallway, Chad led them through a door marked Faculty Lounge. Inside several other teachers chatted at one of the two tables and Chad set his tray on the other.

"Soda?" Chad asked, reaching into the large refrigerator.

"Sure," Jack replied. Chad tossed his friend a diet Coke underhand, which Jack caught easily. On a TV in the corner the CNN headline news reporter, clearly chosen for bouncy, blonde good looks and full lips—a decision highlighted by her low-cut blouse—droned on about stock market trends. Jack slid into a chair and took a big bite of his double cheeseburger.

"Mmmmm." He hadn't realized how hungry he was until that first bite.

Chad took a huge bite of his own dietary sin and rolled his eyes in delight.

"Yeah," he exclaimed with a full mouth. "Being bad tastes pretty damn good, eh, Jack?"

Jack smiled his reply and twisted the top off his Coke. Then something the TV blonde was saying caught his attention—something about Fallujah—and he turned quickly towards the screen. The picture was file footage of Marines advancing through the streets of a war torn and dusty town.

...for the town of Al Fallujah. The fierce fighting continued yesterday, but not without casualties on....

"I think we ought to talk to Anderson about..."

"Quiet!" Jack ordered sharply, his hand outstretched towards Chad. The curt command caused Chad to stop in midsentence, his mouth open, and then he followed Jack's gaze towards the TV.

...numbering perhaps as high as 50 killed and hundreds wounded or captured according to several military sources. Coalition forces suffered yesterday as well, with three Marines reportedly killed and another seriously wounded during a brutal firefight in the city's war-ravaged streets. The names of the killed and injured Marines were not released, pending notification of families here at home. Although military authorities report that coalition forces now control nearly half of the city, they caution that the violence there is far from over. Elsewhere in Iraq, a car bomb has reportedly killed one soldier while four others were wounded in an attack near the town...

Jack's face paled and a cool sweat spread over his whole body. His throat tightened, and he could hear his pulse pounding in his ears.

"Kindrich from Tennessee, Bennett from Texas..." he muttered. Their faces were vividly clear from his dream. And who else? Who was the third? He knew who the wounded Marine was—Sgt. Stillman...Casey.

Jack felt the room closing in on him, and thought he might suffocate if he didn't get somewhere with more air. His throat burned low down, but he didn't have any spit to swallow. He rose and pushed his chair back from the table so abruptly that it tipped over backwards and crashed to the floor. Then he bolted for the door. His stomach churned as he stumbled into the hall.

"Jack! What the hell?"

"Excuse me," Jack choked out over his shoulder as he went rapidly down the hall, towards the light from the glass door at the end. As he got closer to the door, the hallway began to tilt and far off he could hear the sound of gunfire. He was only vaguely aware of someone calling out his name as he pushed through the door and into the cool air outside. Jack sucked in a deep breath as he leaned back against the wall, then he leaned forward as vomit rose in the back of his throat. He dry heaved twice, managed to keep the bite of Sheila's secret double cheeseburger safely in his stomach, and spit the bile taste out of his mouth onto the flowers planted beside the school wall.

Just then a shadow passed over him, and the *thump, thump* of a UH-60 Blackhawk helicopter broke the stillness of the air. He turned his head upward towards the sound, his eyes wide with panic—but the blue sky was empty and silent. A hand on his shoulder made him reel around on one heel, his left hand up defensively, his right reaching behind his hip for his M16A rifle, but he fumbled about grabbing only air.

"Jesus, Jack! Are you ok? What the fuck is going on?" Chad's face was concerned and frightened.

"Mr. Keller?" Two young girls stood a few yards away, their fourth-period books clasped tightly to their chests.

"Everything is fine here, ladies. Get on to class now," Chad said without looking over at them, his voice cracking. The girls shuffled around the two popular teachers and slipped through the door into the school without speaking.

Jack steadied under Chad's firm grip on his shoulders. Then he stepped back gently out of Chad's awkward embrace.

"Sorry, man...I, uh…" Jack felt his mind begin to clear a bit. "Man, those burgers must have been laced with *E. coli* or something. I suddenly got overwhelmingly nauseated. I just about barfed once I got out here. Sorry about all that." Jack managed an awkward smile.

"Sick?" Chad looked unconvinced.

"Yeah...man, I still feel like I might puke," Jack replied, the charade more convincing as it took on comfortable shape.

Chad stepped back without thinking, as folks often do when they think they might get hurled on.

"You do look kinda sick, actually. Jesus, you're pale as shit." Chad seemed to relax a bit. "Maybe you should go home. We'll get one of the subs for you."

Jack shook his head and took a deep breath. He felt better, his face warmer.

"No," he replied. "I think I'm all right. Man, it just hit me all of the sudden." Jack wiped the last of the sweat from his forehead. "Just give me a second."

"Sure, sure," Chad answered. "Take what you need. You want me to hang here with you?"

"No, I'm good now. Get back to your lunch. I'll be in, in a minute."

"Ok," Chad agreed. Then he laughed. "You really scared the shit out of me, man. I thought you knew someone from the news. God, you should have seen old Ms. Foster. I think you might have made her pee herself a little." Chad went back through the door. "Come get me if you need me."

Jack nodded and smiled as the door closed. Then he leaned back against the wall again.

Kindrich, Bennett, and someone else. Why would he know that? What was going on? Jack settled on the only reasonable explanation.

He was losing his fucking mind.

Chapter
3

The rest of the day remained a haze in the background of his thoughts as Jack drove home. Twice during the afternoon periods he had floated off in midsentence, his thoughts in a place that, as far as he knew, he had never been. These had been followed by awkward silence as he drifted back into reality, only to find himself gazing out over a sea of confused young faces—his students, who whispered and giggled uncomfortably. Fifth period was his free period and he spent the entire fifty minutes in the faculty lounge, flipping through the channels to find more information about the Marine deaths in Fallujah. Names. He especially, desperately, needed names. If only the names would be released, he could prove to himself he knew nothing of this place or these people, that his dream and the report were a frightening coincidence. Perhaps he had even heard the story the evening before, and it had rooted in his unconsciousness, coming out as the terrible fantasy later in his sleep. But the news reports barely even mentioned the battle, the loss of three Marines apparently less interesting to America than how the coming Christmas season might affect stock market trends, a huge fire in an empty warehouse in some South Carolina town, and a story run three times about a girl in New Jersey who dumped her newborn in a trash can (the baby survived, the girl was sorry, but was still being charged). The radio on the ride home provided no more help.

Jack knew he was frightened, but unsure of what. Perhaps the idea of being crazy? Wasn't that what you were when you had no control over your own thoughts? He found the returning sense that the world around him was less real than his nightmare—that his whole life felt made up—even more concerning. Try as he might, he couldn't conjure up any emotional details of his life. He had tested himself with curtain colors and the closet door last night, but now those victories seemed more like easily rectified props than evidence of a solid reality. Shit, even a thought like that made him feel his loose hold on sanity might be slipping away. He simply couldn't break from the force that pulled him to some sort of connection with Sergeant Casey Stillman, young leader of Marines.

"Jack?" He startled back to reality to the sound of a tap on the window of the grey Volvo. No, green—his Volvo was green.

Jack looked up to see Pam standing by the car, her arms crossed for warmth. The sun had nearly set, the last haze of autumn pink fading rapidly. He realized the Volvo was still running.

Kenny sang gently on the radio, reminding Jack that there were songs that took him to other places. He grimaced and shut off the ignition and opened the door, grabbing his briefcase.

"What's wrong, Jack? I was calling you from the porch." Pam grabbed Jack by the arm as they walked towards the house. "You've been out here for fifteen minutes, baby."

Jack patted her cold hand.

"Sorry, honey. Really weird day at work. I was just trying to sort things out in my head I guess."

"Well, you can tell me about it over dinner. It's getting cold." They walked into the house where Jack was met with the comfort of warmth and the smell of food. His stomach growled, and he realized he hadn't eaten since breakfast—the nearly puked burger bite didn't count, right?

"Claire is sleeping already. She didn't really nap today and I think she might have a little bug. She was a little fussy all day."

Pam continued on, telling Jack about her day, but he was having trouble concentrating. The grumbling in his stomach grew rapidly, and he felt himself salivate at the smell of a home-cooked meal.

Better than cold MREs behind a sand berm in the dark, that's for fuckin' sure.

Jack ate, nodding and asking questions at the appropriate times, guilty that he had no idea what his wife was talking about. His mind dissected the events of the day and the feelings that he couldn't quite shake. He also debated just how much to tell Pam about his bizarre feelings and his fears about losing his marbles.

"Jack?"

"Huh?" Jack looked up from his nearly empty second plate of ham, mac and cheese, and green beans.

"I said tell me what is up with you today. I'm really worried about you, baby."

"Just that damn nightmare, sweetheart. It haunted me all day long. I just can't shake it." He felt a pang of guilt for not sharing his deeper fears and haunting thoughts with the woman who shared his life.

Pam rose from her seat and sat on her husband's lap. Jack wrapped his arms around her as she caressed his face. Pam kissed him.

"It's just an awful dream, Jack. You're such a sensitive man." She kissed his throat and Jack closed his eyes. "It's just a terrible nightmare in response to the horrible things going on over there. Now," she licked lightly on his earlobe, her breath warm and sexy on his neck. Her voice fell to a whisper. "How can I take your mind off of it?"

Jack felt her hands unbuttoning his shirt as she kissed him deeply this time. His body responded and he kissed her back, his own hands running over her body. Then she stood up and pulled him by the hand towards the stairs.

They made love slowly, passionately. Her touch was warm and gentle, and Jack felt all of his anxiety disappear into oblivion. He lost himself in the wonderful—and more importantly, familiar—feel of his wife's body moving against his. He felt right for the first time since the dream.

Afterwards he checked on Claire. He watched her sleep for several minutes before he picked her up gently. They sat in the glide rocker beside her bed and he rocked her slowly as she slept on his bare chest. The feel of her little hands on his shoulder, the sound of her slow and gentle breathing, comforted him as much as his embrace seemed to soothe her. His heart was so full of love for her that he thought it might burst. After she settled again into a deep sleep, he placed her softly back in her crib. His big girl. Soon she would be ready for a toddler bed. He kissed her lightly on her warm cheek. He stroked her red hair and then pulled her yellow Pooh Bear blanket up over her shoulders.

"Love you, Bear," he whispered.

As he crawled into bed, Pam propped herself up on one elbow and stroked his hair, the sheet falling off her bare shoulder.

"She's fine," Jack said. "Sleeping."

He wrapped his arm around his wife's waist and kissed her.

"Good," she said, her hand finding her way between them and pulling at the drawstring of his pajama bottoms. She leaned in and kissed him deeply again.

They made love again, more urgently this time. Then they fell asleep, wrapped around each other, legs entwined. Jack felt completely at peace. As he slipped into sleep he wondered how he could ever have doubted this reality.

Chapter
4

Jack woke up refreshed and content. Light streamed in through the two large windows, framed by yellow curtains.

Blue and yellow curtains — of course.

He chuckled, then stretched and yawned, squeezed his eyes shut, and reached behind and above him for the reading lamp mounted in the wall. He smelled fresh coffee and heard the chattering of his daughter and wife from downstairs. Jack lay in bed, reliving the passion and comfort from the night before. Yesterday now seemed like nothing more than a bad dream, the anxiety alien and far away. He heard footsteps on the stairs and turned to see Pam come through the door holding a large mug of coffee in her hand. Claire rested on her other hip.

"Morning, my delicious man! Thought you might sleep all day," his wife chided. She looked radiant, gorgeous in the short-cut silk robe he had gotten for her in Okinawa...or...no? Whatever. It didn't matter. She was beautiful and twice as attractive with his little girl in her arms.

Pam set the mug of coffee beside him on the nightstand, sat on the edge of the bed, and put down Claire, who scurried up and onto his chest. She lay there, resting on outstretched arms, smiling.

"Daddy!" she said clear as a bell.

"Hey there, little buddy," Jack answered, leaning forward and kissing her on her chubby cheeks. She giggled the musical giggle that only comes from happy children. The sound was rich in his ears.

"Kisses, Daddy. Kisses!" She plopped down on his chest, her soft hands grabbing his neck. She kissed his mouth with a loud and exaggerated, "MMMMMM MMAAAAA!"

"Tickle bear!" Jack exclaimed and tickled his little girl lightly. He was rewarded with another wonderful, tinkling giggle.

"What time is it?" Jack asked, looking over at his wife and placing a hand on her bare left knee.

"Ten thirty, Rip Van Winkle. Didn't mean to wear you out, old man."

"Oh, shit. I'm late!" Jack exclaimed. He wrapped his arms around Claire and sat up in bed. "I mean shoot," he reminded himself sheepishly and placed his hands over Claire's ears playfully.

"Relax, my absent-minded professor," Pam said. She rolled her eyes and smiled. "Saturday, big boy."

Jack lay back down and rolled on his side, sliding Claire onto the bed beside him and tickling her again.

"Tickles, Daddy, tickles!" she giggled up at him, with her big blue eyes.

Pam picked up Claire and placed her on the other side of Jack. Then she crawled up beside her in the bed. She leaned across their little girl and kissed Jack on the cheek. Between them, Claire cooed.

"Kisses, Mommy!"

Pam kissed her forehead and smoothed the curls of red hair with her fingers.

"Two nights a week like last night and I may just renew your contract, stud boy." She winked at him seductively, and Jack grinned an adolescent grin.

"Maybe I'll give you a down payment this afternoon during nap time in exchange for an off-season bonus."

"Deal!" she laughed and wrapped her arms around both of them.

"Hugs, Mommy!"

"Hugs, Claire Bear," Pam agreed, leaning her forehead against her daughter's and rubbing noses in an Eskimo kiss. "Your Daddy is an insatiable animal!"

"Amimimal," Claire repeated.

Jack reached for his coffee on the nightstand, propping his head against the headboard and taking a cautious sip. The liquid was hot and sweet, and Jack wrinkled his nose.

"Uuuhhh. What's in this brew?" he asked.

"French vanilla creamer and one sugar, Jack. Just like you drink it every morning."

Jack wrinkled his forehead, confused.

"I don't drink it black?"

Pam laughed and rolled her eyes again. "No, Jack. Not in the seven years I've been with you."

"Huh," Jack replied, sipping his coffee again. Not bad, actually.

Pam gathered up her daughter and slid off the bed, pulling her robe around her briefly exposed hip as she did.

"Up ya' go, baby. Let's have some coffee cake and get on with our family day."

They listened to some jazz and nibbled coffee cake in the living room while Claire crawled around, exploring the myriad of toys strewn about the room. The jazz was part of the Pam Parenting Plan, meant to stimulate their daughter's ear for music and make her more creative. Jack remembered fondly how Pam had rested a handheld tape recorder on her belly during her last few months of pregnancy, playing jazz and Mozart and Handel, stimulating Claire and expanding her creative juices even in the womb. She had read about it in one of the dozens and dozens of parenting magazines she had devoured during pregnancy. Pam seemed to love being pregnant, almost as much as she loved being a mom. In the rack between the TV and stereo was a complete collection of the *Baby Einstein* series DVDs. Included in their collection were *Baby Mozart* and *Baby Beethoven*, which combined music with lights and colors, fun animals and toys. Some had poetry instead of music, or word games. They really did seem to stimulate Claire, as she would sit enthralled in front of the TV, rocking to the music and delighting at the animals and colors.

Jack chatted easily with Pam, the way all happy couples do, he imagined. They talked about a mix of nothing and the serious; the soft familiarity of it was comforting. He talked to her about starting an educational IRA for Claire to plan for her college. Jack agreed they should plan now, but he hated to think about anything that implied Claire might actually grow up or, worse, someday go away. He wanted her to stay just as she was right now forever, safe and happy in their loving home. He remembered feeling that way about almost every stage of her development, and then always being delighted that the next stage seemed even better.

After some time at the community party and another bout of lovemaking, Jack worked on lesson plans for the coming week—more cell development, which he outlined from *The Living Cell*, an old text from college. Pam and Claire read books and played in the living room, occasionally coming upstairs to the study to say "Hi" to Daddy. When Jack came down, they were just finishing up a video on colors and numbers. Jack picked up his daughter and hugged her. She gave his nose a tug.

"Whatcha' thinkin' about for dinner, baby? My night if you like," Jack said, as he helped his wife up from the floor.

"How about pizza from Dominick's? Maybe you could get us a movie while you're out?"

That sounded perfect. Jack called in an order for white pizza with chicken and artichokes (he could live without the artichokes but Pam loved them), and then grabbed his jacket, kissing both of his girls on his way out.

Blockbuster Video was a chore that Jack loathed. Too many choices for one thing, and usually he would wander about, indecisive, until he finally settled on a title which inevitably would be out. He had tried the Red Box but the only thing worse than shopping through aisles and aisles of movies, was scrolling through them on the little TV screen. At Blockbuster, he fought that by sticking to the new releases so that he could lessen the frustration somewhat; but nonetheless he still wound up watching the fascinating parade of people who passed by him, picked up three movies in two minutes, and then headed to the check out. Bastards!

Tonight would be easy. He had decided to treat Pam to her favorite genre (with titles he found annoying, though in the end he generally enjoyed the films): romantic comedy. Since he knew nothing of these films, the selection became practically random and thus fairly effortless. Jack parked around the corner (the throngs who found exciting titles in seconds also had a confounding way of finding all the up-front parking spots) and walked through the glass doors into the painfully bright, fluorescent light and marquis posters found in every video store in the world. He headed straight to the back, aiming for the hanging sign Romantic Comedy, which was suspended over two rows of shelves.

An image from a video cover, only half registered and caught out of the corner of his eye, pulled him off course.

The shelves labeled War Films were twice as long as and much fuller than those for Romantic Comedy. Jack figured that the fascination with war was as ancient as mankind itself. It seemed to him that man had written about the wartime experience with a passion beyond that reserved even for love. In fact, some of the greatest love stories of all time seemed to tie the plot to a backdrop of war. Probably even the hunched apemen, who took rock and stick to wall to create cave drawings, spent a great deal of time chronicling terrific battles between man and beast—and all too often, other men.

Jack found himself absent-mindedly wandering down the aisle between shelves packed with volumes and volumes of war films. His eyes drifted slowly over the pictures on the case covers—men battling enemies, guns blazing, flames surrounding them. The men on the covers were grimacing and gripping weapons with amazing strength.

Not at all what it's like, he thought. *Not at all.*

Jack picked up *Blackhawk Down* and flipped it over, looking at the pictures on the back. He was staring solemnly at terrible scenes of destruction, a tear running down his cheek, when a woman's voice caused him to start. Suddenly his pulse began racing and his mouth turned dry.

"Casey! Casey!"

The blood drained out of his face, and he felt the room pulling in on him. He heard the clattering sound of the video which slipped from his fingers and fell to the floor.

A woman moved quickly down the aisle towards him, calling out his name. He was about to answer when something bumped into his leg. He jumped back and nearly stumbled into the video rack, looking down in terror—where all he saw was a boy, perhaps four or five years old. The boy looked up and grinned, and then maneuvered around him. But by then the woman had knelt beside him and grabbed the boy by his hand.

"Casey, shame on you! You know not to run off from Mommy." She looked up at Jack. "I am so sorry."

Then she stood up and turned away, dragging the giggling boy behind her.

"You stay right here beside me, young man. No more horseplay!"

Jack steadied himself with one hand on the video shelf. The color returned to his face and his pulse slowed. He looked at his other, outstretched hand, which he saw had a wicked tremor. He clenched the hand tightly into a fist and closed his eyes.

No!

He would not let this ridiculous nightmare come back to him. He would not give up Saturday, his Family Day, for this insanity. It was a nightmare. Nothing more. Jack decided that his unhealthy obsession with it, and the war, could only be rectified by him. He picked up the video at his feet and replaced it on the shelf, angry and disgusted with himself. He then quick-paced down the aisle towards the Romantic Comedy shelves.

"I am getting a video and heading home to my family," he said firmly, barely aware that he had spoken out loud. Jack felt the stares of several people who no doubt looked at him the way you might look at the disheveled man on the street corner holding a sign announcing the apocalypse and muttering to invisible colleagues. Jack ignored them and scanned the titles briefly, and then grabbed two videos off the shelf without reading them. More random than he had intended, but he marched to the register, paid, and then walked purposefully out of the store.

Jack drove home slowly, determined to work through the ridiculous coincidence from the Blockbuster before settling in with Pam. He stopped on the way and picked up their pizza, even managing a genuine smile when he paid. By the time he pulled into the driveway the time and the smell of pizza worked together with the anticipation of a relaxing evening to push the fear and uncertainty almost completely out of his mind.

I have to decide to let this obsessive shit go.

He said nothing of his anxiety attack (as he had decided to name it on the drive home) and mostly succeeded at putting it out of his mind by the time he and Pam curled up under the couch blanket. They munched on pizza (which Jack casually thinned of artichokes) and watched the video Pam had selected from the two choices. It wasn't bad, actually. Yet another boy-meets-girl-blows-it-and-has-to-win-her-back-again vehicle starring one of the guys from *Friends* and some hot, but unknown, woman star wannabe. He actually laughed out loud more than once. And when the credits rolled, he was again relaxed and happy. He smiled to find that Pam had fallen asleep (as she almost always did at movies on the couch, a constant source of teasing from Jack), so he covered her up with the blanket. He cleaned up the kitchen, woke her gently, and checked on Claire while Pam "readied for bed," whatever that meant. Whatever it entailed was more involved than a leak and a quick brushing of the teeth, which Jack still accomplished in time to slip under the covers before his wife.

They held each other gently and swore their love, then he clicked off the light. They both fell asleep before a few minutes had passed. As he slipped into the comfort of sleep Jack felt content, but unsettled, like something might be waiting for him, just on the other side of sleep.

Chapter
5

He lay in the dark and felt the ground begin to tilt. In the distance he heard the sound of gunfire—or maybe it was close and the distance was an illusion. Battle could do that, he knew. He felt nauseated and tasted bile mixed with blood in the back of his throat. A burning pain spread out backwards over his neck, and a tightness extended into his chest. With each struggling breath he heard a high-pitched whistling followed by a gurgling sound. He realized that it was dark because his eyes were closed and, with great difficulty, he opened them. He looked up into a hazy, purplish sky, heavy with dust. A shadow passed over him and he heard the familiar *thump, thump* of a UH-60 Blackhawk as the fast helicopter passed overhead. A darker shadow enveloped him and someone bent over his face. He tried to force his eyes to focus on the features of the man looking down on him, but couldn't.

"Hang in there, Sergeant. You're gonna be ok!"

"How is he, Doc?"

"I don't know. He's lost a shitload of blood. The left side of his neck is swollen tight. I think he might have gotten his carotid artery." There was a pause and more light as the featureless face disappeared from view. "We got to get him the fuck out of here, Mac, or he ain't gonna make it. He needs to be in an OR, like, five mikes ago."

Doc. That would be Doc White, the young Navy corpsman from New Orleans, now with his platoon. They must have joined up with the rest of the guys. And Mac? Who was Mac? ...Wait,

Mac! That was McIver from Virginia—wanted to be a high-school baseball coach.

"What is that in his neck? Shrapnel?"

"It's a tracheotomy, dipshit. I had to put it in so he could breathe. The bullet tore his windpipe nearly in half. He was drowning in his own blood."

There was movement around him and then another shadow, another featureless face. Casey felt desperately short of breath. He struggled to suck air into his lungs, and the burning grew to an unbearable pitch. He tried to raise an arm, to reach out for Mac, but his arms were dead weight by his sides. He felt a panic grow inside of him and struggled to stay calm.

Why the fuck can't I move?

Casey forced his mind away from his burning pain, from the feeling that tight bands were wrapped around his chest, keeping him from getting air into his oxygen-starved body. He forced his mind to Pam, to thoughts of her body moving against his. He thought of Claire, lying peaceful on his bare chest, rocking in the glider beside her crib. His big girl. With all his might he willed himself away from the nightmare he was living and back home to them, to a place where he could breathe. A place where he wasn't so terrified. A place where he didn't need to be afraid of death.

He sensed more movement beside him and he blinked his eyes to clear them. He managed to turn his head ever so slightly to the left, pain now exploding in his neck to join the burning in his chest, and he forced his eyes to focus on the dark shape beside him in the dirt. Slowly the image sharpened, like someone fine-tuned a pair of binoculars—back and forth, back and forth—and then he focused on the horror only a foot or so from his face.

He opened his mouth to scream, but of course no sound came, just that horrible whistling and bubbling. Then something warm and sticky poured out from the center of his neck. He felt the blood trickle down both sides of his neck and drip off into the dirt.

Beside him in the filthy street, he saw the face of Rich Simmons, the young kid from Albany. Only it wasn't really him. Not anymore. The one remaining eye looked off at an unnatural angle, unfocused, staring out at oblivion. The other eye was gone, as was half of his face and most of the top of his head. The short strands of blondish hair stuck to what was left of his forehead, matted with grey mush, and bits of bone. Casey wanted to turn his head away, but couldn't. Instead he squeezed his eyes shut and, in his mind, screamed again.

* * *

He sat up in bed, tears streaming down his face, gasped for air, and then screamed. His hands clawed desperately at his neck, but found nothing but sweat and smooth skin. Above him, a hazy purple sky was cut periodically with tracers and orange light from distant explosions. The light wind swirled dust around him. It filled his lungs with each heavy breath and burned his eyes. Again, he heard the familiar thumping as the Blackhawk's rotors beat the air into submission. He heard men scream and call out for covering fire. The sounds faded into the distance, as if he was in a silent rail car pulling rapidly away from the battle. As he watched in horrified fascination, the purple sky began to swirl above him like a blackening cyclone. It twisted into tighter and smaller circles, which spun faster and faster, and the edges filled in with familiar white stucco, lit yellow from a pale light behind him. Then, when the swirling black and purple looked no more than the size of a basketball, and the sounds had faded to nothing but memory, the purple circle exploded with a flash of red light and was gone, replaced by a slowly turning ceiling fan.

Jack sat bolt upright, his breathing raspy and fast. Sweat poured off his face and chest. He heard footsteps approaching rapidly, and then a voice which soothed him.

"Jack? Jack, baby, are you ok?"

Pam came in from the hall, the source of the pale, yellow light. She held Claire in her arms, their little girl's eyes heavy and her lip set in a pout.

"Pam?" He felt disoriented and confused. Terrified in fact.

"Jack, what is it? What happened?" Pam sat on the edge of the bed, Claire balanced on her thigh. His little girl started sobbing. "Jack, my God, you're covered in sweat! Are you sick? Do you have a fever?"

Jack took his wife's hand in both of his and kissed it, then held it against his chest, still panting. He tried to speak but found no words.

"Jack, what made you scream?" She started to cry. "Please, say something!"

Jack continued to hold her hand against his chest and cleared his throat, which felt incredibly dry and sore. His heart beat nearly out of his chest.

"I...I, uh..." Jack coughed and tasted the coppery taste of blood in his throat. His tongue burned and he realized he must have bitten it. He could feel his chest tighten and thought he might burst into tears himself.

"N...n...nightmare," he stammered. Then he laid his head over on his wife's leg and the tears came.

"Oh, Jack, oh, baby..." Pam cried harder now, her tears dripping off her chin and into his hair, but he had no energy to comfort or reassure her. "Oh, baby, what can I do?"

"I don't know," Jack choked out. "I don't know... I don't know... What is wrong with me?" He cried hard now. He closed his eyes tightly, trying to force away the image of young Simmons, his face blown off, lying in the dirt beside him. It didn't help. He could still taste the dust in his mouth, still smell the gunpowder and blood.

Pam rubbed his shoulder and kissed his hair. "It's ok, baby... Everything's ok." Claire sniffled more softly, her head on her mother's shoulder. "It's ok, Jack. I'm here. I've got you, baby. We're gonna get you better."

Jack stayed for a long while like that, holding his wife and daughter and crying in the night.

Chapter 6

Sunday morning started off quiet and awkward. Jack tried pointlessly to pretend that everything was okay—because, he supposed, he desperately wanted it to be. He felt terrified by the nagging thought that he must be going crazy, but was more frightened by thoughts of what Pam must be thinking about him. A big part of him had lost all doubt that he was losing his mind. The nightmare seemed so vivid again, so real. In some ways more real than sipping coffee (vanilla creamer and one sugar) quietly at the kitchen table, wincing as it stung his bitten tongue.

So it was Simmons—the third death in the firefight—twenty-year-old Simmons from Albany, with his dirty blond hair, always a little longer than the rest of the guys (and a source of constant hazing from his squad leader, Sergeant Casey Stillman). He could see him in his mind's eye in better times, sitting back against a sand berm before the assault on Fallujah, shoveling cold MREs into his mouth with a plastic spoon (Jambalaya, dry crackers with a packet of jalapeno cheese, and water from a canteen). He was talking about a girl, Beth maybe, from home. A girl he wanted to marry at the NCO club when they got back to Pendleton.

Well, Rich wouldn't be marrying Beth now, would he? Not in Pendleton or any other goddamn place. Rich from Upstate was leaving half his grey matter in a dusty street in Fallujah, thanks-just-the-same, and the other half would be planted in a hole near the VA in Albany. There would be taps, and flowers, and crying parents.

But he couldn't really know that could he? He couldn't possibly. Any more than he could know that he, or, no, Sergeant Stillman, was the mortally wounded man in that same firefight. And then a more terrifying thought occurred to him. What if he continued to have these nightmares? And what if, as they continued to unfold the horrible story, he—the Sergeant Casey Stillman "he"—died from the horrible wounds to his throat? What would that mean for Jack? He remembered as a kid, turning around with his friends the myth (or was it?) that in those frightening dreams where you fell and fell, that if you dreamed the part where your body splattered onto the pavement, instead of waking up with a start, that you would die in real life. How would that old wives' tale apply to him now? The answer felt, for a fleeting moment, to be terribly important for him and his family.

Jack shuddered uncontrollably at the kitchen table, an uneaten English muffin cooling on the paper towel in front of him. He wasn't sure which frightened him more, the idea of going crazy or the thought that he wasn't. That both realities, his and Casey Stillman's, could both be true seemed so insane that he couldn't even begin to get his head around it. But neither could he shake the feeling that the answer to all of this lay somewhere in that notion, as inconceivable as it seemed.

Pam had rented a movie once. They had sat on the very sofa where they had just a day ago made love, and watched it together (some of it—she had slept in his lap by halfway through, of course). It was about a woman who saw things through a killer's eyes in her dreams. He couldn't really remember the story, but as he sat there now, he vividly remembered its premise. The woman had believed, as he did at that moment, that she was losing her mind—until stories in the paper (it was never in the TV news in these stories) started to tell of the murders she had seen. He thought it ended with her teaming up with the cops and catching the killer. How could Jack's story end, if indeed he was able to see a battle in Fallujah through the eyes of a real Marine sergeant there? How could he make this mean something, be something other than a personal terror?

Jack picked up his cup and freshened and diluted away some of the sweetness with coffee from the pot. Then he walked into the living room, listening as he did for his wife and daughter. He heard them upstairs, where Pam was changing Claire's pull-up from the night into big girl underwear and a pair of farmer's overalls with Minnie Mouse on the front pocket (he knew this for sure, for some reason). He sat on the couch and picked up the remote, clicked it and brought the idiot box to life. He sat and sipped his coffee (much better now) and flipped through the channels, looking for the talking heads who might help him sort out what was going on in his mind. He settled on Fox News when he saw the red banner with *Update in Iraq*, printed in boldface across it, along the bottom of the screen. A retired army general critiqued the offensive in Fallujah, rattling off statistics and military acronyms, as he talked about the battle as if he himself had led the charge. Jack snickered and shook his head.

You don't know shit.

Jack listened to the arrogant general praise the troops and in the same breath detail how he would have done things just a bit differently. Fallujah was a tough battle, the general told him, against an enemy determined to fight to the death against the great Devils of the American Marines. He listened to a story, which angered the shit out of him, about insurgents who had shot from behind a white flag, wounding a Marine on a rooftop and killing another soldier acting as an interpreter. Then the anchor cut to a live feed from the streets of Fallujah in Iraq, and asked the correspondent embedded with the Marines there, for his impressions of the battle.

Jack leaned forward, straining to see the scene behind the reporter, wearing a green flak jacket and a Marine desert cammie Kevlar helmet. Jack paid little attention to his droning monologue on the fierce firefight that had occurred there. He instead shifted his head back and forth, as if that would help him see the street behind the reporter on the two-dimensional television screen. Jack's pulse quickened and he could feel his heart beat in his temples and arms as the reporter shifted left and looked behind him.

…where Marines engaged a fierce contingent of insurgent combatants recently. The Marines here were hopelessly outnumbered, and suffered multiple casualties. Three Marines were killed here yesterday, and several others were wounded…

The street looked so fucking familiar. A different angle from that which he had appreciated in his mind's eye, but it was definitely the street, wasn't it? Something wasn't right, but he felt sure that this was the street. The reporter turned forward and blocked his view again.

Goddamnit!

"Move your ass, dickhead!" Jack hollered at the TV. His coffee sloshed in his mug (I Love My Daddy) and dribbled down his hand onto the carpet.

"Jack!" Pam's voice rang harsh, and a little frightened, from behind the couch. She leaned over, Claire clinging to her arm from her right hip, and viciously snatched the remote from his hand. She clicked the TV power off, and then dropped the remote to the floor.

He could see tears in her eyes, and he stood up and came around the couch.

"Hey," he said and smoothed the hair out of her eyes and then kissed Claire on the cheek. "It's ok, baby. Just a little editorial for the news." He struggled to sound more together than he felt. Pam pulled away.

"No more news, Jack. That idiot box is the fucking problem!"

He had only heard her use that word once since he had known her.

"Baby," he began and she turned to face him, her face more scared than angry.

"No, Jack. I'm serious. You are obsessed with this goddamn war. You have to stop thinking about it!" She moved closer and looked at him pleadingly. "It's not healthy Jack. It's an obsession with you. It's giving you horrible nightmares. You've been so absorbed with it!"

"Honey," he began again, but didn't know what to say next. How could he explain? He didn't understand himself what was going on. He needed the information from the news to help make sense of all this, didn't he? And he hadn't been obsessed with all this before the first nightmare the other night. At least he didn't remember that he had been. In truth, everything seemed kind of hazy before two days ago. He looked again at his wife. He had to tell her. To make her understand that he was losing touch with who he was—that the lines between his dream and reality were becoming blurred. He had to explain it to her.

"Ok," he said instead and squeezed her hand. "You're right, Pam. We'll both take a break from all this for a while." Pam smiled and hugged him tightly.

"I'm sorry Jack. I am just so worried about you."

"I know, honey. It's ok. I'm fine." Jack hoped his wife believed the words more that he did.

They dressed for church while Claire played on the bed with her talking Elmo doll. Jack made an attempt at senseless conversation while they dressed. Pam chatted about Claire's playgroup, but her voice sounded tense and nervous. Jack struggled to keep his mind from wandering to the street scene on the TV.

It was the street, wasn't it — the street where Casey took a bullet to the throat?

The angle seemed all wrong, like maybe the footage had been shot from the corner down and to the left, so that left and right looked reversed. If the reporter had just moved his fucking head Jack felt sure he would have seen a low, tan wall with a hole ripped in it from an RPG round. In front of it would be a pool of dark blood where Kindrich had taken a bullet into his head and collapsed in a heap beside him.

"Jack?" Pam's voice sounded worried.

"Yeah?" he said and shook the vivid image of Kindrich, his helmet in the dirt and the back of his head an empty black hole, from his mind.

"I said do you know where my black shoes are? The ones with the little bows?"

"Bathroom," he answered fondly.

"Oh, here they are," Pam said from behind him as he tied his tie in the mirror behind the door.

"Elmo!" Claire said.

Pam's hands wrapped around him from behind, and she smiled at him over his shoulder in the mirror.

"Next to the bed," she said.

"Hmmmm?"

"The shoes, Jack," she said and kissed him on the neck. "Beside the bed, not in the bathroom."

Jack chuckled. "Sorry."

He saw a hint of worry in Pam's eyes.

"Watcha' thinkin' about, Jack?"

Jack turned around and kissed her cheek.

"Where to go for brunch," he answered easily. Then he picked Claire up from the bed. "How about Drake's? They make those cool Mickey Mouse pancakes for Claire."

"Which you always finish, piggy boy," Pam laughed. Her voice seemed like hers again and she grabbed his arm tightly. "Sounds yummy."

The three of them walked together down the stairs, Claire pulling on Jack's ear. They piled into the green Volvo and headed off to church.

Jack did a fair job of following along with the service, holding Pam's hand lightly throughout. He mouthed the words to all the hymns. Jack hated the sound of his voice and was sure that others around him would, too. So he did everyone the courtesy of keeping his singing voice to himself, and enjoyed instead the soft sound of Pam's voice as she sang along with the congregation. It felt strange when they were all asked to say a special prayer for the troops in Iraq. Pam squeezed his hand tightly, and he sensed that she looked at him, though he kept his own eyes closed. He tried to think about school, unable to believe that at this moment God could possibly understand his prayers.

After a big brunch Jack was full to bursting, as always, having finished his own eggs Benedict and Claire's barely-touched Mickey Mouse pancakes. They stopped briefly for a swing in the community park, but because of the cold they didn't stay long. At home, while Claire napped, they stayed busy straightening the house. Jack sensed that they were avoiding talking about things, which was fine with him, actually. Pam mopped the kitchen floor while Jack busied himself organizing the playroom their living room had become. He found himself glancing frequently at the TV, his urge to turn it on and surf the news channels almost more than he could bear. Finally, when the TV's calling nearly overpowered him he went upstairs and cleaned the shower with the special cleaner Pam insisted he always use (he found the "scrubbing bubbles" just made the rinse take forever, which maybe was the whole idea). He let his mind probe the TV scene from Fallujah, careful not to think about it directly. Instead he let his brain sort of wander around and sneak up on the thought casually, like a college kid trying to strike up a conversation with a pretty girl at a party that he knew was out of his league. It didn't shed any new light, however, and he finally forced his mind away.

The afternoon was relaxed and comforting in its normalcy. He played with Claire and then the three of them watched *Elmo Goes to the Firehouse.*

"Elmo! Elmo!"

By the time dinner was over Jack felt pretty much himself again, and he sat on the couch reviewing his lesson plans while Pam got Claire ready for bed and tucked her in. He was absorbed in his lesson about DNA and RNA, when abruptly he felt the call of the TV again. The picture of Fallujah leaped back into his consciousness and, feeling guilty as hell, he listened intently for the sound of his wife reading a story to his baby girl. Then he picked up the remote and turned on the TV, madly mashing the volume button until the sound of the Fox News reporter was little more than a whisper. Feigning indifference (for whom he didn't know), he flipped again through his lesson plans while the reporter droned on about some battle in South America he couldn't give less of a shit about. He listened intently though, for the music which would herald another *Update from Iraq* segment, his eyes unfocused as he shuffled his papers around for the benefit of the empty room. Another meaningless story—something about a spending bill which a bunch of suits were arguing about in D.C., but *this* reporter was sure it would pass. Then the music came.

And now another update from Iraq.

Jack dropped his papers, some of them fluttering unnoticed to the floor, and sat forward on the couch, ready.

...in a roadside bomb just outside Al Najaf. There was no official information on casualties in that attack, but confidential and reliable Fox News sources inside Iraq tell us that two Iraqi security officers were killed and one American soldier was wounded...

Come on, come on. Get to Fallujah.

Jack stole a guilty look over his shoulder towards the stairs and then leaned farther forward, the remote in his hand, thumb at the ready to tickle the volume up a bit, should he need. The scene shifted, but not to Fallujah. Some other idiot was talking nonsense from a street in Baghdad.

"Come on, for Christ's sake," Jack muttered.

Suddenly the remote was torn from his hands. He spun around on the couch, his remaining papers hitting the deck, and turned to face his wife, a kid caught flipping through his dad's *Penthouse*, shorts around his ankles.

"P...Pam," he stammered.

"Enough, Jack! Jesus, what are you doing!" Her lip quivered. She clicked the TV off with an angry flourish, then sagged her shoulders and dropped her head. "Enough," she whispered again, then turned on her heel and walked out of the room into the kitchen. She sobbed, her face in her free hand. Her other hand continued to grip the remote.

Jack set his pencil, a remnant of his illusion of indifference to Fox News—apparently now his own personal heroin—gently on the table in front of him and leaned forward, elbows on his knees, face in his hands. He felt tears of frustration in his eyes. He had to have some answers.

Didn't she fucking get it?

He had to know what had happened to his men. He had to know whether he was having some bullshit, armchair posttraumatic stress, like the psychiatrist on *The Today Show* had warned Katie Couric of (*"So much violence and death coming into our living rooms, Katie."*) or if he were losing his mind, or if...well, if it were something more frightening. He didn't know how he thought Fox News would help him find those answers (hearing familiar names wouldn't really answer that question, would it?), but goddamnit he had to find answers somewhere.

He rose slowly to follow his wife into the kitchen, knowing somehow the way Pam would suggest he find his answers. He didn't know why it made him feel angry, but it did. He stopped in the doorway to the kitchen and watched his beautiful wife slapping left over fruit cocktail from a Thomas the Train kiddie plate into a clean margarine tub (poor man's Tupperware, she called it). Her body shook, with fear or anger—maybe a little of both. He knew even from behind her that tears streamed down her cheeks, and he felt guilty as hell.

"Pam?"

His wife stopped punishing the fruit chunks and leaned her hands on the counter, her shoulders sagged and her head dropped, a blue plastic spoon clutched in her right hand so tightly that her knuckles were white. She said nothing. Jack didn't see where the remote had ended up, but saw that the tall plastic trash can's lid was up and had a pretty good guess. From upstairs, he could hear Claire talking to herself as she often did before she drifted off to sleep, happily oblivious that Pop was losing his marbles. Her voice was soft and far away, and held an innocence that could only mean she didn't know that daddy should soon be wrapped giggling in a sheet on his way to a padded room somewhere and the peace of mind dulling, psychiatric drug therapy. Jack waited a moment then cleared his throat nervously.

"Baby?"

Pam turned around slowly, the blue spoon still clutched in her hand, fruit syrup dripping onto the linoleum floor. Jack shifted his weight nervously and looked at his feet. How could he make her understand? Pam sighed heavily, her eyes red and her cheeks wet with tears.

Jack's chest tightened when she dropped the plastic spoon to the floor and covered her face with her hands, fruit cocktail syrup smearing on her cheeks. Her body shook and so he walked heavily across the kitchen towards his crying wife and took her into his arms. Pam pressed tightly against him and laid her head against his chest, still crying. Not sure what to say or what else to do, he just rocked her gently. After a moment she pushed softly away from him and turned her anxious eyes up to meet his. Her beautiful face looked frightened and eager for comfort. Jack kissed her forehead and she closed her red eyes again.

"It's gonna be okay, Pam," he said and closed his own eyes, hoping he sounded more convincing than he felt. He opened his eyes and saw she watched him expectantly.

"I'm sorry, baby," she said, her voice full of anguish and fear. "I'm so sorry, Jack. I'm just very scared and confused." Pam gripped Jack's hands tightly in her own. She blinked the tears from her eyes.

Here it comes.

"Baby," she said, then paused and sighed heavily. "Jack, I need you to do something for me." Her eyes held his.

"Anything," Jack said as he stroked her cheek, reading his lines and playing his role perfectly.

"Please, Jack," she sobbed a little again. "I want you to see someone, a counselor or something. Please, baby. I'm so scared for you. Please, let's go and see someone. Someone you can talk to." Pam leaned against her husband, not able to look him in the eyes anymore.

"Ok," Jack sighed heavily. "Ok, Pam. I will. I promise I will."

He knew it wouldn't help. What in the hell would he say? How could he possibly explain to a stranger how he felt, the awful things he saw in his sleep, and sometimes even when he was awake. How he could tell them things he couldn't even tell his wife? He realized Pam was still talking.

"…therapist. Or maybe a psychiatrist. I heard about this on *Good Morning America*. Post stress, or something, it was called. It's from all the shit on the TV. All the horrible things right in our living room." She held his face in both her hands now, looking at him, her eyes pleading.

"No," Jack said and pulled away a bit. Pam's eyes filled with tears again. "Not a shrink. I…I…Pam, I couldn't tell this to a stranger. I need…" he sighed heavily. "Maybe the battalion surgeon."

Pam's face wrinkled in confusion.

"The battalion…" Jack realized his mistake. "Our doctor," he corrected. "Our primary care guy?"

"Oh," she said leaning back against the counter. She unconsciously wiped syrup from her sticky hands onto her jeans. "Doctor Barton," she said and her eyes locked on his again. "Soon, Jack?" she asked, her voice unsure.

"I'll call tomorrow," Jack said and turned away, leaning an arm against the wall. Pam came up from behind him and wrapped her arms around him again, hugging her head against his back.

"Thank you, Jack," she said. "I love you so much."

"I love you, too, baby," he answered without turning around. He thought of Claire, by now asleep in her bed. "I love you both so much."

Chapter
7

He slept soundly—or at least he had no memories of dreams—but he woke up tired and achy, his muscles tense like he had slept curled up in a knot. His hands, in particular, were sore and he saw that he had deep purple, crescent-shaped bruises in his palms from where his nails must have dug into his flesh. He dumped his pale, sweet coffee into the sink and filled a travel mug to the brim with steaming black coffee before he headed out to his car, kissing his daughter and wife on his way out.

"I love you," Pam said, her voice tense with worry. Jack felt her eyes studying his face from her seat beside Claire, a spoonful of oatmeal in her hand.

"I know," he answered tightly. "Me, too." He wanted to give her more, to say something magic to erase her anxious look, but he had nothing.

He drove to work listening to a Dierks Bentley CD, trying to think about the words to the songs—anything other than the images of Fallujah that flashed in his tortured mind. Instead the images became a slide show set to country music.

Bentley sang about a hot girl in a tank top...

Click.

Kindrich, his brain blown out the back of his head, his face frozen in surprise.

Bentley wanted to kiss the hot chick...

Click.

Simmons lying in the dirt beside him, his face a gory mess of missing skin and bone. That horrible, one remaining eye staring at nothing, the other socket a ragged oversized black hole.

Bentley wondered what the hell he had been thinking...

Jack knew what the fuck he was thinking. He was thinking about how it felt to be starved for air, sucking too little air through a bloody hole in his neck. The terror of not being able to lift his arms, the feel of dust on his face and in his lungs, and the sound of a Blackhawk, kicking up dirt around him.

Thump thump thump thump...

The sound of a horn made him open his eyes. Green light. His hands were tight and white knuckled on the steering wheel and his palms ached. He pulled through the intersection and ignored the angry face of the driver pulling around him, mouthing the word "asshole" as he sped by, his middle finger up in an irritated salute.

Jack mashed the forward button on the CD player, tired of thinking about what he was thinking and where the night might lead. Dierks slowed it down with an angry tune about throwing his girlfriend's love letters into the river and flipping over his mattress. He wanted to be able to burn the pictures in his head and get on with his life, too.

I hear ya' Dierks. I hear ya', buddy.

His first two periods went by in a blur. He felt distracted, but able to keep a train of thought loosely focused on his lesson plans. His students seemed unusually sedate and asked few questions, doubtless reading the heavy mood of one of their favorite teachers. Chad came by in between to make sure his friend was ok, and seemed somewhat satisfied with Jack's reassurances that he felt much better. Jack told him he was heading to the doctor later "just to be sure." Chad said he would check on a sub for his last class so Jack wouldn't have to come back after his free period.

Third period started out normal enough. Jack was talking away about how DNA wrote out recipes for the cell to make things they needed, and how RNA carried the recipes in code to the "kitchen" workers, so that they would make the right stuff. He enjoyed his lesson, actually, and relaxed just a bit as he let his mind focus on cell biology, a nice break from the war in Iraq.

Halfway through, Jack felt a growing sense of dread that he couldn't explain. Something was going to happen, something bad. His mouth became suddenly dry and he couldn't stop his eyes from frequently scanning the back of the room. He pushed on with his lesson and forced his eyes to his notes and his mind to the cycles of the cell.

Something is coming. Something bad.

"We're coming for you, Sar'n," Simmons' boyish voice told him, clear as a bell. In his head, right? Jack scanned the room again, his eyes full of terror. He had stopped in midsentence. His students shifted uncomfortably, looking around the room to see what had taken their teacher's attention and, from the look in his eyes, filled him with fear. They saw nothing and so they looked at each other with growing discomfort.

Sar'n? a sleepy voice asked.

"Yes?" Jack answered to no one, his voice cracking.

Come back, Sar'n. You belong here with us. Don't leave us, Casey.

The voice came from nowhere and everywhere. Jack dropped his hands to his sides, his lesson plans fluttering to the floor. He stared intently at the door in back of the room. Was there movement?

As he watched in horror, his pulse pounding in his temples, a figure passed by the doorway in slow motion. He was dressed in filthy Marine digital desert cammie pants and a torn green T-shirt. Dog tags danced on his thin chest as he walked, limping slightly. He paused briefly in the doorway and turned to Jack, smiling. As he turned, Jack saw that the other side of his face was gone; a black bloody hole gaped at him where the eye and cheek should have been. The smile ended halfway across his face in a twisted mass of scattered teeth and bone. Simmons winked with his one remaining eye and raised a thumb in greeting.

"Hey, Sarge," he croaked with a thick, black tongue, his missing lips turning "Sarge" into "Sarze." When he did, dark blood spilled out over his dirty chin and spattered onto his T-shirt. Two teeth twisted loose and fell out of his deformed mouth, which he caught easily in the palm of his dirty hand. He shrugged, embarrassed, popped them back into his mouth like hard candy, and then shuffled on, disappearing past the doorway. Jack felt a dusty wind swirl around him, and coughed as the dirt filled his mouth. He looked up towards the sound of the Blackhawk passing overhead and saw, without much surprise, that the ceiling had swirled its way into a purple sky. He heard the *whump* of an outbound mortar shell, and then seconds later the loud explosion of the shell as it found its mark. Jack dropped instinctively to the ground, balanced on one knee, an arm over his head.

The room tilted nauseatingly to the left, and Jack struggled back to his feet and steadied himself on the desk in front of him. Then he pushed back, stumbled, and fell painfully to his knees again. He scrambled back to his feet and bolted to the door. As he passed the first row of students, his hip slammed into the corner of a desk, sending a textbook and sheets of handwritten notes to the floor and nearly knocking the young girl there out of her seat. Jack continued on, oblivious to the muted scream of the student, and gripped the doorframe with a hand as he skidded past it into the hallway. His eyes darted back and forth as he looked for the dead Marine he knew would be there.

Empty.

But he heard a click as the door at the end of the hall snapped shut. Jack sprinted full speed down the hall and slammed his full weight into the horizontal bar across the door, twisting his right wrist painfully as he did. The door exploded open and Jack found himself outside in the cold air. He panted and his eyes darted around, searching in all directions for the corpse of his friend.

"Simmons," he hollered.

But there was nothing there. No one. The sounds of gunfire and yelling faded quickly away, and he heard only the sounds of traffic on the street beyond the thin tree line around the school. Jack dropped in a heap to the sidewalk, sitting Indian-style on the cold concrete, and began to sob.

He had no idea how long he sat there. A fairly long time, he thought, long enough for him to begin shivering from the cold, and for his tailbone to start aching from the hard concrete. He didn't have a single linear thought. Instead he had a series of disjointed and emotional thoughts, which alternated between the terror of what had just happened, guilt over how all of this was affecting Pam—and doubtless soon Claire—and extreme anxiety over what it all meant. He was vaguely aware that the school door opened twice; he heard the hushed murmur of voices, and then it closed again.

His most consuming thought was the debate over what was real. He felt most terrified by the way his mind kept insisting that it was Casey—and Kindrich, and Simmons—who were real. That would make him the lie, right? His life here, his job, and his home were the fantasy. His brain whispered to him that the horror of his nightmares, that Simmons walking past with his face blown off, that his dying as Casey Stillman, in the dirt in a street in Iraq, were all real. That thought instilled in him the most horrifying fear he could imagine.

Worse than being fucking insane?

That was a close contest, actually.

When his shivering became uncontrollable and his ass ached past the point of being ignored, he struggled slowly to his feet, wrapped his arms tightly around himself for warmth, and sighed. Then he turned to the door, opened it slowly, and went back inside.

Time to face the music.

His classroom was empty except for Chad, the school nurse (a gigantic, sweaty woman who always looked pissed off about something) and, of course, Stuart Anderson, the John F. Kennedy High School principal. They clearly argued about something, but fell silent immediately when Jack walked in. Chad rose at once and came to the door, wrapping his arm around Jack's shoulders.

"How are you, buddy?" Chad spoke slowly, like you might to an Alzheimer's patient who has just had yet another stroke, or a child who you knew was destined for long rides on a short bus to the special classes in the trailer behind the school.

"I'm fine, Chad," Jack said patiently, fighting the urge to shove him violently to the ground. "Where's my class?"

"Well," Anderson began, and then cleared his throat. "We had to send them down to join Ms. Gillespie's class, Jack. But that was quite a while ago. It's well into the lunch period now."

Jack pursed his lips and nodded his head slowly. Of course, his look said. That would be the prudent thing when the biology teacher totally loses his shit in front of 35 teenagers.

Off to Ms. Gillespie's class, kids. We'll come get you after we are done picking up your teacher's marbles and packing them in a ziplock baggie for the trip to the loony bin. Hurry up now! And don't step on Simmons' bloody tooth, there.

Chad led him gently to a chair, flipped up the half desk, and helped Jack slide into the seat. One more helpful hand from his friend and Jack decided he might break his jaw.

Mr. Anderson watched him uncomfortably, arms crossed as he leaned back against Jack's desk. Nurse Cratchett (Jack had no idea of her real name, and couldn't have cared less) stood sweating the chronic perspiration of the morbidly obese and looked disinterestedly at her fingernails. Her face said she had seen it all before in her long career in health care.

Doubt it, Jack thought. *If you knew what the hell you were doing you'd be able to get a real job instead of pushing thermometers into kids' rectums with your fat sausage fingers.*

Mr. Anderson cleared his throat nervously.

"Jack," he began and then paused. He shook his head and uncrossed his arms, apparently preferring to pace. "What's been going on, Jack?"

Not much. Just a little unnerved by the dead kid who dropped by for a visit. And how the fuck are you?

"I've been pretty sick, Mr. Anderson." Jack began. No problem convincing them of that. Jack knew his face must be pale, his hands trembled, and he figured he looked like he might pass out at any minute. "I apologize for the little problem here. I think I spiked a fever," he shot a glance at Nurse Cratchett.

Don't get your hopes up, Nightingale.

"And I felt like I was going to pass out. The whole room was coming in on me, and I guess I just needed to get out." Jack sighed heavily and gave Anderson his best 'I'm way too sick to go to school today, Mom'look.

Anderson looked skeptical and stopped his stroll across the room. He put a hand to his chin and looked at Jack critically, dissecting him with his eyes.

"Everything okay at home, Jack?"

Jack started at that, and looked indignant, which wasn't hard. Still he had to be careful here.

"Everything is fine with Pam and Claire, sir. I truly have been very sick. I actually have an appointment with my doctor today." Jack looked at Chad, hoping for confirmation.

"We already arranged a sub for his afternoon periods, Stu," Chad chimed in on cue.

"Look," Jack said as he wiped perspiration from his forehead. "I really am sorry. It was a mistake to come to work feeling as shitty as I do. I just didn't want the class to get behind." He held Anderson's doubtful look. The principal's gaze softened. In fact, he looked relieved.

Just sick. Not nuts. Thank God.

"Well, no apology necessary, Jack. We just want to be sure you're okay." He looked stern again. "But go home, Jack. Rest up for the doctor's appointment. And stay home until you are well enough to be here."

Anderson walked over to Jack and clapped him gently on the back.

"Try and take care of yourself, Jack. No one is indispensable for just a few days. But we can't afford to lose anyone for the year."

A threat or just worry?

Anderson glanced at Cratchett, his look signaling her that they were done, and the two walked out. The nurse gave him a once over as she passed. Then she looked away impassively and followed the principal out, leaving the door open behind her.

Chad stayed behind, watching Jack with genuine concern. Jack met his eyes for a moment, but then his eyes fell.

"I've got to find my students and explain what happened," Jack said.

"Jack, I'll take care of it. We're interchangeable to those kids."
He smiled. "How about if I call Pam to come and get you?"

Jack shook his head.

"No, please don't, Chad." The thought of Pam hearing this
story was frankly more than he could stand. "I don't want her to
worry. I took some Tylenol for the fever. Give me a half hour to
get my stuff together and leave a lesson plan for the sub, then I'll
be a good boy and head home. And Chad…" Jack held his friend's
eyes with a pleading look. "Please don't say anything about this to
Pam. She's pissed enough that I refused to go to the doctor on the
weekend."

Chad laughed.

"Women!" he exclaimed, relieved that his friend seemed to be
himself. Then he left and closed the door behind him.

Jack slumped down in the little chair. What the hell was he
going to do? He sure as hell couldn't go home. What would he say
to his wife? That dead Simmons walked by his class and made
him lose his shit, scaring the hell out of a room full of kids?
Should he tell her that the ceiling had spun into a purple sky, that
he could taste the dust and feel the grit on his teeth?

Not a chance. He would instead stop by the Starbucks out on
Route 143 for coffee and a snack, and wait for his appointment
with Dr. Barton.

They had a TV there, didn't they?

Chapter
8

The coffee house had a TV, but it was tuned to some ridiculous talk show where two middle-aged women chatted about being middle-aged women with semi-celebrities. Jack ate a plain croissant chased with two cups of black coffee, and sat in a corner alone with his thoughts. He mostly thought of how and what to tell Dr. Barton about what was going on with him and, frankly, that scared the shit out of him.

What if Barton told him he was crazy? Jack sure as hell couldn't tell him, their family doctor, that he was having waking hallucinations—visions of dead buddies he never actually knew stalking him at school. That would be a one-way trip to inpatient therapy, locked in a room and heavily sedated. Sane people just didn't chase dead Marines down the hall in front of kids they were entrusted to teach.

You belong with us, Casey. Come back Sar'n. We need you.

Jack felt the shudder which was becoming way too familiar.

Jack tossed back the last lukewarm swallow of coffee and headed back to his car, parked on the street in front of the coffee house. Worse than the short drive to Dr. Barton's office was the wait in the clean waiting room. After signing his name on the clipboard at the front desk, Jack settled into an uncomfortable vinyl-covered chair. Fidgeting in his seat, Jack flipped through a *Woman's Day* magazine, afraid that *Time* or *Newsweek* would contain an article or picture from the war that would flood him with images, or worse, bring his friend back for a visit. It wouldn't help his cause to lose his shit in the waiting room, to scream at invisible ghosts in front of the woman with a two year old in her lap. He looked over at the old man who stared at him suspiciously. Jack smiled at him uncomfortably but the man turned away and then coughed and spit green snot into a handkerchief, which he wrapped up carefully and slipped back into his jacket pocket like it was some valuable gem. Jack glanced back into his lap at the article about coping with period depression (*I should have your problems, lady*), his leg bouncing up and down nervously.

Barton greeted him like an old friend, although he had probably only met the doctor a handful of times and couldn't really remember the last time he had been here. It seemed strange, but the young doctor really did feel like a friend of sorts, and Jack relaxed as they chatted about Pam and how great little Claire was doing. They sat beside each other in plastic chairs, Jack avoiding sitting up on the exam table like an actual patient. Finally Barton plunged in.

"So what's up, Jack?" he asked, a friendly hand on Jack's shoulder.

As he knew he would, Jack kept the school encounter with Simmons and the anxiety attack from last Friday to himself. He confessed to the nightmares and admitted that they haunted him during the day. It seemed more okay to be haunted by nightmares about bloody corpses than by *actual* bloody corpses, right? He told Barton about the anxiety he felt, and even his burning need to watch the news, hoping to catch images of the war, knowing it would fill him with fear. He didn't mention that he was hoping to hear the names of the dead from Fallujah, and his certainty that he would recognize those names. No sense in pushing it.

Jim Barton ("Relax, Jack. Call me Jim"…yeah, like that would help) reassured him that his anxieties were not unique, and that many people were deeply affected by the war that flooded into their lives through newspapers and TV (Katie Couric nodded knowingly in his mind). He was not the only one who had trouble coping with those images. Barton claimed to have several patients with similar nightmares.

Any of them getting visits from theirs at work?

Doc Barton told him that it was a "bit" out of his field and gave him a referral to "a good friend of mine, really good at this stuff." He also gave him a prescription for Effexor to help with the anxiety.

"Isn't that an antidepressant?"

"Well, yes, but we use it for lots of other things, too."

Yeah, right.

The other prescription was for Ambien to help him sleep.

"Ambien won't disrupt the normal sleep and dream patterns, Jack. You'll rest, but won't feel hung over in the morning."

Jimmy definitely didn't get it. He could get to sleep just fine, thanks very much. The truth was he didn't want to sleep. Not tonight. Not ever again. He was terrified by the thought of falling asleep.

Got a pill for that?

The Doctor put his arm around Jack's shoulders just like Chad had done—maybe like everyone did when they thought they were dealing with the deeply disturbed—and showed him politely out of the exam room.

"Hey, thanks for everything, Doc...I mean Jim."

"No problem, Jack. Just try and relax and make sure and call Dr. Lewellyn today. I'll call him, as well, so he'll see you right away."

Jack shook the offered hand and hurried out of the office. Then he sat in his car with the engine running and Today's Country blaring on the radio for nearly twenty minutes, tears running down his face, his prescriptions wrinkled and clutched in his fist.

On the radio, Dierks Bentley seemed excited to see where the night might lead.

Fuck you, Dierks!

He pulled out of the crowded parking lot and headed home, with a quick stop at the Rite Aid.

Jack walked into his house with his very best forced smile and "everything is fine now" look on his face. He had a small white paper bag, full of little oral bullet solutions to all his problems, clutched in his right hand. He realized he held the bag unconsciously out in front of him like he was carrying a little bag of dog shit, and dropped his hand to his side, trying to look more relaxed. He was greeted by his smiling little girl (gratefully oblivious to Daddy's slipping sanity) and his beautiful wife, her forced smile in no way masking the concern in her eyes. Jack dropped his bag of cure on the coffee table as he hugged his wife and kissed Claire on the forehead.

"Hey, guys," he said. Pam held him a moment longer than usual.

"Hey, baby, how was your day?"

Did Dr. Barton purge your demons? Did he rescrew your head on?

"Okay," Jack answered as he collapsed onto the couch, fingers pulling on his tie. Pam dropped Claire into Daddy's lap, her squirming feet kicking into the soft spot in his crotch and earning her a painful grunt instead of a hug.

"Kisses, Daddy…MMMMM…MAAAAAAA!" Her mouth was wet on his cheek and smelled of fruit cocktail. It was wonderful in a way that only a parent would understand.

"Kisses, Claire Bear," Jack responded, kissing his baby on her soft cheek. He looked up at his wife, who watched him tentatively, not wanting to ask. Jack shifted Claire to his knee and unconsciously blocked another foot shot to his package.

"Well, good news," Jack said more casually than he felt. He Eskimo kissed Claire, who giggled. "Daddy's not crazy, little buddy."

Pam grimaced. "No one thought you were crazy, Jack," she said, shaking her head as she joined him on the couch. "What did Dr. Barton have to say?"

"Well, you were right, baby. Doc says he has several patients with this same problem. He says that it's a reaction to the flood of war images coming into the house, just like you said." Claire grabbed his nose. Jack kissed her little fingers gently.

"Noze," she said.

"That's right, buddy! Nose—Daddy's nose." He looked at Pam, who waited patiently for more.

"He gave me some head-shrinker pills to help me with the anxiety, and some sleeping pills." Jack felt his left eye tick a bit at that. Pam nodded and waited for more.

"He thinks that will help?" Her voice sounded full of hope.

"Yep! Says it will." Jack kissed Claire on the ear. "Ear—Claire Bear's ear!"

"Air," she answered, delighted. Jack continued.

"He's also got me an appointment with a Dr. Lewellyn, a friend of his who kind of specializes in this sort of thing." Pam hugged her husband tightly and Claire squirmed to hug them both.

"Thank you, baby," Pam sighed, her relief palpable.

"Thank you, honey," Jack answered, breaking the group hug and kissing his wife gently on the mouth, tickling her upper lip with his tongue. "Thanks for sticking by me."

Pam chuckled a light "don't be silly" chuckle.

"Yeah, well, I guess I love you a bit," she said, kissing him on the forehead. "You can pick your friends, but you're stuck with your family." She rose from the couch to head for the kitchen, and Jack grabbed her hand. She turned to face him and he looked her in the eyes deeply.

"Seriously, Pam. Thank you. I love you so much."

Pam closed her eyes gently, embarrassed by the attention, then looked back at her husband.

"I love you too, Jack." She squeezed his hand and headed for the kitchen.

Jack held his daughter up in front of him, her legs kicking joyfully in the air.

"Belly!" he announced and pressed his lips to his little girl's soft tummy, blowing a ripping belly fart.

"Beddy! Beddy!" Claire answered, squealing with delight. Jack hugged her tight and his gaze fell on the little bag on the coffee table. He closed his eyes tightly, his face changing to a grimace.

"Love you, Bear," he said. He held his little girl and tried desperately to ignore the subtle smell of Iraqi dust and the far off sound of gunfire.

* * *

Maybe the Effexor helped. It sure as hell wasn't the Ambien, which Jack had taken from the pillow where Pam had left it for him, and flushed it down the crapper—feeling a twang of guilt—when he went for his pre-bed piss and brush. Whatever it was, he had slept the dreamless sleep of the righteous, that was for sure. In fact, he awoke in the exact same position he had drifted off to sleep in, his back aching and his throat dry, like waking up after a second bottle of wine before bed.

Jack had slept well, but he realized he hadn't slept long. Before slipping into a deep sleep, he lay in bed staring in the dark at the shadowy shape of the spinning ceiling fan for several hours, begging the night not to let it morph into the powerful blades of a UH-60 Blackhawk. He lay still in the dark, not wanting to disturb his sleeping wife, who had watched him quietly for a while before falling off to sleep, her arm across his chest, her leg across his waist. He had nearly woken her up after the first hour, thinking the distraction and subsequent relaxation of wild sex might help take his mind away from his dread of sleep and what the night might hold in store for him. In the end he had concentrated instead on the rhythmic musical snore that only sexy women can pull off, and thoughts of his pretty little girl, sleeping the deep sleep of the innocent down the hall. And then somewhere in the night he had drifted off to sleep.

He woke ten minutes before his alarm, glancing at the clock and silencing it before it could shake the quiet with its jarring whine. Pam had rolled on her other side sometime in their slumber, and he rolled stiffly onto his own side and wrapped his arms around her, feeling the soft curve of her hip against him in all the right ways. He pressed gently against her, feeling a comfortable stirring, and she squeezed his arm.

"Mmmmm," she sighed. "I guess I know how you are feeling." She rocked her hips backwards against him, and he pressed into her again, his hand pulling her into him as he caressed her belly gently. Pam rolled over to face him, raising her head to look at the time. Satisfied with what she saw, she pulled his hand down between her soft thighs, which she opened slightly, and closed her eyes. "How'd you sleep, baby?" she asked, her own hand now drifting slowly down his hip, then turning inward.

"Great, actually," he answered honestly, then closed his eyes and moaned as her hand found her way to him. He rolled over onto his back at her gentle urging, and she straddled him, pulling her nightgown up over her head.

*****

While Pam went to start the coffee, her face glowing and happy, dressed in one of his T-shirts and a pair of postsex "granny panties" (as she called them), Jack went to get Claire. She had started cooing for them and talking to herself before they had finished making love.

"Daddy!" she announced as he picked her up from her crib.

"Hey, big girl," Jack said as he laid her on the footrest of the rocker and pulled off her damp pull-up. He dressed her in his favorite outfit, big girl Levi's and a pink Polo pullover. He loved how much she looked like Pam dressed like that. Then, he swept her up and carried her downstairs.

He walked into the kitchen with his baby in his arms, tugging on his "Air," and was greeted by the smell of fresh coffee and frying bacon. He came up behind Pam and playfully reached under the oversized T-shirt, squeezing her gently.

"Jack!" Pam laughed. "My lord, man of mine, are you never satisfied?"

"I am ALWAYS satisfied," he answered, kissing her neck and then turning to put Claire in her high chair. "Each and every time. That's what keeps me coming back." He winked at her and she blushed. Jack poured himself a cup of coffee, aware in a detached way that he added nothing to it, and then sat at the table beside Claire.

"What's with the big breakfast, honey?" He glanced at his watch. "I don't think I really have time. I'm running a little late already."

Pam slid a bowl of cereal with milk and a baby spoon in front of him.

"Not anymore, baby," she said, turning back to her stove and carefully flipping the sizzling slice of bacon. "Stuart Anderson called and asked how you were feeling. I said fine, but he said to tell you to take one more day, that they already had a sub."

Jack felt his face flush red with embarrassment and guilt. He waited for the inevitable question, but it didn't come. He turned to look at Pam, fully anticipating an expectant stare, but instead she was happily whipping eggs and milk together in a bowl. When she turned to him, she looked content.

"You want cheese in your eggs?"

"Sure," he answered. He was about to say something, anything about what happened at school, and then another thought occurred to him. "I didn't hear the phone ring," he said instead.

"Huh?" Pam turned to him, her face confused, then smoothed out with realization. "Oh, the call. Yeah, I was on the phone with Bev when he called, and I clicked over." She sprinkled grated cheese over the cooking eggs.

Jack sat quietly for a moment, feeding spoonfuls of cereal into his daughter's mouth with little thought.

"Those nightmares really had me spooked at school," he started. He had to say something, right? Pam said nothing, but still seemed all right, folding his omelet over on itself. "I couldn't stop thinking about them. Anyway, Chad and Stuart both noticed, and I guess I told them I was sick. I didn't know what else to say." He looked up at Pam now, milk dripping from the little spoon onto the table. Claire strained to reach the bite but failed. Pam slid the omelet onto a plate, cut it in half and slid one half onto a second plate. Then she added strips of bacon and toast to both. She slid one in front of him and sat down beside him in front of the other.

"Bev was going to watch Claire at her house for a while, so I could go shopping." She poured some juice into an empty glass in front of Jack. "Since you're home today, do you want to watch Claire, or go to the store with me?" Apparently his wife was unconcerned by his in-school breakdown. Or maybe Anderson had not told her much. Either way, Jack felt relieved.

Jack decided to go shopping with Pam. Rarely did they get much time just the two of them these days, and Jack thought it might be fun to hang out together like old times—maybe grab lunch out somewhere nice. Pam was delighted by that idea, and started planning their morning outing while he fed Claire and nibbled at his breakfast, still distracted by the lack of reaction his wife had to the news he had left school "sick" yesterday. In the end he decided he was married to the greatest woman in the universe (a fact he'd long suspected) and let it go from his mind, instead getting excited by the thought of an adult day together.

They spent the early morning playing with their daughter, sitting together in a circle on the living room floor and going through a picture book learning the names of animals. Claire fussed a little at being dropped off at Pam's friend's house, but the novelty of the attention from Beverly's two older girls distracted her enough to keep her from crying. Then they headed to the mall, where Pam told Jack they were going to find him some new slacks and shirts.

Jack was not generally a shopping kind of guy, but he had to admit he had a great time. They cruised around the mall and Jack chatted comfortably with his wife about everything and nothing. The morning flew by. He particularly enjoyed sitting in the comfortable armchair outside the dressing room at Hecht's, watching his beautiful wife playfully model outfit after outfit, while he looked her up and down. He delivered the deciding thumbs up or thumbs down to each look, like a Roman emperor deciding the fate of each gladiator. Those outfits condemned to death were piled up on a counter, while Jack got the job of collecting the growing pile of survivors in his lap. He loved the way she flirted with him while she strutted and spun in front of him in each new look.

They ended up at Bennigan's for lunch, where Jack ordered a beer and Pam a glass of wine. She expressed a fleeting moment of concern, asking Jack if he was allowed to drink on his medication. Jack assured her Dr. Barton had not said anything about any restrictions.

"I guess we'll find out, huh?" he laughed, taking a big slug of cool beer from his frosted Pilsner mug. He didn't have a seizure and his head didn't explode, so he guessed he was all right. Together they looked over the menu, planning their meals together so they could share them, like they almost always did.

"Surf and turf," Jack announced. And so Pam ordered the skewered shrimp and he the blackened New York strip. They also split a salad and soup and both managed to consume another drink as they ate from each other's plates. They talked and laughed like they had when they were dating and the time flew by. When the waitress came to clear their plates, Jack felt warm and relaxed, mostly from the company of his one true love (as he liked to remind her, even now) and partly from the two 16-ounce beers. Jack began to feel a surge of hope that his cynicism towards Dr. Barton's "magic bullet" had been unfounded. He sure as shit felt great right now, and he had slept through the night hadn't he? Jack saw that Pam stared at him, trying to read his look.

"Don't worry, baby," Jack said before she could ask. "I was honestly just thinking how great I feel." He squeezed Pam's hand, and she responded by putting her hand warmly on his knee.

"You do seem more your old self, Jack." She kissed him on the cheek.

"Yeah, well, I *am* having a lunch date with my one true love," he answered.

"And playing hooky," Pam laughed.

"Yeah," Jack agreed. "That helps too. I guess ol' quack Barton knows something after all." He paused for a moment and then looked her deeply in the eyes again. "Thank you for making me go, Pam."

Pam looked down. "Hey, I was just trying to get a good night's sleep."

The waitress came back, looking a little uncomfortable at interrupting. "Anything else?"

"Nothing for me," Jack answered, "but the lady would like a piece of raspberry cheesecake with two forks, and two coffees with Bailey's."

Pam shook her head in mock embarrassment and wrapped her arms around his.

"You are a bad man."

Jack kissed her full on the mouth, a long and passionate kiss that made Pam look around, her embarrassment more real now.

"Jack!"

"You love me because I'm a bad man," he said playfully.

They talked about going to a matinee at the mall, but instead headed home. Claire would be in midnap by now and they agreed to spend an hour or two at the house, just hanging out. They wound up lying together, arms wrapped around each other on the couch, one of Pam's favorite HGTV decorating shows on the television. After only a few minutes of watching total strangers make big changes to their homes on a shoestring budget, Jack's breathing deepened and he relaxed to the feel of Pam's fingers running lightly through his hair. He felt perfectly content.

Chapter
9

Jack had no idea how long he slept, but he awoke still tired and achy from being in one position too long. He was alone on the couch, a blanket across him, and his head at an awkward angle on a thin pillow against the armrest. He stretched his arms and rubbed his stiff neck, then sat up. The light from the kitchen had taken on a reddish hue, and Jack realized it must be close to dusk, his nap having lasted most of the afternoon.

"Pam?" Jack called out. He heard no movement from the kitchen and the TV was off. Jack rose and headed slowly to the kitchen. His mouth was dry and he became suddenly aware that he needed to pee. "Baby, are you here?"

No answer. She must have headed out to Beverly's to pick up Claire. Jack veered off course from the kitchen, the pressure in his bladder outweighing his thirst, and headed for the bathroom a few steps down the hall. He stepped into the dark room and unzipped his fly without turning on the light, his full bladder now calling to him with true urgency. Jack shifted uncomfortably back and forth as he fumbled with his boxers, and then aimed in the general direction of the can, hoping the lid was up. He was immediately gratified by the sound of urine hitting water, and smiled as his urgency dissipated, happy he wouldn't be cleaning piss off the floor and toilet lid. Relieved, Jack repacked his pants and zipped his fly, then turned to the sink to wash his hands.

His sight adjusted somewhat to the dim light from the hall. As he turned on the faucet, Jack found his eyes drawn to a peculiar dark pattern in the sink, shadows in the dim light playing tricks on his slowly acclimating vision. He rinsed his hands unconsciously, his mind fascinated by the changing dark pattern, swirling now in the water running off his hands. Suddenly Jack felt growing anxiety rise inside him to compete with his curiosity. Something wasn't right. His eyes remained locked on the changing patterns in the sink, his right hand groping behind him for the switch on the wall.

The light clicked on and Jack froze in terror. Swirling in the sink was dark blood, lightening in color as it mixed with the swirling water. The water was pink, backing up slowly in the sink, seeking an exit around the chunks of bone and grey tissue that collected around the drain. A scream stuck in his throat and came out instead as a high-pitched grunt. Jack became aware, in a detached way, that dark blood was spattered on the walls and mirror as well. He stumbled backwards and heard a nauseating crunch beneath his shoe. He looked down and lifted his foot slowly. Beneath it was a cracked and grimy tooth in a puddle of blood. He saw bloody footprints from his own feet in front of the toilet. Then his eyes were drawn to the toilet itself, his urine pink, mixed with blood; the seat spattered with drying blood and his own still wet piss.

As Jack backed slowly out of the horror show that was his bathroom, he became aware that his right hand was warm and sticky. The wall beside the light switch was thick with dark blood, and the switch plate had a dark handprint pressed in the gory liquid. As he looked at his hand coated with black blood, he stumbled over his own feet and fell backwards out of the bathroom, landing sharply on his ass in the hallway. The impact unlocked the scream trapped in his throat and he heard his own horrified voice echo throughout the house. Jack's feet kicked backwards, slipping in the trails of blood which extended out into the hall, and propelled him with a crunch into the wall behind him. Jack scrambled up the wall, his hands leaving more bloody prints on the clean plaster behind him. His shoulder sent a picture from the wall, Jack and Pam smiling behind the blue-eyed infant in front of them, crashing to the floor. The glass broke and exploded out of the frame. He remained in a crouch, his back pinned against the wall, unable to tear his eyes from the bloodied bathroom. Then he spun on one foot. He stumbled as he slipped again on the bloody floor, then caught himself and ran from the hallway to the kitchen, his right hand waving wildly in front of him.

His knees slammed painfully into the cabinets beneath the kitchen sink as he stuck his bloody hand beneath the faucet. His clean hand spun the handle madly until clear warm water spit out. He held his hand beneath the running water and watched the blood wash away, then swirl pink down the clean kitchen sink. He became aware of his own voice in his ears, a childlike chant escaping from his tightened throat.

"Nuh...nuh...nuh..." Jack closed his mouth to silence the sound. Then he felt his throat tighten, the vomit and bile trapped low down in his chest. The room started to spin, and he felt incredibly hot. Suddenly another thought gripped him.

Pam!

He spun around, frantically searching the room for evidence of his wife, terrified he would see her mangled body slumped against a wall.

"Pam!" he screamed, his throat still tight and burning. He felt the bile escape his chest and arrive in the back of his throat. He bent over in a spasm of coughing, hands on his knees. His stomach contracted painfully, and he vomited onto the clean linoleum floor. Chunks of blackened steak and skewered shrimp tumbled away from the liquid and slipped beneath the cabinets.

Large spatters of blood marched a trail across the kitchen floor and out the screen door, which he only now saw was open, and into the backyard. Jack stood up slowly, unaware that he still whimpered softly, puppy-like, and walked in a haze towards the open door. His eyes remained glued to the sticky droplets of drying blood, afraid to look up beyond the next spatter. The trail led down the brick steps and across the concrete patio. As he followed it slowly, tiptoeing carefully so as not to step on any of the large puddles of half-dried blood, he noticed something in the middle of one sticky pool. He poked it gently with the toe of one shoe. A bloody tooth stuck to his shoe, causing him to shake his foot back and forth until the tooth flipped free. It pinged against the gas grill and then flipped into a bush along the side of the patio. Jack kept his head down and wiped his toe along the patio, trying to smear the blood from his shoe, his efforts painting a reddish-purple pattern of modern art on the concrete.

"Hey, Sar'n," a raspy voice said.

Jack froze, his leg bent, his foot in midsmear. His head stayed down, but his eyes darted back and forth in panic. Then he raised his head and turned towards the sound of the voice.

Just past the edge of the patio, Simmons sat Indian-style in the grass (*criss-cross apple sauce*, Pam would say to Claire). His dirty green T-shirt was spattered with fresh blood, which trickled down his chin and dripped off into his lap. He was bent over, his attention on an open khaki bandana in his lap. He poked at something on it with one finger. Jack walked over, arms hanging limply by his sides. When he got within a few feet, he stopped, and Simmons stopped his prodding at whatever was in his lap. Jack saw that the bandana was bloody and that Simmons' fingertips glistened with blood as well.

At first Simmons didn't look up, but a grin spread across his face, revealing bloody teeth. He turned his head to face Jack, revealing his missing eye and the side of his face missing flesh and bone. The ragged teeth Jack remembered from the hallway at school were gone. The missing cheek and lips left a gory hole which revealed only ragged gums.

"Jush gettin' my shish together, Sar'n," Simmons said. The horrible, gaping hole flapped ragged flesh as he spoke. He held up his bloody bandana, which Jack now saw contained a half-dozen ragged bloody teeth. "Droppin' like fly'sh," he laughed. Then he was wracked with a rattling cough, fresh blood spraying out onto his desert cammie pants and boots. Jack stood motionless, unable to speak or move.

"Sit down," Simmons said, gesturing with a dirty hand, his fingertips coated in blood like he had taken a gory pedicure soak ("You know you're soaking in it," Madge said from the old TV commercial). With his missing face his words came out "shit down."

Jack felt bile rise again in his throat, but instead of barfing he belched a wet acidic burp. He felt himself pale and he began to sway gently, overcome with dizziness. He felt sure he would pass out. Finally he spoke, his voice a harsh whisper.

"Nightmare..." he said. That felt right. Jack closed his eyes tightly and willed himself to wake up. He opened his eyes, but Simmons still sat there, grinning too widely. He opened the side of his mouth that could close and laughed a choking, raspy laugh, which spilled more dark blood onto his chin. He reached his fingertips into his mouth, pulled out another ragged tooth, and considered it critically for a moment. The left side of his mouth frowned, the right side grinned a ghoulish, jack-o-lantern grin of bloody gums.

"Shun of a bitsh, eh Sar'n?"

Jack closed his eyes again, his fists balled up at his sides.

Wake up, goddamnit! Wake up!

* * *

Jack sat up, his eyes wide open and his hands still tight fists. He was in his bed, the room dark and his body soaked in a cool sweat. His eyes darted madly around, but he saw nothing, unable to penetrate the darkness which engulfed him. He was aware of the sleeping figure beside him—heard Pam's deep rhythmic breathing. Jack had no memory of coming to bed, or any other part of the evening. He remembered falling asleep on the couch, the horrible nightmare about Simmons, and now he was awake in bed in the middle of the night. It was dark and he was in bed with his wife.

What the fuck!

Jack felt tears spill down over his cheeks. The image of the bloody bathroom, the horror of Simmons in the yard, and his panicked confusion of waking up here in bed with no intervening memory—all combined to rob him of any remaining hope that his mind was under his own control. He cried out loud and his hand trembled as he searched out the light switch on the wall. But he found nothing. The reading lamp somehow escaped his grasp. He fumbled instead on the end table, found the lamp, and flipped the switch.

Jack sucked his breath in, making a high-pitched hissing whistle. He was lying on top of the covers, his naked chest and belly covered in sweat, mixed with dirt and drying blood. He wore dirty, desert cammie pants, bloused at the ankle over filthy tan combat boots. The covers beneath him were covered in sand and dust, which swirled around him in a light breeze. Jack held his breath in, frozen in terror. Then he reached beside him for his wife, but his hand froze in midair, above the shoulder of the sleeping figure.

The covers were pulled up nearly over the head of the body in bed with him, but he knew immediately that something was wrong. The sheet on the back of the motionless figure was soaked in blood, the circle growing as he watched. The breathing of his wife changed to a harsh, wet snore, and the body beneath the covers shook badly. Jack slowly reached out a trembling hand for the stained and dirty sheet. He saw his own hand was filthy with black grime beneath the broken fingernails. He wanted to stop his reach, but couldn't. The events unfolded outside of his control, and he watched in disbelief as his dirty hand grasped the corner of the sheet. He watched the shaking hand pull the cover slowly back to reveal what he already knew was there.

The back of the head was gone and a gaping hole stared back at him, rimmed with jagged white bone and ragged scalp. Inside the hole, reddish-grey brain matter gaped back at him. Blood spurted in little arcs from a small pumping blood vessel in the center of the gory crevice and onto the back of his hand, dripping in puddles onto the sheets.

Kindrich.

As he watched, his hand frozen in midair, clutching the sheet, the sand and dirt began to swirl around him, faster and faster like a growing cyclone. It became thicker, spinning a dirty tornado around his head which blinded and choked him. Jack looked up at the ceiling and saw, without much surprise, that it was gone. The bedroom walls remained in place, but opened into a purple sky above. The twisting sand grew thicker now and the dust obscured the sky, until he could see nothing except a wall of spinning sand, twisting around him faster and faster. The sand filled his mouth and lungs, suffocating him. He felt a burning grow in the center of his neck and then felt the bed get softer beneath him. He tried to scream, but there was no air. The bed disappeared beneath him entirely, and he collapsed slowly into the center of the swirling dirt. It sucked him downward and his hands clawed out, looking for something solid. But the downward pull became more violent, sucking him into the vortex of madly spinning sand. He felt his body begin to twist and spin in the cyclone of sand as he was pulled down farther and farther, like unseen hands pulled him into a spinning grave from below. His body whipped around in circles faster and faster, until finally the earth stopped twisting and swallowed him up. It closed in on top of him and he was buried beneath the now still sand.

And then it was still. And quiet.

And dark.

Like a grave.

* * *

Jack struggled to open his eyes again, fighting the darkness and the sense of being buried alive. Thick clouds of dust and sand swirled around him, kicked up by the blades of the helicopter. The blackness continued to envelop him, although he felt quite certain that his eyes were open now. He lay flat on his back, uncomfortable in his body armor. His Kevlar helmet was off, his head in the dirt, but he didn't really care. He was only vaguely aware of the sound of gunfire, like noise on a TV in another room. He could also hear voices and was aware of activity all around him. Someone held his hand. He could feel a horrible burning in the center of his throat and heard a raspy gurgle whenever he sucked in a breath.

"They're coming around this side."

"Clear that space as a path."

"Hold his head! Hold his head!"

"Corporal, light up that fucking window and silence that Hadji sniper!"

A burst of gunfire.

Screams in the distance.

"Dustoff in 3 minutes, sir!"

"Casey! Hang in there, bud. Helo's coming! ...Casey!"

Casey? He was unsure why that sounded wrong, somehow. He felt a squeeze from the hand in his and he tried to squeeze back, but couldn't be sure if he had. He saw spots of light in the dark—small, but bright. He felt that should mean something to him. He wiggled the fingers of his left hand and felt them move.

"That's good, Sar'n. I'm here, buddy. We're gonna get you out of here."

Casey tried again to talk, but his effort brought only frustration and more pain deep in his throat. This was all wrong. Casey thought of his wife. What would she be doing right now? What time was it there? Was it day or night at home? He wasn't sure. He only knew that he wanted desperately to be there. Where was the dusty tornado that was supposed to take him home? Casey was unsure what that meant, but it seemed both right and important.

Pam wanted him to get out of the Corps. She wanted him to go back to school with his GI Bill, and to stay at home with her and Claire. He remembered the tearful conversation, how she had said she would even go back to work if he wanted. But Casey couldn't imagine going to school, having his wife working, and a young child at home. Plus the Corps had become like a home. He loved being a Marine, especially now. Now he was a sergeant. Now he had a shot at making the Corps a real career. He had stood out as a leader, and the Corps had been there to let him try and reach his potential. How could he explain it to this woman, whom he loved so dearly, so completely? He wanted desperately to be at home with his girls, to sit with them, to watch them, to play with them. He hated being away—hated it more that he could ever make his one true love understand. But being a Marine was no longer what he did. It had become who he was. He couldn't imagine what he would be without the Corps, not anymore.

And here I am in this dusty-ass country, dying in the street seven thousand miles from home.

What had he done? How could he make her know? He loved them both so much. He had to get to them. He needed so much to tell them that he never loved anything more than them, but that he believed in what he did. That he did it for them as much as for the rest of the country. More. It was for them that he was fighting.

Pam, Claire…I love you so much!

"Bird's on the ground."

"Great." Doc's voice. HM2 White, the Navy corpsman. "Doc Barton on board?" Barton, the battalion surgeon.

"He's here."

Another squeeze on his hand. He felt so fucking weak, but squeezed back. His mouth was so dry. He wanted a drink of water—wanted it with desire bordering on hysteria. Casey blinked his eyes as he saw red lights approaching. Flashlights. Then there was a loud explosion, close this time, and he felt Doc White lean over him to keep the blowing dust from settling on his face.

"Shit! Jesus, where did that come from?"

"No! Goddamn it, no. Check left! Check left!"

He heard short bursts of M16A rifles, then the loud burp of a squad assault weapon letting loose a ten- or fifteen-round burst. There was shouting as well, farther away.

"Holy shit! How long has his neck been that big?"

Barton's voice? He felt fingers probe the left side of his neck, which sent a shocking burst of pain up into his jaw and head.

"Goddamn. Got the carotid artery for sure. If that thing lets loose we'll sure as hell lose him."

"Doc, he's awake. He can hear you."

"Sergeant Stillman? Casey? It's Doc Barton. You're gonna be ok, buddy." He felt a squeeze on his left shoulder, but was not reassured. Casey felt a strong terror growing inside him. He didn't want to die here in this shit hole. He didn't want to die at all.

"Pam...Claire," he mouthed the words but there was no sound. He had to get back to his family. He had to tell them how much he loved them. Casey felt the world getting dark again, felt again like he was tumbling, falling to the left. It was nauseating and he felt a horrible sharp pain grow in his left temple. He could also feel tears run out of his eyes and down his grimy cheeks.

I just want to go home. I want to go home to Pam and Claire. I just want to go home.

Then he felt himself being pulled down into a warm darkness, like the night was wrapping around him in a comfortable blanket.

Pam.

Chapter
10

"PAM!"

It was a bloodcurdling scream, and it came from his own throat. Jack sat up, clawing at the air. Again his heart pounded in his chest. Again he was bathed in sweat and his breathing came in harsh, raspy grunts. Again his eyes darted around madly, looking for his Marines, for Doc White, for Simmons, for the enemy.

The house was quiet as his scream faded away. It was light and he was on the couch, a blanket over his thighs, the TV off. He was home, home with Pam and Claire Bear. Jack got slowly and stiffly to his feet, letting the blanket fall to the floor in a heap. He walked to the hall bathroom and shuddered as a chill ran up his spine. The light in the bathroom was off, and he reached awkwardly around the corner searching for the switch, afraid to go inside until he found it and clicked it on.

Normal. No blood in the sink or on the walls. No grimy tooth on the floor. No urine or gore in the toilet. He felt a bit more calm and walked through the kitchen and found the back door closed. He looked cautiously out the window, lifting the frilly blue curtain with a finger. Nothing. No young Marine sat in his yard, grinning his toothless grin from his half face. No red trail.

Jack leaned his forehead against the window and enjoyed the cool on his face. Then he heard the front door open and felt a moment of growing panic. Simmons?

"Jack? Baby, we're home!"

Pam.

"Daddy!" Claire squealed as he walked as casually as possible into the living room.

"Hey, guys," he said, kissing Claire on the cheek, then Pam lightly on her lips.

Pam looked at him critically, concern again in her eyes.

"Are you ok, baby? You're pale."

"Fine, honey. I'm fine." He hugged his family tightly. Then pulled back and looked at his wife. "I just missed you guys."

Pam kissed his chin.

"We missed you, too, Jack." She placed Claire into his arms and he Eskimo kissed her, making her giggle. "I need to fix her dinner, okay?"

"Sure," he said. Pam frowned.

"You sure you're okay? Did you have a nightmare? You weren't watching the news channels were you?"

Jack squeezed her hand and they headed for the kitchen.

"No, baby. Just woke up and you weren't here. I'm great now."

Jack followed his wife into the kitchen, his baby girl warm in his arms. Thoughts of Iraq, of Simmons and Kindrich, of the horrible pain in his neck and throat, swirled around his head like ghosts. He did his best to shake them off, but felt their pull no matter what he tried.

His fantasy that all he needed was a pill in the mornings to dissolve the nightmares slipped through his fingers. He needed more—much more—if he was going to save his girls from this horror. Tomorrow he would take another day off. He would call this Dr. Lewellyn and try to get an urgent appointment. Tomorrow he would try and make this madness stop.

Chapter
11

Jack sat uncomfortably in the waiting room of the slick and expensive-looking office and flipped through a magazine without seeing the pages. He was hot. The dark leather chair looked luxurious but felt uncomfortable, at least to someone nervous and fidgeting. Every time he shifted positions, which he did frequently, the chair made an obnoxious farting sound that made him glad he was alone in the small room. He had filled out the patient information sheet (Do you have thoughts of suicide? Have you ever had thoughts of harming someone else? Are there any sexual problems? How much alcohol do you drink per day/week? Do you use any recreational drugs? Why are you here today?) and set it on the armrest. He briefly fantasized of bolting from the room and taking his soft yellow patient information sheet with him. Only his need to get his insurance card back kept him in this little room, fidgeting in his large farting chair.

And the need to save my family from my madness. Let's not forget that one.

The door cracked open and the sharply dressed receptionist poked her head in.

"Hi, Jack," she said softly, as though they shared some secret. "Dr. Lewellyn is ready for you now."

"Thank you," Jack said and followed the receptionist down a short hall, lined with expensive-looking and brightly colored art, intended no doubt to fill him with happiness. They came to a dark wood door with "David Lewellyn, Ph.D." engraved on a gold plate at eye level. The receptionist opened the door quietly and ushered him into a well-lit and spacious office.

"Dr. Lewellyn, this is Jack."

David Lewellyn looked a bit younger than he had expected. He was very fit and dressed in expensive dark slacks, a white dress shirt, and a yellow tie. He was smiling broadly, his hand outstretched.

"Hi, Jack. Come on in."

Jack took the outstretched hand and shook it, the grip firm and confident. Dr. Lewellyn looked familiar somehow, at least in the way that the smartly dressed models in *GQ* looked as if you had seen them shopping in the mall.

"Please sit down." Lewellyn motioned vaguely towards the two chairs and couch. Jack stood there a moment, unsure.

"Where?" Jack asked.

Dr. Lewellyn laughed warmly and clapped Jack on the back with his well-manicured hand as his receptionist closed the heavy door behind them.

"Wherever you're most comfortable, Jack. It's not a test."

Jack smiled, embarrassed, and felt himself relax a little. He walked over to the couch and sat down awkwardly. The psychologist sat in the large chair closest to him and crossed his legs. He pulled out a pen and picked up an expensive-looking leather folder, but didn't open it. Jack wondered how he had known where he would sit, but then noticed that the little wood and marble tables next to the other chair and at both corners of the couch all contained identical folders. Clever. Lewellyn smiled softly.

"So," the psychologist said, and looked at him expectantly.

"So," Jack answered, unsure what else to say, then felt like an idiot.

Dr. Lewellyn leaned forward, still smiling.

"Jack, relax. I'm not testing you or trying to analyze you." He sat back again. "Just think of me as a friend with a helpful education. Maybe I can help you sort some things out. The way this works is I am just here to talk to. Together we'll help you figure out for yourself what we can do to help you feel better." He smiled that warm smile again. "Okay?"

"Okay," Jack said, not much relieved. He looked around the office awkwardly, not wanting to meet the doctor's eyes.

"Well," Lewellyn said, "I'll start. Jim Barton tells me that you're having a lot of nightmares. But I want to start with what made you call today. You seemed quite eager to come in." He looked at Jack again, his notebook now open in his lap, his pen ready to turn Jack's mind into scribbles on his legal pad. He looked relaxed, but expectant.

Jack had decided yesterday, after the terror on the couch, that he needed to commit to complete disclosure with the psychologist. He needed one person he could tell everything to, and it might as well be someone who could help make sense of all this crap. Doc Barton trusted this guy, and he liked and respected Barton. No more putting it off. If he was nuts, he was nuts. But better to know and let the chips fall where they may.

"Well," he began, shifting, grateful that the leather couch was less fart prone than the chair in the waiting room. "Jim says he has several patients with this kind of thing," he felt pretentious calling Doc Barton "Jim," but no going back now. "I have these bad dreams—"

"Nightmares?"

"Well, yeah. Nightmares, I guess. Jim thinks it's some kind of stress thing, I think he called it, related to all the war shit I've been watching on TV, in the paper— you know."

"Let's start with the first thing that happened that caused you distress. The first time you felt there was a problem. When was that?"

"Last week," Jack answered. He liked this better. Simple question and answer. Hard to fuck that up, right?

"When last week?"

"Thursday. Or maybe Wednesday, I think."

"Okay, what happened?" Lewellyn watched him again, still patient, unhurried. Jack tried again to relax.

"Well, that was when I had my first dream—nightmare, I guess."

"Okay," the doctor scribbled again. "Tell me about the nightmare as best you can."

And Jack did. He tried his best to give every detail of the late afternoon in Fallujah. He began slowly and with difficulty, trying to read Dr. Lewellyn's expression (there was none, really), but as he told the story he relaxed, and it poured out of him more easily and more and more quickly. He told about Kindrich taking a round in the head which split his team and drove him, Bennet, Simmons, and the others behind the wall. He gave a detailed description of Bennet taking a round then dying beside the wall. He told Lewellyn of his plan to get his guys across the road to join up with the rest of his platoon and of the RPG round that had buried Bennet's body. A few times the doctor interrupted him for a brief moment, trying to catch up on his notes. Then he would nod and look at him without speaking. He seemed fascinated by the story. During the pauses Jack became aware of the tears that streamed down his face, of the tremor in his voice. He didn't care. Now that he'd started, there was no stopping. It was all he could do to pause briefly while Lewellyn caught up his notes, then his trembling voice would begin again, and out it would come. He told him every detail of the bullet he took in the chest, of struggling back to his feet, and then the feel of the second round that tore open his throat. He wept openly now as he told of the terror of not being able to speak, of the burning pain, of the fear that he was dying. He told him about wanting desperately to get to his wife and daughter. When he was done, he collapsed backwards, exhausted.

Dr. Lewellyn finished writing and sat back as well, watching him without speaking. The pause seemed eternal, and Jack felt himself grow more uncomfortable again. He began to fidget and looked around the room nervously.

"What happened then?" the psychologist finally asked.

"That was it," Jack answered, uncertain what else to say.

"You woke up?" Lewellyn watched him, but his expression remained soft and sympathetic.

"Yeah, sort of, I guess."

"What do you mean, sort of?"

"Well," Jack was unsure how to explain it, "I mean I woke up, but I was confused. I wasn't sure where I was. I wasn't even sure who I was. I mean, I think I knew who Pam was—"

"Your wife?"

"Yeah, I mean I knew it was Pam, but I didn't know who the hell I was. For a moment, I mean. I was scared, terrified really. I fell out of bed. The room seemed unfamiliar. It scared the shit out me. And something else."

Jack paused again. He was going into scary territory now, but he was more afraid of keeping things back than he was that David Lewellyn might think he was crazy. He had to get help, had to know what the hell was wrong with him. He needed this classy but seemingly compassionate man's help. He needed help to make this shit stop.

"Well," he began, "it was like part of me was still there, you know, still in Fallujah. Like the ceiling seemed to be missing—"

"What do you mean missing?"

Jack felt more frightened than ever. He had forced his mind away from these thoughts the last week. This was the stuff that felt crazy. But it was too late to stop, so he continued.

"Well, I looked up, and I could see sky, you know, instead of a ceiling. And I could still hear shouting. And gunfire."

Dr. Lewellyn considered this for a moment and jotted something in his notebook. Then he looked up again.

"How long did that last?"

Jack thought a moment. "Just a few minutes, I think, maybe even seconds, I'm not sure. Then the ceiling just kind of, I don't know, filled in or something. Maybe I was still kind of half asleep?" He desperately wanted some reassurance.

"That's not really very unusual," Lewellyn said, crossing his legs again. "Sometimes when we awaken from a really terrifying dream, it lingers in our mind. It can be very distressing."

"Terrifying," Jack corrected.

"I'm sure," Dr. Lewellyn agreed. "Go on. What happened next?"

"Pam was scared."

Lewellyn nodded and started writing again.

"She was crying on the floor beside me. I had a cut on my head that was bleeding a little. She didn't know what the hell was wrong. Then Claire—"

"Your daughter?"

"Yeah, our little girl. She started crying and I was better."

"What do you mean better?"

Jack thought a moment. What did he mean? Better how? He was himself again, he thought. He was Jack, and not Casey Stillman.

"I sort of figured out who I was—and where. Her cry—I knew it was Claire, and it just sort of, I don't know, oriented me or something." Jack was tired. He felt perspiration on his forehead. The telling had taken a lot out of him, and he had a long way to go. There was the incident in the school lounge when he had seen the report on the news. There was fucking Simmons and his two ghastly visits to him. He had been awake for those for sure, hadn't he? How could he explain that, a dead Marine visiting him at work? There was the bloody bathroom, and the tooth. Mostly there was the calling, the pull he felt, to go back to his Marines in Fallujah.

Come back, Sar'n. You belong here with us.

Jack doubted he had the energy to go on. He looked up and saw that Dr. Lewellyn was watching him patiently. He said nothing, but held the doctor's gaze, wondered if the fear and desperation were obvious in his eyes. The doctor leaned back in his chair.

"Can we switch gears a second?" he asked.

"Sure," Jack answered, relieved. "But there is some other stuff. Strange things..." Jack's voice trembled again, and he felt tears well up again in his eyes.

"I'm sure, Jack," Dr. Lewellyn said softly. "And we'll get to all that. I want to talk about your family a moment. Is that okay?"

"Sure," Jack said. He felt more like a passenger now, an observer as this kind man worked to twist the top off of his head and peer in. Dr. Lewellyn stood up and placed his leather folder in his chair.

"What else do you have going on today, Jack?" he asked as he walked over to his desk.

"I took another sick day," Jack answered. "I'm yours as long as you need." He tried to screw a smile onto his face, but failed. "I just want this shit to stop." Another tear spilled out onto his cheek and wound its way to his chin, where he wiped it away with the back of his hand.

Dr. Lewellyn picked up the phone on his desk and called his receptionist to clear the next hour, as well. Then he came back to his chair and handed Jack a small box of Kleenex, squeezing his shoulder as he passed. He resumed his position and opened his notebook, getting his pen to the ready.

"Tell me a little about your family, Jack," he said.

And Jack did. He didn't know how long he talked, was unsure if he could even summarize what he had said. He painted a picture of Pam, his one true love, and the powerful force her love had been in his life. He talked about her unconditional support, how he felt most like himself only when he was with her, how he believed he was a better person because they were together. He talked about their ability to communicate with just a look from across a room. And how they could spend an entire afternoon, just sitting and talking about nothing and everything, and have more fun than he thought most people had on a Caribbean vacation.

"She is really everything to me," he concluded.

Then he talked about his little Claire Bear, his joy, the physical product of his love for Pam. He found himself telling stories like a proud dad, going on and on, and apologized.

"Don't be silly, Jack. It sounds like you have a wonderful family and a very healthy, loving relationship with Pam." The psychologist was smiling.

"I'm very lucky. I know that." Jack wiped another tear from his cheek, unsure why the hell he was crying now. "I feel bad that I've kept some of this from her."

"What have you kept from her?" the psychologist asked.

"Well," Jack paused. "The bad stuff. I mean, some of the things we haven't talked about yet." Dr. Lewellyn nodded as if he understood and jotted something in his notebook. Jack thought again of how he was afraid to tell Pam about Simmons visiting him at school, of his "breakdown," and meeting with Stuart Anderson and the school nurse. Worse, he thought about his lie about the nightmare on the couch the day before, seeing the bloody bathroom and Simmons in the backyard.

"Can we talk about the war in Iraq for a minute?" Lewellyn asked.

"Yes," Jack said, but he felt his stomach flip. "But I really think I should tell you about some other things—some very disturbing things. You asked why I felt compelled to come in today. Well, these other things, these things that happen when I am *awake*, are the reason." Jack realized he was pleading. He had come in unsure if he could even talk to this stranger, and now he was begging to tell him the most frightening part. Once he had opened it up, he had to get it out, like draining pus from an abscess.

Dr. Lewellyn pursed his lips and thought a moment.

"Ok, Jack. Let's talk about the things you see when you're awake."

So Jack spoke again without pause, except in response to Dr. Lewellyn's occasional, "Hold on, Jack." He told his story in as much detail as he could recall, his voice cracking at times, tears running down his face again. He spoke freely, holding nothing back, interjecting at times his emotional responses—not just his terror, but his feeling of connection to these men he felt he really knew. He talked of his desperate need to tune into the news, hoping to catch the names of the men who had died in the street in Fallujah, and his haunting belief that he would know not only the names, but also the faces. Bennet, Kindrich. Simmons, and of course, Sergeant Casey Stillman. He talked fondly of his men and gave some of the details of their lives. He spoke of his particular fondness for Simmons, the carefree boy from Albany. He (or Casey) had taken Simmons under his wing, hoping to train him to be a truly tough and career-oriented Marine. Then he cried when he again relived the visits from Simmons, and the way he had been calling him to come back to them, to his men, his Marines. He talked of the bizarre guilt he felt that he was not there.

When he was done, he laid his head against the back of the leather couch, exhausted again. He looked at his watch and was amazed to see that he had been talking for over an hour. He looked at Dr. Lewellyn, who was flipping back through many pages of notes in his tidy leather notebook. Jack said nothing more as the psychologist reviewed what he had told him. He had expected to feel great anxiety about what the doctor would think. Instead, Jack felt only a tired sense of relief that he had gotten the story out—he had purged himself in some way. He closed his tired eyes and waited.

Finally he opened his eyes in response to the sound of Lewellyn setting his leather-bound collection of Jack's madness on the wood and marble table. Dr. Lewellyn's warmth masking any judgments he might have formulated.

"Would you like something to drink, Jack?" he asked.

"Sure," Jack answered quietly.

"Coke okay?"

"Great," Jack answered, though he really preferred Sprite.

Dr. Lewellyn walked stiffly over to a small refrigerator next to his desk and got two cans of soda out. He walked back and handed one to Jack, then took his seat, sipping his own soda as he did. He sat quietly for a moment, apparently thinking about where to go next in his evaluation. Jack drank deeply from his own can and realized his throat was dry as a bone. The first swallow burned as it went down. Then he waited patiently.

After a few minutes Dr. Lewellyn looked at Jack and smiled.

"What do you think of the war in Iraq, Jack?"

Jack felt confused by the question.

"What do I think?"

"Yeah," Lewellyn said, setting his Coke on the table. "What do you think? Are we right to be there?"

"Well, it's not really for me to decide," Jack answered without thinking. "I mean, we follow orders. The commander in chief makes the call. We're there as a force to project his policy."

Lewellyn considered this a moment.

"Jack, who in your family is in the military?"

"No one," Jack answered. "My dad was in the army in the early seventies, but never went to Vietnam. My mom was always home with us."

"Do you have any close friends in the military? Anyone you know who is over in Iraq? Have you ever considered a military career?"

"No," Jack answered honestly. It felt funny somehow, like it wasn't quite true, but he didn't know why.

Lewellyn considered this for a moment. Then he did something else that surprised Jack and made him a bit uncomfortable. He got up and sat on the couch beside Jack, leaning forward, his elbows on his knees. He rubbed his face. Jack was again overcome by how familiar he looked. Then the psychologist put a hand on his shoulder.

"You're not crazy, Jack." he said plainly. "You know that, right?"

Jack shifted uncomfortably again. He sure as shit did not know that. It was, at the moment, his biggest fear other than falling asleep or seeing a dead Marine in his backyard.

"I guess," he said. "Doc, I just want this to stop. I feel like it *is* driving me crazy. And it's killing Pam, too." His voice was pleading.

God, please make this stop.

"I know, Jack," Lewellyn said, confidence in his voice. "And we will. We'll stop it together." He leaned back on the couch beside him and stretched out his back. Then he looked at him again. "Jack, Barton is right. You do have a terrible stress disorder, like PTSD that soldiers get after combat. I don't know why," he said honestly, causing Jack to grimace, "but we'll figure it out. Together."

Dr. Lewellyn got up and headed for his desk where he grabbed a piece of paper from a book like a prescription pad.

"Jack, if you can take another day off I would like you to come back tomorrow at ten a.m. Can you do that?"

"Sure." Jack answered, his voice nervous but full of hope. Dr. Lewellyn handed him a slip of paper and Jack looked at it. It was an appointment card.

"In the meantime, I'm going to phone Jim Barton and ask him to call in a prescription for you. It'll help you sleep and you shouldn't have any nightmares, okay?"

Jack sighed heavily, visibly relieved and closed his eyes. "Thank God," he said.

"Now the only problem is it's likely to make you feel a little hung over in the morning, okay? You'll sleep, but you won't dream much, and that'll make you feel poorly rested."

"No problem," Jack said enthusiastically. He didn't care if he got cancer from the damn thing, as long as he didn't go back to Fallujah, riding in the body of a dying Marine. Jack thanked the doctor profusely, shook his hand, and then picked up his insurance card from the receptionist and left. In the hall he leaned back against the wall and felt tears well up again, though he was unsure why. He cried quietly in the hall for a few minutes, then collected himself and headed for the elevator.

He was going to be all right. David Lewellyn would help him, and he would be fine.

As the doors closed on the elevator, Jack felt the tug of familiarity again. He definitely knew this guy, but had no idea from where.

Chapter
12

The pill worked. Whether by placebo effect, or by activating—or inactivating—some chemical pathway in his brain, Jack didn't know or care. After an awkward evening where he promised his crying wife that the psychologist would be able to make everything all right, Jack slept without dreaming. When he woke up he still felt tired and had a vague headache, but those side effects did little to diminish the relief he felt that another night had passed without a visit to his personal purgatory. He found himself stiff and uncomfortable in the same position he last remembered from the night before.

Jack lay beside his sleeping wife, lost in thought. The sigh of her breathing had an amazing and calming effect on him. He lay beside her, stroked her hair, and thought again about his meeting with Dr. Lewellyn. He decided he trusted him, that he liked his easy style and the way he let Jack lead the conversation. He still felt anxious and unsure, still terrified truth be known, but he was also filled with hope. If a few more painful and emotional hours with the psychologist would help him put all this behind him, it was well worth it.

As he lay there, he let his mind drift back to the images of Fallujah. He tried to let the pictures from his dreams unfold like a remembered movie. He tried to pick out some detail he had missed, which might give him a satisfying "Ah-ha!" of insight as to the root cause of his nightmare. He thought a lot about Dr. Lewellyn's words, that they could find what caused his obsessive thoughts about a war seven thousand miles away, and that the insight might help him make it stop. True, he was horrified by the images of the war that came via the talking heads into his safe and quiet world, but weren't millions of others? He hadn't seen many of them chasing visiting corpses down the halls of the neighborhood school. Why did he feel so personally connected to all this? He came up with nothing, but he was haunted again by the unsettling feeling that he was indeed a part of it somehow; that it owned him. He belonged there for some reason.

Come back, Sar'n. You belong here with us. We need you.

Jack shuddered. Simmons' words—young Simmons from Albany. Jack closed his eyes and let his hand run over Pam's warm, soft shoulder. She stirred and sighed.

The evening had been difficult for Jack, but worse, he sensed it had been a strain on Pam, as well. She needed some reassurance that he had been unable to give her. He told her in very general terms of his meeting with Dr. Lewellyn. He shared with her what he had told him about his dreams and his obsession with the news. He emphasized Lewellyn's confidence that he could help with Jack's "stress disorder." Jack cringed as he imagined their next meeting starting with "so, tell me about your mother…were you breast fed?"

Pam didn't ask for more and seemed content that there was hope in this Dr. Lewellyn, but Jack was sure it must bother her that there were things he didn't share. His description of the meeting fell way short of accounting for the intense three hours he was with the doctor. Jack wrestled with a heavy guilt that he didn't share more with the woman with whom he had shared everything, but he couldn't bring himself to talk with her about his breakdown at school, or worse, his visits from Simmons. If Lewellyn thought he was crazy, so be it. It was his job, if he thought that, to fix it. But there was no way he could bear the thought that his wife might begin to believe that her husband had slipped the chains of reason and gone over the edge, into some pit of madness. So he kept that part to himself, despite the fact that he needed his wife's support now more than ever. He had never kept anything from Pam—not ever.

Jack rolled over now and wrapped his arm tightly around his wife's waist and hugged her. The smell of her hair and the feel of her against him filled him with peace and joy, as they had since the day they first lay down together.

"I love you so much, Pam," he said, soaking in the warmth of her.

She squeezed his arm gently.

"I love you too, baby," she said sleepily. "I'm so proud of you."

Jack held her like that for a long time and watched as the pale light through the window grew into an orange sunrise. Then he slipped quietly from their bed. He padded softly down the hall in his bare feet to Claire's room and stood beside her crib. He watched her beautiful face as she slept in the growing morning light. He loved his little girl so much, and he felt happy tears run down his cheeks as he watched her. How could he ever bear to be apart from his girls? How did those young Marines possibly stand the separation from family, and the fear of never seeing them again? He didn't think he could ever do it. If he was ever separated from his girls he could never give up on getting back to them, no matter what it took.

Claire stirred slightly and Jack bent over, picked her up, and cradled her head on his shoulder. Then he went to the rocker and sat down. He slowly rocked his baby girl against his chest. He kissed her hair and stroked her cheek as he sat there, thinking about the painful morning ahead of him. No matter what it took, he would sort this out and come back, healed, to his family. No nightmare, no Hadji bullet, would keep him from his family.

Jack was stirred from his thoughts, and the comforting feel of his daughter, by the feeling of someone watching him. He looked up to see Pam leaning against the door, watching him and smiling. She looked gorgeous, her face glowing in the morning light, her eyes happy and full of love. Jack smiled back and reached out a hand to her. She came to him, took his hand and kissed him gently on the cheek.

"How long have you been there?" he whispered.

"Just a few minutes," she answered then sat in front of them on the small ottoman, specially built to rock back and forth with the chair. "You are so beautiful, sitting there holding our baby," she said, and then kissed his hand. "Would you like a nice breakfast?"

"I would love one," he answered. "Let me put her back and see if she'll stay down and I'll help you."

Pam rose, kissed him again, and then held her hand for a brief moment on his cheek.

"I'll meet you in the kitchen."

Claire stayed peacefully asleep as Jack laid her back in her crib, covered her to her waist with her blanket, and kissed her on the cheek. He stared at her for a moment more then headed downstairs to join his wife.

Pam was still pouring water into the coffee maker when Jack shuffled in. They had long ago given up what had been an every morning conversation about how they should program the machine and fill it at night so that they could wake up to fresh coffee. Jack hugged his wife from behind and kissed her neck. Then he opened the refrigerator and got out juice, milk, and eggs.

"Eggs okay?" he asked over his shoulder.

"Sure," Pam answered. She took the juice from him and poured them each a glass, while Jack continued his search for ham or bacon. Finding neither, he grabbed some Italian sausage instead.

"Spicy okay?" he asked. He turned and looked at his wife who looked amused. He gave her an unconscious "What?" look.

"Spicy is fine," she said softly. "You slept last night? No nightmares?"

Jack placed his ingredients on the counter and started slicing open the sausage casings as he spoke, dropping the spicy meat into a pan, to which he added a splash of olive oil.

"I did sleep," he answered as he worked, "and no nightmares."

Pam looked satisfied, and kissed him on the cheek. Then she stood beside him, grating cheese and bumping him playfully with her hip. When the sausage was simmering in the pan and the rest of the ingredients were ready to pour in, he added the eggs and cheese to the pan, and mixed it all together. Pam often told him with a chuckle that if there was no folding, there was no omelet, and you really just had "cheese eggs," which was fine with Jack.

As Jack whipped his sausage and cheese eggs around in the pan, he was distracted by thoughts of things he had held back from his wife. Even as they worked together in the kitchen, Jack felt a distance between them, at least in his mind, created by untold fears and unshared experiences. Pam had been there for him, had stood by and loved and cared for him, true to their vows. Could he really repay that by holding back from his partner—from what truly was the better half of the one person they had become—the things that frightened and worried him most? Did he really want to go this alone, without his one and constant source of strength and courage? He looked at his wife, who sat glowing at the table, and in that moment he decided that he wanted that wall gone. He would tell her everything—the gunfire, the missing ceiling, the visits from dead Marines—everything. Most importantly, he would share his fear that he might be going crazy. He would tell her also of his overwhelming feeling that in some way he was a part of all of it, that he was a Marine.

He scraped their breakfast onto two plates, his stomach fluttering. He doubted he would even be able to stomach the breakfast that moments ago he had hungered for. He turned to her, a plate in each hand.

"Juice?" he asked.

"Got some for both of us," she said and pointed at the two full glasses on the table. Jack placed the plates down and slid into the seat beside his wife. He took a couple of anxious bites despite his wrenching stomach, and then felt Pam's hand squeeze his knee. He looked up at her.

"What is it, Jack?" She looked at him softly, knowingly. This was a woman with whom he could have conversations from across a crowded room with just their eyes. She knew him.

"I have some things I want to tell you," he said. He looked at his plate instead of his wife. "There are more things than just dreams. Scary things," he said and waited for her response.

Pam looked at him, her face anxious but without judgment.

"You can tell me anything, Jack."

"I know," he said.

He started with the waking visions he had after his nightmares, telling her of the smell of dust and gunpowder that lingered in their room, the sound of the Blackhawk, seeing the smoke-filled sky instead of the ceiling. He told her of the day after the first nightmare and how he had what he called an "anxiety attack" in the faculty lounge, and of the sounds he had heard behind the school. Then he hesitated.

"What did Dr. Lewellyn say?" his wife asked, showing no apparent concern that these things might be evidence that her husband was nuts.

"Well," Jack said, grateful for the delay before he came to the visits from Simmons, "He wasn't that worried. He said that nightmares can linger, and the anxiety can produce some hallucinations, more like memories, when we're awake."

Pam considered this a moment. Jack watched her closely, worried what he might see. All he saw was love and concern. No fear and no judgment.

"Did that make you feel better?" she asked.

Jack smiled. All these terrible things that he brought into their lives, and still she seemed concerned only that he was all right.

"Yes," he replied, "but there's more."

And he told the rest. He told her of seeing Simmons in the hallway, and how he had chased the phantom out of the back door of the school. He spared her the gory details, but was candid about the reaction of Chad and Anderson. Then he told her the worst part, of the bloody bathroom and Simmons in their backyard, and how he told him again that he belonged with them—with his Marines. He told her of being sucked down in the cyclone in their bed after finding himself lying beside the bloody body, and how he had again ended up in Fallujah, just another shot up Marine dying slowly in the dusty street. When he finished, he studied her face, looking for signs that this was just too much. But again, there was none.

"Well that part sounds like just another dream, right?" She asked. She laid her hand on his arm gently. Her hand felt warm and comforting. He could tell how desperately she wanted to believe everything was all right or to make it all right if it wasn't.

"Well, yeah. I mean, I guess so."

Jack thought for a moment. He hadn't really thought of that event as a dream. It just seemed too damn real. More like a haunting. But she was right, wasn't she? He *had* woken up on the couch afterward. It had to be a dream. How bizarre that it hadn't occurred to him until Pam said it.

Pam squeezed his arm and pushed her now cold plate of breakfast away. Then she took his hand in hers.

"Jack, I love you. I love you no matter what." Tears rimmed the bottoms of her soft eyes, but not enough to spill out onto her cheeks. "Honey, there is nothing you can't share with me. I'm here for you. I just don't want you to go through this alone."

Jack forced himself to hold her eyes with his, which now welled up with tears of their own. He swallowed hard, and asked the question he had to hear an answer to. His voice trembled.

"Do you think I'm crazy?" he asked. Tears now spilled down onto his cheeks.

Pam rose. Her hand tightly gripped his arm and she slid into his lap at the table.

"Oh, God, Jack, no!" she said and hugged him tightly. She held him and stroked his hair as he clung desperately to her, crying out loud now. "No baby, not at all. I love you so much."

Jack pulled her off his shoulder and looked into her face, feeling warm.

"I keep thinking about that movie," he said, actually thinking about it just now for the first time. "You know the one, with the guy from *Gladiator*? The one where the guy is a mathematician and thinks he works for the government? In the end it turns out the people he sees aren't real and he's just crazy. Schizophrenic, I think."

"*A Beautiful Mind*?" Pam asked.

"That's it," Jack answered. *"A Beautiful Mind.* That guy saw things and he had schizophrenia, remember? Maybe that's what I have. Isn't that having split personalities?"

Pam hugged him again, tightly. "Oh, Jack," she said. "Baby, you're not crazy. You have some sort of stress disorder, but you do not have schizophrenia." She pulled back again and looked at him, wiping the tears from his face. Then she smiled. "Baby, I love you no matter what. Forever. We will get through this, darling," and she kissed him lightly on the lips.

Jack let out a heavy sigh. He had so underestimated this wonderful woman, and he vowed he never would again. Far away, Jack heard the happy chatter of his little girl. That, combined with the soft touch of his wife's hand on his cheek, filled him with happiness and hope.

It really was going to be all right.

As long as he had his girls.

Chapter
13

The familiarity of the little waiting room, and his comfort with Lewellyn, did little or nothing to relieve his anxiety as Jack sat and waited for his next visit with his doctor. He did feel much better after his talk with Pam, as he should have known he would, and the hour and a half spent playing all together on the family room floor had helped even more. But now he felt incredibly anxious. He felt like he was waiting to be dissected, his mind opened by the sharp blade of the psychologist's probing questions. He was terrified, just like the first day.

What the hell will we find today?

Lewellyn had relaxed him the day before with his blanket pronunciation that Jack was not crazy, but what else could he say, really? It wasn't like they would tell you outright. *"Well, Jack, you are clearly and totally insane. Open and shut case. Can you come back tomorrow at ten?"* Just what did you say to a crazy person, anyway?

Jack flipped the page on the three-month-old *National Geographic* and tried to force the thoughts from his mind. He had been given hope, first by Lewellyn and then by Pam. He couldn't sit here and let his obsessive fears steal that away now. They would figure this out together, the doctor had told him, and that was what he would hold onto.

"God, it's nerve wracking, isn't it?"

Jack's breath caught in his throat, and he smelled him before he turned his head to look, feeling like he moved in slow motion.

The smell of Iraqi dust assaulted him, but he turned slowly anyway. He knew what he would see. It would be Simmons, with his horrible, bloody death grin.

He was wrong.

Beside him, his legs crossed casually at the knee and a *People* magazine open in his lap, sat a Marine officer. He was older, his close-cropped hair grey, his face tan and lined with crow's-feet. His digital cammies looked clean, but the boots beneath the bloused pant legs were worn and coated with dust. The rank insignia on his collar indicated he was a lieutenant colonel. Jack stared at him, his mouth open. The man smiled back.

"I said its nerve wracking isn't it?" the man repeated, leaning in a bit, as if perhaps Jack had not heard him.

This was insane!

He had fallen asleep again, that was all. He was asleep in the chair and having a dream, though this one certainly had a new twist. Jack closed his eyes tightly, balled up his fists, and willed himself to wake up. He opened his eyes again, but the man still sat there, his face now amused.

"Not that easy, Casey. Sorry." He held out his hand. "I'm Commander Hoag," he said, and Jack reached out and shook his hand as if in a trance. He looked more closely at the man's uniform and saw that, sure enough, it said Navy instead of Marines. The Navy provided medical, dental, and religious support to the Marine Corps, which lacked its own such services and was, after all, a part of the Department of the Navy. Jack wondered how he knew that. The man sat back, and closed the magazine in his lap. "Sergeant, I'm the regimental chaplain for First MEF. How are you hanging in there, Sar'n?"

"I'm Jack," Jack responded numbly.

"Yes, well," Commander Hoag took off his round glasses and cleaned them on the bottom corner of his uniform blouse. "That's what we need to get into, don't you think?" He replaced the glasses on his face and looked at Jack patiently.

"Get into?"

"Yes," the commander answered. "We don't have time now, of course. But before you go in there to talk to your friend, I wanted to ask you what you thought this was all about."

Jack felt tears well up in his eyes. He should be getting used to that sensation.

"I don't know," he answered. "Me going crazy, I guess."

The Navy chaplain shook his head and watched him softly.

"No Casey, you're not crazy," he said. "Not at all. It's about Pam. It's about your love for Pam and Claire. That's what keeps pulling you to this place."

Jack felt that the chaplain's words held some terrifying meaning, but he couldn't quite grab at it. What about this was so horrible? What the hell was this ghost of a man talking about?

"What do you mean, pulling me? What the hell does that mean?" Jack felt his thin grip on control slipping away. He was sliding down a slippery slope here, and what waited below was something his mind knew of, somewhere deep and unavailable. He felt panic grip him, and his throat tightened. He realized that he didn't want to hear the answer—that he didn't want to hear another goddamn word.

The door opened suddenly. Bright light from the hallway exploded into his softly lit room and Jack jumped to his feet. He felt like a teenager caught touching himself to his mother's fashion magazine as the receptionist stuck her head in the doorway.

"Dr. Lewellyn is ready for you, Jack."

Jack jerked his head back and forth between the attractive receptionist and the Navy chaplain, who sat quietly with his legs crossed, smiling and watching him. The girl didn't react at all. She just looked at Jack, puzzled, maybe even a little concerned.

"Sir? Jack?" she corrected herself. She was probably taught to call the nut jobs by their first names. Soothing. "Jack, are you all right?"

Jack twisted his head, his body so tense he felt a tearing pop in his neck, and looked at the empty chair where the chaplain had just been.

She didn't see him. How in the fuck?

Fade to Black

Jack dropped heavily back into the oversized leather chair, rewarded by a ripping fart sound that in other circumstances would have made him laugh. He shook his head, trying to calm down.

"Do you want me to get Dr. Lewellyn?" There was real and unmasked worry in the receptionist's voice now.

"N...n...no...just...just hold on." Jack struggled for control. Of course she hadn't seen him, because *he* hadn't seen him either.

Just another goddamn, terrifying, fucking nightmare, right?

There had never been anyone in the room but him. Jack clamped his jaw tight and when he did he accidentally bit his tongue. A familiar, coppery taste filled his mouth. Then he looked up at the receptionist, his face more controlled, despite the sweat that now ran down to his neck from both his temples.

"No, I'm fine," he said and rose. He forced an awkward smile. "I was, uh...well I fell asleep and had a helluva nightmare again, to be honest. I'm ok now, really."

The receptionist looked skeptical.

"I'm sorry I scared you. Dr. Lewellyn is treating me for these damn nightmares." The quiver was gone from his voice now and he sounded more convincing.

"Okay," the girl answered. "Well, Dr. Lewellyn is ready to see you. Are you ready now?"

"Absolutely," Jack answered and followed her out of the room. He glanced over his shoulder as he did, looking again at the empty chair. His eyes caught a glimpse of an open *People* magazine, out of place on the floor beside the empty chair, and he shuddered. Then he followed the receptionist down the carpeted hall to the dark door with Dr. Lewellyn's name on it.

The psychologist greeted him warmly and shook his hand, his grip firmer than the chaplain-ghost. Jack mumbled a greeting in reply and walked heavily over to the couch where he assumed his position. Lewellyn sat in the same chair as before and crossed his legs.

"You ok, Jack?" he asked, his gaze soft and patient.

Jack squirmed a bit on the couch, unsure how to proceed. "Uh...yeah. I'm uh..." his voice trailed off. He hung his head and

~ 106 ~

took a deep breath. Then he leaned back and tilted his head up. He looked at the ceiling, halfway expecting to see a purple sky and tracer rounds overhead. "I'm not so good, Doc. Something…well I had another nightmare. I mean, I think it was a nightmare."

Jack proceeded to tell Lewellyn about the Navy chaplain and their brief chat in the waiting room. Lewellyn listened quietly and then folded his hands in his lap. For a moment he said nothing.

"How is Pam doing?" he asked finally.

Jack was stunned for a moment. What the hell was wrong with this guy? Had he not heard what he just said? Jack had just had a conversation with an imaginary Naval officer in his waiting room, and all he had to say was, how is your wife? What the fuck was going on here?

"Doc, don't you think it's a little fucking weird that I just saw another ghost in your waiting room?" The irritation was sharp in his voice.

The psychologist uncrossed his legs and leaned forward on his elbows.

"Jack," he began softly, "I know that these dream images are very disturbing to you. But the cure is not in obsession. It's in understanding the root cause of the images and what they represent to you. Central in everything you have shared with me is your love for Pam and a desire for your family to remain intact. Now," Lewellyn leaned back again and recrossed his legs. "How is Pam?"

Jack's mind still reeled. Was he supposed to believe this was all about Pam? He was having horrific nightmares and hallucinations about dead Marines that he believed he knew because he was in love with his wife? He sat back, resigned. He was just along for the ride again.

"Pam is fine," he answered flatly.

There was a long and uncomfortable pause during which he felt like Lewellyn was again sizing him up, deciding where to head next.

"Jack, what do you think you should do next?" the psychologist asked after a long while.

"I think I should see a psychologist," Jack snapped, more sharply than he intended.

Lewellyn watched him impassively, not reacting to the harsh dig. He waited patiently for Jack to continue.

"I'm sorry," Jack said, looking at his hands. "I didn't mean it like that. I'm just frustrated." Jack looked up at the doctor. "I do trust you, Dr. Lewellyn."

"It's okay, Jack," Lewellyn said sincerely. "I know you're frustrated." Then he shifted in his chair. Jack noticed his little notebook was again open, his pen at the ready. "I know we have a lot to cover, Jack. There's a lot more background we need to delve into, but I want to start a little differently than I had planned."

"Okay," Jack answered, trying to relax and allow himself to shift into a more open frame of mind.

"Jack, what do you think these images represent?"

"Images?" Jack asked, confused.

"Yes," Lewellyn answered. "The images of the Marines from Fallujah. The Navy chaplain you saw when you fell asleep in the waiting room. What do you think they represent?"

Jack thought hard for a moment, but he still didn't really fully understand the question. To him his Marines and now this Navy chaplain were like demons, pulling him into a nightmare world of death—his death, as Casey Stillman. They were calling to him, trying to lure him away from his safe world of Pam and Claire, trying to pull him into insanity.

"They're like ghosts," he answered.

"Ghosts?"

"Yeah, or demons maybe. It's like they're begging me to go with them into these nightmares. Like they're trying to convince me that I belong there with them and that my whole life is just a fantasy." Jack looked down at his shaking hands again. "Maybe I *am* crazy. Or schizophrenic or something." There. He had said it. His cards were on the table. No more bluffing.

"Jack," Lewellyn said. Jack could hear him setting his notebook on the little table. "You are not crazy. We need you to stop worrying about being crazy." The psychologist leaned forward with his elbows on his knees, as he had the other day.

"These images are, to me and my way of thinking, voices from your own subconscious trying to tell you something important about whatever the underlying stressor is in your life. Maybe you should try and find a way to listen to them and hear what they have to say."

Jack shivered as a chill washed over him. Had he heard right? He looked up at his psychologist, unable to conceal his shock and amazement. He realized he was looking at his therapist as if he had a horn growing out of the middle of his forehead. He felt his confidence in Lewellyn slip along with his hope that he would be okay.

"What do you think, Jack?"

Lewellyn waited patiently, either unaware or unconcerned by the way Jack stared at him.

"Are you suggesting I sit and chat with a hallucination? That maybe me and an invisible dead Marine, with half a face, stroll through the park and work out our differences?"

Lewellyn ignored the sarcasm and anger and leaned back again.

"Jack, your unconscious is trying to tell you something. And unless we find a way to listen to it, I don't know how you will ever be able to identify the problem so that you can find a healthier way to cope with it." For a moment the doctor seemed lost in thought. Then he continued, "Jack, we're going to work hard today, and every day you can get here, to find a conventional way to root out your problem and deal with it. In the meantime, I'm not suggesting you sit in a restaurant and talk to yourself. I am just suggesting that if you accept that these images are your own subconscious trying to find a way up to the front of your mind—to tell you something you need to deal with—that maybe you can fight off the fear and dread they cause enough to listen to what they're trying to tell you. Accept that they are *not* real, but that they represent your own voice trying to help you find the solution on your own." The doctor stared at him for a moment, as if he expected a response. "Is that a more comfortable way to think about it?"

Jack leaned forward, elbows on his knees, and thought about Lewellyn's words. It sure as hell made more sense said that way. His problem, so far, had been his uncertainty about whether the images really were just hallucinations, or ghosts, or something real and even more terrifying. Their calling was so powerful and so convincing. Of course it made more sense that the power of that call came from his unconscious mind somehow.

"Yeah," he answered finally. He looked up from his hands and held Lewellyn's patient look. "Yeah, that makes sense, Doc."

Jack sat back again and forced a smile onto his face. "Just promise me that if I get locked up for talking to myself in the park, like some kind of bag lady, you'll come and bail me out."

Lewellyn laughed an ice–breaking, and natural, laugh.

"I promise, Jack," he said. Then he picked up his little notebook, making Jack stiffen unconsciously, and opened it again in his lap. "Well, Jack, I am afraid we have at least an hour of monotony. I need to get a good psychological background on you, and I am afraid there is really no way around some trite questions." The psychologist clicked open his pen. "Let's talk a few minutes about your parents and your childhood."

Jack sighed heavily and leaned back his head on the large leather couch.

"Okay."

Here we go.

Chapter 14

Jack strolled slowly down the street, a few blocks from Dr. Lewellyn's downtown office. His right hand unconsciously thumbed the pocketed card that Dr. Lewellyn had given him as he'd left. On the front was an appointment for two p.m. the next day, and another for four p.m. on Monday.

"I have to get back to work by Monday," Jack had told the doctor.

"I don't see a problem with that, Jack. Hopefully tomorrow we will get you some psychological tools that will lessen your anxiety about going back to school," his therapist had reassured him.

On the back of the card were two telephone numbers—one for David Lewellyn at home and the other, his cell phone. At first Jack had felt flattered that the psychologist cared enough to provide him with personal contact information. But now, as he walked slowly down the block peering absently into shop windows and fingering the card in his pocket, he worried that it meant something more ominous. What was it the doctor thought might happen? Why would Jack need to be able to contact him day or night? Was Lewellyn worried about Jack losing his shit— being found mumbling to himself in an alley, curled up in the fetal position, the card in his pocket the only link between the cops or paramedics who found him and the utter madness inside him?

Jack forced the thought from his head.

Ridiculous!

If Lewellyn had those kinds of worries he would arrange to have Jack hospitalized or something, right? He sure as shit wouldn't have smiled, shook his hand, and sent him home to his wife and little girl. And he wouldn't have reassured him that he could return to school in a few days either, right? Still, the very idea that he was somehow in a position where he might need to call a psychologist at home, or on his cell phone, was terrifying. How in the hell had he ever gotten here? What was it his psychological demons were trying to tell him?

Jack considered for a moment that, as Dr. Lewellyn had suggested, his hallucinations and nightmares really were some inner voice, trying to give him clues to his mind's struggle. If he could listen to those images, then maybe he might identify what was screwing with his mind. He wouldn't really be listening to ghosts or demons, after all. He would just be listening to himself, right? And could that lead to a cure? He felt skeptical, even though it all made sense psychologically. Maybe, but Lewellyn didn't live in these dreams with him. He couldn't know the horrible intensity of them, or the incredible reality of them. He couldn't know the way his life felt like a lie after he awoke.

Real or imagined, in those moments I really am Casey Stillman.

How could he explain that to anyone, even Lewellyn? He wasn't sure he had made Pam understand, who often knew him better than he knew himself.

It's about Pam. Your love for Claire and Pam. That is what keeps pulling you to this place.

Commander Hoag's voice, clear as a bell in his mind. But what did that mean? Pulling him to what place? Did he mean to Dr. Lewellyn's office or something deeper, or worse, more sinister? Jack got the sense that the answers were so close, like a familiar word on the tip of your tongue.

Jack realized he had walked the whole two blocks and that he now stood in front of his car, parked at a metered spot by the curb. He also realized that he needed more time to think about the things he had talked about with the psychologist. Not that Pam wasn't a great support. God knows she was. But he felt he needed to sort things out a bit more before he could go home and talk with her. Besides, he had a powerful feeling that he was slowly picking the lock on an important door here. That he was close to something, though he had no idea what. He looked at the shops along the block on his side of the street. There were several small clothing stores, a shoe store, and one that advertised "Electronic Miracle," whatever the hell that implied. He turned his gaze across the street, where his eye immediately caught a green neon sign that announced the Tenth Street Bar and Grill. Underneath was a smaller sign which bragged "Best Sandwiches Downtown" in bright red script. Perfect. He realized he was starving, and a cold beer wouldn't hurt either.

Jack dropped four quarters into the meter by his Volvo, checked the traffic, and crossed the street, smirking at the irony of the Armed Forces Recruiting Station sign on an overhanging marquis on the corner. Beneath the sign hung four small flags; one for each of the four branches of the military. He felt a lump in his throat at the sight of the red flag in the middle, the yellow eagle, globe, and anchor of the United States Marine Corps emblazoned in its center. Jack tore his eyes away, confused by the tightness in his chest and tears in his eyes, and pushed through the glass door with a fancy brass bar handle into the restaurant. He breathed in the aroma of hot sandwiches and French fries. There was a small podium in front of him, with a college-aged girl dressed smartly in a pants suit.

"Can I help you, sir?"

"Yeah," Jack answered. "Table for one."

The girl smiled. "Certainly, sir. I can seat you in the dining room, or would you prefer to sit at the bar?"

Jack looked to his left and saw a large, old-fashioned wood bar with a brass railing, glasses hanging upside down above it. Scattered around it were several tall wooden tables with barstools around them. The bar was fairly crowded, mostly with men in suits conducting business or just having a quick drink on their lunch break from their downtown offices. Too many people, he thought.

"The dining room, I think," he answered. "A booth if you have one." To his right he peered into the dining room, with high-backed dark wood booths surrounded by scattered four-top tables with green table cloths. The restaurant was a bit more upscale than he had expected from a bar and grill, no doubt catering as it did to the downtown business crowd.

The girl grabbed a menu and led him through the maze of tables with a crisp "Right this way, sir."

She sat Jack in a corner booth towards the back, sensing he wanted some quiet, he supposed, and announced that Ethan would be his waiter. He slid into the booth and rubbed his face with both hands, scanning the large lunch menu the hostess had placed in front of him. He guiltily skipped over the salad section that Pam would love for him to order from, and decided that a hot turkey Rueben and French fries would hit the spot.

When a large glass of water with a wedge of lemon was slid in front of him, a familiar voice caused him to look up.

"Here's your water, Sar'n," a young voice with a southern Tennessee drawl said.

Jack felt the blood drain from his face as he looked into the face of Jason Kindrich. The boy smiled and his hair was longer. More importantly, his head had no hole in it. But it was definitely Kindrich. Jack pushed back reflexively from the table, scurrying deep into the corner of the booth, and his hand knocked over the glass of water as he did.

"Oh, shit!" he exclaimed, more from the shock of seeing Kindrich than from the cold water that now soaked his lap. He grabbed the green cloth napkin and used it to dam up the remaining pool of water on the table, keeping more of it from pouring into his seat. The waiter grabbed another napkin from the table and began soaking up the water.

"Here let me get that, sir," he said, his voice now deeper and without any trace of southern accent.

Jack looked up in shock at a man closer to forty than twenty, with close-cropped dark hair and an earring. He looked nothing like Kindrich.

"What did you say to me?" Jack stammered.

"Sir?" the waiter responded, confused.

"When you put the water down. What did you say?" Jack demanded.

"I …uh," the waiter looked completely baffled now. "I think I said, here is your water, sir." He used a green napkin to slide the ice and much of the water onto his tray. "Are you okay?"

Jack nodded. He also tried to shake off the now all too familiar I-am-fucking-nuts feeling that he suspected the waiter would agree with at the moment. He was just tense and obsessed with thoughts of his demons. He had let his imagination go wild, maybe. The hostess arrived with a large cloth, which she used to begin cleaning up the remaining spilled water.

"Is everything ok here?" she asked, seeing Jack's wild look. The waiter looked at her and shrugged, his eyebrows arcing as if to say "I don't know what the hell is going on."

"My fault," Jack said quickly. "I'm afraid I was lost in thought and got startled. I knocked over the water glass." He looked at the completely unfamiliar waiter with a sheepish grin. "I'm sorry, Ethan," he said, remembering the name the hostess had told him.

"No problem, sir. My fault," the waiter said, though they both knew it was not. "Let me clean this up and get you some more napkins for your trousers. And then I'll get you a fresh water."

He and the hostess scurried away, no doubt to talk about the strange guy in the corner booth. Jack looked down at his wet lap and sighed heavily.

Jesus, Jack! You've got to get your shit together. If you don't calm down you will indeed be calling Lewellyn from the ER, or maybe jail.

He dabbed at his wet lap with the damp napkin and tried to calm down. The demons were bad enough. He couldn't afford to let his imagination become his enemy, too. Slowly, he felt himself begin to relax. The tremor in his hands diminished and the pounding pulse in his temples disappeared. What had triggered that bullshit? Jack decided to blame his therapy session. Probably that shitty conversation about his ghosts and the thought of "trying to listen to them and hear what they have to say" had made him even more paranoid.

When Ethan returned, Jack did his best to hide his embarrassment and ordered a hot turkey Reuben with French fries and a tall Foster's lager. The thought of food made him realize he was starving, and the anticipation of a nice meal distracted him momentarily from the obsessive thoughts about his problems. He was aware of the strange way the waiter looked at him, and imagined murmuring from the other diners about the crazy guy in the corner booth. Jack shuddered and tried to force his mind away from the paranoid thoughts. He focused his thoughts instead on the things he had come here to try and sort through. He knew he was delaying going home to his girls, but he really needed to organize his thoughts. He shoved the guilt out of his mind and thought again about his session with Dr. Lewellyn.

The remainder of the session had been fairly uneventful. They had talked a lot about his childhood, his relationship with his family, his education and job. Jack was surprised to find that his memories of his college years were somewhat vague and disjointed. Most of the memories that were vivid involved Pam—their early friendship and later courtship, falling in love. The time around his sophomore year things seemed again somewhat staged and artificial. He had mentioned his thoughts of joining the Navy or the Marines, mostly to help earn money for the rest of his education. Lewellyn had stopped him there.

"I thought you said you never considered a career in the military?"

That had caused an uncomfortable pause in Jack's train of thought. He *had* said that, hadn't he? In their first session. He hadn't lied. He simply hadn't recalled any desire to join the service until he had begun his free association rambling about his years in college.

"You were with Pam then, right? How did she feel about you joining the military?"

Jack had considered that a moment. He remembered very clearly their conversation about the Marines. They had been at Paul's, a Greek deli they hung out at a lot, eating sandwiches, just the two of them on a Saturday afternoon. They had skipped the football game with their friends to have lunch alone together (private moments were a rarity back then, much like since Claire had arrived). He had told her of his plan to join, probably the Marine Corps, to get the GI Bill. He had already gotten a brochure online and talked to a recruiter on the phone.

Pam had made it clear that she would support any decision he made, and had offered to take a break from school, also, so they could be together. He remembered she had been worried, though not as much about his safety. There was no looming war then, and the chance that he would not return to school, thereby giving up his plan to be a biology teacher, was small.

"What happened then?" Lewellyn had asked.

Again Jack remembered feeling uncomfortable and unsure, though he didn't know why the memories seemed so vague after that.

"I decided not to do it, I guess," Jack had answered.

"Why?"

Jack didn't really know. He had told Lewellyn that he thought it was because of Pam's concerns, but he really wasn't sure why he changed his mind. In fact he couldn't really even remember the end of their conversation that day. It felt like a gap in his memory at that point. Not in the memories themselves, but more in their clarity. They seemed broken and vague, somehow, like trying to remember a story you had been told instead of one you had experienced yourself. He had graduated a few years later and started his job at JFK High several years ago. He and Pam got married, which he had clear emotional memory of, but again he had trouble with the details of the wedding, which he felt should be crystal clear. Jack remembered getting anxious again during this discussion with Lewellyn. He had been very disturbed at the thought that so much of his memory after the day at Paul's Deli was superficial. Especially frightening was the fact that he could not conjure up clear memories of his wedding, arguably one of the happiest days of his life. He couldn't even picture the wedding party, though they must have a picture album that recorded the day. He remembered his dad, shaking his hand. He remembered the breathtaking sight of Pam entering the back of the church in her gown. He remembered their first kiss as a married couple. But it was these fragments that he was left with, rather than a clear recollection of the whole day.

Ethan brought him his sandwich and fries, interrupting his thoughts about his emotional memory gap, and asked if he wanted a refill on his beer. Well, of course he did, so Ethan hurried off to get another lager, and Jack dug into his sandwich and fries. God he was hungry!

He had very clear memory of the birth of Claire, however. He remembered every second, including all the warm emotions associated with it. He could picture Pam's face, tired and sweaty, and her smile when they had laid little Claire by her head, the two of them just staring at each other for the first time. Pam had cried, he remembered. And then he had cried as well. He kissed both of his girls and stroked Pam's hair. They were a growing family.

Jack started in on the second half of his sandwich and chomped a few more fries, washing them down greedily with his beer. Across from him by the window, a table of men and women in suits drank white wine and argued loudly about some new account with the city hospital, for whatever it was they made or sold. He heard laughter from the bar.

So Claire was born and then what? Jack felt his stomach tighten at the realization that he again had only fragmented, picturelike memories after that. The three of them in the park. Claire's first birthday. Swimming together in a pool. Bits and pieces that didn't seem linear, like he was reading one out of every ten pages in a book. Did he have some bizarre form of traumatic amnesia? Was something in the missing memories the key to his so-called stress disorder? The only really clear memories he had after the birth of Claire were of the last week, most especially the nightmares. What the hell did that mean? Jack felt a growing panic, and felt himself resist his mind's pull towards the answer, which he felt in some way he already knew. It was like looking down a long hallway at a door he knew he should go through, but being too paralyzed with fear to take the first step down the hall.

"Anything else, sir?"

Jack jumped at the voice, startled out of his thoughts.

"What?" he asked, looking up at Ethan.

"I'm sorry, sir. I didn't mean to startle you," Sarcasm? "Do you need anything else? Another beer perhaps?" Jack sensed the waiter was condescending to him. Or was that just his paranoia again?

"No...no, I'm good," he answered, wiping his mouth on the cloth napkin. "Just the check. Actually..." Jack felt an urgent need to get the hell out of this place, to get home to his girls. It was sudden and overpowering. He fumbled for his wallet and pulled out a credit card. "Just go ahead and ring this up. I'm in a bit of a hurry."

"No problem, sir," Ethan answered politely. "I'll be right back with this." The waiter grabbed his empty plate and glass as he left.

Jack again rubbed his eyes with the palms of his hands. No more thinking right now. It was time to go home. Ethan was back in record time, no doubt as anxious for Jack's departure as he was. Jack left a generous tip and thanked him, then slipped his card and wallet into his pocket. He slid out of his booth and headed for the door. As he passed by the booth next to his, a voice stopped him.

"How was your lunch? You must be starving!"

Jack turned, but he recognized the voice before he looked. Sitting in the booth was Commander Hoag, regimental chaplain, First Marine Expeditionary Force. He was dressed smartly in his dress blue uniform this time, his white combination hat on the otherwise empty table in front of him. He looked at Jack kindly through his round glasses. Jack felt his right leg begin to shake and he fought the urge to bolt for the door. Instead he looked around the room to see if anyone was staring at them, then returned his gaze to the Navy chaplain.

Maybe you should try and find a way to listen to them and hear what they have to say.

"I thought we might chat a moment, Casey."

"No," Jack shouted louder than he meant to. "No, I'm not ready..." Then he strode quickly for the door. "YOU'RE NOT REAL!" he screamed over his shoulder as he reached the hostess stand. He spun around to look at the Navy officer again.

But the booth was empty. The room was quiet and the crowd of business people spread out at several tables stared at him in stunned silence.

"I'm sorry," Jack mumbled and pushed through the heavy glass door and out into the cool November sunshine on the street.

Jack leaned against the wall and breathed the refreshing air deeply, open mouthed. It felt good, the way it tightened his chest and chilled him. The cool air made him feel alive, which was more than a trite saying these days. Jack realized he was more angry than scared. Perhaps he should have done it. Perhaps he should have listened to what the "image" had to say.

Jack shook his head. What the hell was he supposed to do? Sit down in an empty booth in a crowded restaurant and have a conversation with this image, this voice from his mind? They would haul him away giggling and wrapped in a wet sheet to a place that Lewellyn would get a phone call from. No, there had to be a better way.

Jack looked down the street to the corner, where the recruiting station flags still fluttered in the breeze. All he really needed was to prove to himself that Casey Stillman and his friends weren't real, right? Once he did that, the rest would be easy. How could he focus on finding a psychological root for his problem when he still couldn't shake the belief that THIS was the fantasy? How should he deal with the sense that his nightmares of Fallujah felt so much more real than his real life, except for Pam and Claire? Everything about his dream was vivid, yet he couldn't picture in his mind his own fucking wedding day! It might piss off Lewellyn, but Jack had to prove to himself that he was wrong about the Marine Corps, about Fallujah, about Bennet, Kindrich, Simmons, Stillman, and now Commander Hoag. He had to prove to himself that none of it was real. He didn't have a plan how to do that, but maybe this could be a start.

Jack headed down the block towards the row of flags.

Chapter
15

The United States Marine Corps Recruiting Station was colocated in the first floor office space with the recruiting offices for the other three service branches. Jack went through the glass door emblazoned with Armed Forces Recruiting Station and found himself in a small lobby with a single desk at which a civilian receptionist sat reading a magazine in front of a bank of quiet phones. The walls were covered with large pictures of jets flying over the desert, ships at sea, a SEAL team coming up a beach, tanks rolling up a road, and other staged scenes of America's military might in action. On the wall behind the receptionist were four recruiting posters, asking visitors to be an Army of One, to be one of the Few and Proud, to Aim High, and another one that just said Navy. Jack felt a familiar stirring when he looked at the picture of a Marine, standing in full-dress uniform in front of an embassy somewhere in a faraway place. He also felt anxious.

"May I help you?" the receptionist asked pleasantly.

"Uh, yes," Jack said, and then hesitated. What the hell was he afraid of? That the recruiter would recognize him? That the office would be full of dead Marines, chatting and telling war stories in their dirty and bloodstained digital cammies?

"How can I help you?" the receptionist asked patiently after an uncomfortable pause. She smiled knowingly. Maybe everyone was a little nervous in this office, Jack thought.

"I'm sorry," Jack said, and shook his head clear of images of his dead buddies. "I'd like to talk to someone in the Marine Corps office." Jack realized with some dread that he had no plan at all for what he wanted to talk to them about.

"Certainly," the woman said, and she snapped a piece of paper on a clipboard and handed it to him over her desk. "Can I just get you to fill out some information for us?"

Jack held up a hand, unsure why the idea of writing out his demographics was unnerving. It was hard enough just being here without a paper trail of information on his visit. Hell, the last thing he needed was a bunch of recruiting brochures to show up at the house.

"Uh, actually I'm not here to join. I just have a few questions." Then he added, with a sudden brainstorm, "I'm a teacher at JFK High, and I'm looking for a little information for a class I'm teaching on current events." Brilliant! Things just got a lot more comfortable now. "I can make an appointment and come back if this is not a good time."

The receptionist placed the clipboard with its blank form back on the desk. "Let me see real quick," she said holding up an index finger to Jack and dialing the phone. Jack heard the chirping of a phone down the hall, and when it stopped she spoke again. "Hi, Staff Sergeant. There's a teacher from the high school here who wanted to talk to you for a minute if you have time...okay, sure." Then she hung up the phone. "Staff Sergeant Perry will be right out."

"Thanks a lot." Jack stepped away from the desk and started casually scanning the pictures on the walls. This was perfect! He could ask some background questions without looking like an asshole. Why had he not thought of this before?

Jack leaned in and looked closely at a picture of a Coast Guard helicopter with a rescue diver jumping out into the water below it, but he didn't really see it. Instead he sorted things in his head. What did he want to know from this Marine? More importantly, what did he think he already knew that he could confirm or prove wrong with the recruiter? He would ask about the 3/1, the Third Battalion, First Marines. They were a part of First MEF, right? They were out of Camp Pendleton in California, near San Diego. The CG, or command general, was a Major General Owen Thomas, his memory (fantasy?) told him. Their light armor element was the First LAR, which was remotely located at nearby Twentynine Palms. They owned the LAVs that Stillman and his platoon had been clearing the road for in Fallujah. If only the LAVs, with their 25 mm guns and crew-served weapons and mortars had been closer, maybe Simmons and Bennet would be alive, and Casey would not be dying in the dark while he sucked blowing sand through a hole in his neck. Jack shuddered at the images.

Actually, Simmons had originally been with LAR and had come to them at Kilo Company just before deployment. He hoped to go back to them on their return. Might Jack be able to confirm a few names, even? His pulse quickened at the thought. Then he realized that he was unsure what answers he hoped for. A part of him almost wanted to find that the names were real, despite the terrifying questions that would leave.

"Hoorah, sir. I'm Staff Sergeant Rusty Perry." A strong and confident voice said behind him. Jack turned and saw a poster-perfect Marine in crisp dark green trousers and khaki shirt and tie. His blond hair was cropped skin tight on the sides and back, only slightly longer on top—a so-called high and tight haircut. On his sleeve were three red chevrons, the bottom one joined by an arcing rocker with a pair of crossed rifles in between, indicating he was a Staff Sergeant, an E-6, in the United States Marine Corps. His hand was outstretched and Jack took it, shaking hands with the squared-away Marine.

"Hoorah, Staff Sar'n," Jack replied easily. "Thanks for giving me a few minutes of your day."

"No problem, sir." Perry answered then gestured down the hall. "Why don't you come on back to the office?"

Jack followed the Marine down the hall to the first office on the right. Perry pulled a chair out from the wall and placed it beside a cubicle-style desk with neatly arranged folders, paper work, and a computer on which a screen saver boasted "The Few, The Proud." The Marine sat at the desk and motioned for Jack to take a seat.

"How can I help you today, sir?" Perry asked and leaned back in his chair.

"Well, I'm teaching a current events class," Jack lied, crossing his legs and folding his hands in his lap, "and I was hoping you could help me get a little information on the Marines and what they are doing now in Iraq." Jack held the eyes of the enlisted Marine recruiter and hoped his anxiety was not evident.

"Anything to help, sir," Perry responded. "What can I tell you?"

"Well," Jack was unsure how to start. "The Marines we see on TV, the ones fighting in Fallujah—where are they from?" Jack felt his anxiety rise, suddenly aware that he already knew the answers. He felt certain now of that.

"The Marines fighting in Fallujah now are mostly West Coast-based units," Perry answered. "We set up rotations where the East and West Coast units swap out deployments, together with the Marines in the Pacific, and at present it is the California-based units who are in theater."

"That's the First MEF, right?" Jack asked.

"That's right, sir," Perry answered. "Elements of the First Marine Expeditionary Force from Camp Pendleton are currently conducting operations in Iraq. There is some overlap, though, so some forces from Third MEF are also still in theater."

"Third MEF is Hawaii and Okinawa?"

"That's correct, sir."

"So they're still completing the RIP?" Jack asked.

"That's right," Perry answered. He looked more closely at Jack now, apparently intrigued by his knowledge and use of Marine jargon. Jack made a note to try and be more careful. "The RIP is the overlap period where the existing unit turns over responsibility of the AOR to the incoming units."

"I see," Jack answered, not sure how to feel about knowing that or where to go next. "Were you ever with First MEF, Staff Sar'n?"

"No, sir. I was Twenty-fourth MEU with Second Marines out of Camp Lejeune."

"Long way from North Carolina, Staff Sar'n," Jack said smiling.

"Yes, Sir," Perry answered. "Recruiting tour is a nice way to round out your package for promotion. I'm actually from Ohio, so makes no difference to me." The Marine seemed more relaxed. He obviously loved talking about the Corps.

"Hoping to make Gunny this year?" Jack asked, referring to promotion to Gunnery Sergeant.

"Just might make it, Sir," Perry answered.

Jack sat a moment, trying to think of a way to get to the real questions. He couldn't just ask outright about individual people could he? Even if he did the OPSEC rules, operational security, would prevent Perry from telling him anything. So now what?

"Is General Thomas still the CG over at One MEF?" he asked casually. The CG was the commanding general, in charge of all the units that made up the expeditionary force. Jack's pulse quickened and he realized he was squeezing his hands together in his lap so tightly that his left hand had begun to tingle. He tried to relax under Perry's scrutiny.

"Who were you with, sir?" he asked after a moment.

Jack was confused for a moment. Had he gone too far?

"I teach at JFK High," he answered.

Perry reached for a coffee cup on his desk, a pewter bull dog with a drill sergeant's cap on its head decorating the front, the unofficial mascot of the Corps.

"No, I mean when you were in?" He looked at Jack with a knowing grin, sipping his black coffee. "I can always spot a fellow jar head."

Jack felt himself beginning to panic. The last thing he wanted was to look like a fool in front of this Marine staff sergeant. He shifted uncomfortably in his seat, his mind reeling. Why in the hell would this guy think he was a Marine?

"I was never in the Corps, Staff Sergeant," he answered, unaware that his hand was now numb. "One of my best friends is in, though. I kind of lost touch with him the last two years," Jack swallowed hard. No going back now, so what the hell. "Casey Stillman. Ever meet him?"

Perry looked a little disappointed that he had missed the call, but didn't look particularly suspicious, Jack thought. Why would he? The staff sergeant looked up at the ceiling, apparently in thought. After a moment he looked back at Jack.

"Doesn't really ring a bell, sir. Was he East Coast?"

"Not really sure," Jack lied. He knew exactly where Stillman was—bleeding to death in Fallujah, somewhere in the night. He decided to take one more shot. "What about Rich Simmons? Young kid, kind of lanky?"

"Don't think so, sir," Perry answered without much thought. Jack sensed that he had become unsure of him and was being more cautious now. He decided to shift gears.

"Well, anyway," he said lightly, as if those names, his real reason for coming, meant nothing, "let me just get a little quick background, and I'll let you get back to work."

Jack proceeded to ask a few innocuous questions about training and assignments. He asked about the relationship to the Navy and how the Marines got around. He even made a show of borrowing a piece of paper and jotting down a few notes, for his lecture on current events. After a few minutes he rose and stuck out his hand. He tried to conceal his deep disappointment. This had been a waste of time, other than showing him and Staff Sergeant Perry that a biology teacher from the high school had an unusually detailed understanding of how the Marine Corps was set up. What the hell did that prove?

"Thanks a lot, Staff Sar'n," he said. "This is a real help. I'm sure the kids will find this stuff interesting, especially with all they see on the news these days."

Perry rose from his chair and shook his hand firmly. "No problem, sir. Happy to help. If any of the kids want more information, especially the seniors, have them give me a call." He handed Jack a stack of business cards.

"You bet, Staff Sar'n," Jack replied, slipping the business cards into his pocket. Then he turned to leave, but turned back as Perry spoke again.

"By the way, sir," he said from his chair. "You were right. General Thomas is still the CG at One MEF."

Jack stopped. He felt the blood drain from his face. How in the fuck could he possibly know that? How could he know any of this shit? The walls seemed to be closing in on him and he felt his throat tighten. For a moment he thought he smelled the all too familiar stench of the dusty Iraqi desert.

"Thanks again," he said over his shoulder as he headed out of the office.

As Jack walked to the front door, with a courteous wave and thank you to the smiling receptionist, he stopped, his eye caught by the little newspaper stand by the old couch where nervous applicants waited to talk to their recruiters. On one stack was a newspaper called *Marine Corps Times*. On a whim Jack grabbed the top copy and folded it under his arm as he left the office.

A few minutes later, Jack sat in the growing warmth of his Volvo and listened to Julie Roberts singing softly on the radio, apparently hoping she wouldn't run out of gas.

I sure would hate to break down here.

Jack wiped the frustrated tears from his cheeks and shifted the car into gear. He maneuvered the Volvo out of his spot by the curb and carefully into traffic. Then he headed home to his girls, his *Marine Corps Times* unopened on the seat beside him and his head full of more questions than answers.

* * *

Jack's dark mood and deep confusion lifted instantly when he walked through the door of his home. The smell of the house, the scattered toys, the sight of his wife, all combined to melt away the pain of the last few hours. He felt his shoulders drop as his tension evaporated.

Pam sat on the couch, legs tucked up underneath her. As he came through the door, her face lit up and her eyes pulled away from the TV and whatever the gang was making on HGTV. Jack felt a surge of guilt as he saw that she was eating peanut butter toast off a paper napkin.

"Hey, baby," she said, reaching a hand out to him without getting up. Her face looked so beautiful, smiling as she was. Jack took her hand, then leaned over and kissed her. Peanut butter. He felt bad again. "I tried to wait for you, sweetheart, but I got too hungry."

"That's ok, Pam," Jack said, plopping onto the couch next to her. "I'm sorry I took so long. I had to sort out some of the things we talked about in the session. I grabbed a bite downtown." He looked at his wife, who still looked happy to see him. "Sorry I didn't call you," he added.

"Don't be silly," Pam said, shaking her head. "Claire Bear is napping." She slid up closer to him, wrapping her arms tightly around his and leaning against his shoulder. "How did it go, Jack? How do you feel?"

Jack considered a moment. How much should he tell her about the restaurant? What would she think about the recruiter visit? It didn't matter, Jack realized. He would tell her everything. Telling her all the missing details the other morning had set him free somehow, or given him strength. She was there for him, as he would be for her whenever she might need him, and he wasn't going to lose that. Jack squeezed her arm and kissed her cheek.

"Well, it's been an interesting day," he began.

He told her every detail of his morning and early afternoon, and felt the bond he shared with his wife as he spoke. His worries that she would judge him or be frightened drained away, and he wanted her to be with him for wherever this was taking them. He started with his session with Lewellyn, and shared with her his surprise and fear over the idea of confronting his "images."

Pam held him tightly during this, her arms wrapped around him.

"Do you think it would help you, Jack? Do you think you could do it?" she asked. "You have to admit, it kind of makes a lot of sense."

"I don't know," Jack answered honestly, his head leaning against hers. "It seems kind of flaky, talking to a hallucination."

"But wouldn't you really be just listening to yourself?" she asked, turning to look him in the eyes. "I mean, isn't that sort of what Dr. Lewellyn is saying?"

"Yes," he replied, feeling himself tense up a bit. Pam had an uncanny way of seeing right to the heart of the matter. "But it's still scary. I mean there is a part of me that still feels it's all so real. And these images," Jack shuddered unconsciously, but his wife felt it and hugged him tighter. "Well, they can be pretty horrifying."

Pam leaned against his arm again and said nothing. Jack continued, talking briefly about the review of his childhood and then told her of their conversation about her. How they had fallen in love in college, and most importantly, how she and Claire meant everything to him. She sighed at that part; a content and happy sigh. Then he talked about their conversation about the Marine Corps at the deli one Saturday during college.

"Do you remember that?" he asked, his voice hesitant.

Pam thought a minute. "Sort of," she answered. "You talked about it a lot during college."

"I did?" Jack asked, surprised. Pam seemed confused by his reaction.

"Sure, Jack," she said. "You talked a lot about serving your country and giving something back, that sort of thing. You still talk about it sometimes." She had laid her head back on his shoulder. "What else did you guys talk about?"

Jack hesitated. Why could he not remember that he had talked often about the military? In his mind he remembered mostly that it was an opportunity to help earn money for college. His memories of them when they were dating revolved mostly around his burning desire to be with her always, to have a family and grow old together. Well, and to get in her pants—they had been nineteen at the time, after all.

"Well, the thing that bothered me the most was how, I don't know, sort of fragmented my memories are after that. It's like I only remember big picture stuff." Jack closed his eyes, picturing some of those images that he treasured. "You holding Claire, her birthday, how beautiful you were at our wedding, that sort of thing. But it's sort of disjointed or something." Jack sighed heavily. "I don't know, baby. It's like somewhere in there is the answer and I can't get to it."

"Or you're afraid of it," Pam finished for him without looking up.

"Yeah," Jack said then paused. What on earth was in there that scared him so? How could he lose such blocks of their life? And why did Pam seem so okay with that?

Jack shook the weird, ominous feeling off and continued. He told her of his lunch and the mistake with the waiter. By now he felt relaxed and comfortable, and when he told her of the "image" of Commander Hoag in the booth, he wasn't even aware that he no longer hesitated or thought at all that the story would make Pam pull away from him. He told her of yelling at the empty booth on his way out the door.

"That must have been a sight," she said with a smile and hugged him again. He heard no worry or fear in her voice. If she was concerned about her husband's sanity, she was doing a helluva job concealing it, Jack thought.

"Then I did something that may have been stupid," he said, and pulled back from her so he could see her face and gauge her reaction. "Or at least I think it would make Lewellyn mad," he said, but of course he was really only worried that it would upset her.

"What's that, baby?" Jack thought he saw a glimmer of concern in her eyes.

"Well," he began. "It was kind of impulsive. There was a recruiting station on the corner downtown, and I guess I kind of went there." He paused again and studied her face.

"You went to a recruiter, Jack?" There was a mix of confusion and worry in her face now. "What on earth would you do that for?" Pam still held his arm, but she pulled back to see him more clearly.

"I don't know," Jack said, embarrassed now. What the hell had he hoped he would get from Staff Sergeant Perry? "I think I just needed to see if the details that my mind keeps telling me about the Marines were just made up, or if I really do know this shit. I mean why would I know these things, Pam?" Jack realized the question was in no way rhetorical. He really needed to hear her thoughts on this.

"Jack," Pam said softly, holding his hand now, a patient parent with a slow child. "You read dozens of brochures about the Marine Corps a few years ago. You devoured information about the military when you thought it might be a career choice for you. You know how you are, baby. You learn everything about things that interest you. You haven't thought about these things in years, but those things are still rattling around up there." She tapped his temple gently. "Then, when whatever it is about this goddamn war grabbed you like it has, it came back to you."

It seemed so simple the way she said it, so obvious. Jack looked at the floor and thought hard for a moment. That wouldn't really explain knowing who the commanding general of First MEF was, though. But, Jack supposed, he could have just picked that up from the news, maybe, and tucked it into his memory without knowing it. Pam could be right. He wanted to believe that, wanted desperately to believe anything that meant he wasn't crazy. Or worse, trapped in a very real but horrifying world, where dead buddies visited you in a dreamed reality you created for yourself. Yes, Pam had to be right, but of course, none of it explained why he was having nightmares and hallucinations in the first place.

"So what did you find out, Jack? What did Sergeant Perry tell you?"

Jack snapped out of his thoughts. What had she said? Sergeant Perry? Jack was sure he hadn't told Pam his name. He didn't think he had told her any detail of the visit yet, in fact he knew he hadn't. What the fuck? Jack felt his anxiety grow, and a fear he couldn't understand. Something was very wrong here. Very fucking wrong! Pam's reactions were too perfect, too controlled. How could she not be upset by the things he was telling her? He had talked to a fucking ghost in a crowded fucking restaurant for Christ's sake! If she had told him that, he would have been mad with worry. And fear, too, probably. Not for himself, but for the woman he loved, and maybe for their child. Jack was gripped even tighter now by fear and the feeling that this, all of this, was somehow very wrong.

"Jack?"

Jack looked up, almost sure he would find himself holding hands with Simmons, his faceless grin and bloody gums staring back at him.

Come back Sar'n!

But it was Pam, her face full of worry now, her eyes clouded.

"Jack, what is it? What's wrong, baby?" She was holding both of his hands now and her voice trembled.

"I...I...uh..." Jack stammered. This was insane! He was paranoid as hell and now he was letting it hurt Pam. He gripped her hands tightly and closed his eyes, squeezing them until there were white flashes in his vision.

Stop it, goddamnit! Stop this shit right now!

He opened his eyes and looked at his wife, the most real thing he had ever had in his life. Then he smiled at her tightly.

"I'm sorry, baby," and he kissed her cheek. "Just another flash of something. I'm so sorry." Jack leaned over and took his wife in his arms, her head on his shoulder, and rocked her gently. Pam clung to him.

"Everything is ok, Jack," she said, the tremor gone from her voice. "I love you so much, baby. I am so proud of you and I love you so much."

He held her like that for a long time, neither saying a word, their eyes closed. Jack had no idea where to go from here. *God, please let Lewellyn have some ideas tomorrow.* Then Pam broke the embrace and stood up.

She still held his hand, but stood beside him now. The light from the kitchen silhouetted her from behind, and Jack had the distinct feeling again that he was looking at an angel. His angel. God, how he loved this woman. Jack felt a lump in his throat.

"Jack," she said, her voice soft and soothing, her hand warm in his.

"Yes?" he said.

Please, say something that will make the fear go away. Please, help me.

"Claire will be napping for another hour or so, sweetheart." Her eyes seemed almost glowing. "Will you come upstairs with me? Will you lie with me and let me take you away from all of this for a while?" She squeezed his hand.

Jack rose and hugged his wife tightly, feeling her arms around him, breathing in her scent again. What on earth could possibly be in his mind that would take him away from this woman and all her love? Jack broke the hug and kissed his wife deeply, his tongue exploring her mouth as she pressed against him. And again, the feel of her and the love in her eyes took all of the nightmare far, far away; back to some deep recess in his hurting mind.

"Lead the way, honey," he said. "I place myself in your very capable hands."

Together they nearly ran up the stairs, hand in hand, to their bed and sanctuary from his madness.

Chapter
16

The afternoon gave Jack a renewed sense of hope. It was not just the lovemaking (though that was fantastic) and the closeness and vivid sense of reality it had brought. It was just as much the simple things that the day provided. The time spent playing with Claire in their bed. The walk to the playground hand in hand, their little girl pointing at squirrels from her stroller, squealing with delight. It had been the trip to the grocery store with all three of them together (though he wondered briefly if Pam was afraid to let him go out alone, and had to shake the feeling off). It had been laughing and teasing each other while they made dinner together, Claire looking at picture books in her high chair. It had been sipping wine over a simple spaghetti dinner, and cleaning Claire's spaghetti sauce clown face off while they all laughed. When Claire was asleep again in her crib, after Jack read her stories ("Rainbow fish went into a scary cave"), they had cuddled on the couch together. They finished their bottle of Shiraz and talked about the future, neither even trying to follow the senseless sitcoms on the TV. Jack had not felt at all afraid. He had been full of hope.

Now, lying in bed beside his wife, her sleeping head on his shoulder and her soft arm across his chest, Jack fought desperately to hang on to those feelings. His mind kept pulling him to the fears of his day and doubts about the future they had planned on the couch. It was hard not to be haunted by thoughts of tomorrow and what it would bring, with his looming session with Lewellyn and all the burning questions his mind tried to raise. The things Pam had said earlier about his knowledge of the Marine Corps made perfect sense, but still seemed off somehow for reasons that were hazy, like shadows in the dark.

Jack yawned a deep and tired yawn. He had taken his magic pills and sleep was pulling at him. He allowed himself to collapse and to give in to his exhaustion. He would think about these things tomorrow. He kissed Pam lightly on the lips.

"I love you, baby," he said, and let his heavy eyes close.

"Mmmmm," Pam replied.

In moments he was fast asleep beside her.

* * *

Jack dreamed, despite the medicine that Lewellyn and Barton had given him, but this time he dreamed without fear.

Jack walked along the sand berm in his tennis shoes and jeans, shivering slightly in the cool desert air. Despite the night, the half-moon made it surprisingly easy to see, and Jack maneuvered along the berm towards the hushed voices farther up the large wall of sand and rock. Just over the berm, Jack could see a rim of light in the distance.

Fallujah.

He kind of expected to feel a rush of fear or anxiety. He felt nothing but calm. Maybe it was because he knew he was dreaming. Or maybe because in this dream he was himself, Jack, instead of a dying Marine sergeant who couldn't get enough air into his bleeding lungs. He knew his beautiful wife slept beside him seven thousand miles away and that their daughter slept just a few steps up the hall in her nursery. They were both safe. Or maybe the medicine, the Effexor, did something after all. Maybe that was what made it all tolerable. Whatever the reason, he actually felt pretty damn good, a new feeling but he sure as hell liked it. Jack smiled a little in the dark.

As Jack got closer to the hushed voices they became more discernible, more like talk than just noise, and he could see a group of young men huddled together against the berm, leaning back, legs stretched out in the dirt. A few orange cat eyes bobbed around the group, glowing ash from lit cigarettes that a few of the Marines smoked as they talked and laughed in hushed whispers. When Jack got a few feet from them, he stopped, and sat cross-legged (*criss-cross apple sauce,* Claire giggled in his mind) in the dirt and listened to the young men.

"Rich, you would eat the ass out of dead rhino," a voice cracked. That had to be Bennet, Tex to his Marine buddies (like every Texan in every Marine platoon, Jack thought).

"Fuck you, man," Simmons answered, his neutral upstate New York accent contrasting sharply with Bennet's slow drawl. "I'm telling you this shit is good. This is the best MRE they give us."

"God, Rich, you say that about every fuckin' MRE meal." Jack wasn't sure at first if he could place the voice, but then realized it sounded like Ballard, a lanky kid with bad acne from Ohio. Probably the best shot in the platoon. Jack (Casey) had taken him off the SAW, the M249 machine gun, and put him back on an M16A, but with a laser scope, early in the deployment. "You even said that about that 'Captain's Country Chicken' shit, remember Mac?"

"Yeah, I remember," McIver answered. "That Yankee will eat any goddamn thing."

"Captain's Chicken is ok," Simmons defended, "You guys just don't crush up the crackers and add hot sauce."

"Captain's Chicken don't come with friggin' crackers," an unknown voice said.

"Bullshit it don't," Simmons answered.

"Hey, Rich if you'll eat anything, why don't you crawl over here and eat me?"

"Fuck off, Tex," Simmons laughed. "Anyway, I'm too hungry for that little snack."

They all laughed.

"Noise discipline, guys," a familiar voice said. Then Jack caught his breath as he realized why it was familiar. It was his voice.

"Sorry, Sar'n," Simmons said, his voice now a lower whisper. "Casey, don't that chicken thing come with crackers?"

"Shit, Rich, I don't know," Stillman answered in Jack's voice. "But I'll tell you guys one thing." There was a pause.

"What's that, Sar'n?" Kindrich asked with his Tennessee accent.

"Simmons will eat about any goddamn thing!"

And they all laughed in hushed giggles.

Jack listened as his men continued to tease each other, smoking in the moonlight—except Simmons who was still eating, and McIver who was dipping Skoal and spitting onto the sand berm. He still felt pretty content, if anything.

"Good bunch of kids," a voice said behind him. Jack didn't jump. He had expected the voice. Why not? It was just a dream, right? His dream. And he felt, for the first time, very much in control.

"Yeah, they are," he answered and turned slowly to look over his shoulder, already knowing that Commander Hoag would be there. "I think I love them all," he said. Then he considered the statement and added, "Or I would, if they were real."

Commander Hoag sported his clean digital desert cammies and dirty desert boots again. He sat down beside Jack in the dirt, groaning as he did, like all middle-aged men eventually come to do. He looked at Jack in the moonlight.

"What makes you think they aren't real?" Hoag asked with a patience that reminded Jack of Dr. Lewellyn. Jack smiled. Not this time. He was in control here. It was his mind who created Hoag, and his decision to summon him here for some reason.

Listen to what your mind is asking you.

"Well," he said leaning in towards the Navy chaplain, "For one thing, I'm dreaming."

"I see," Hoag answered, looking up at the moon, as if he were thinking that one over. "And because you are dreaming, this can't be real?"

"Well, it's real in one sense, I guess," Jack answered. He leaned back now on his outstretched arm, content to play the game. "I mean, my mind is real, my thoughts are real. I came here to this place in my mind, this dream, to find some answers, I suppose. Answers to some real questions about some real problems I'm having. Those guys," Jack gestured in the direction of Casey Stillman and his squad of Marines, "are from my nightmares. They're real to me, I guess. Sometimes too fucking real," he laughed. "But they exist only here, in my mind." He tapped his temple like Pam had done and felt very satisfied with the answer.

"You're sure?" Hoag asked quietly. "Sure that this place is the dream?"

Jack felt anxious at that question. Wasn't that the real question he had been asking himself all along? Wasn't that the crux of his deepest fear, that this was real and his home, his life and job, his girls, were the dream? "I'm sure," he lied.

Hoag shifted in the sand, lying back against the berm, and gazed up at the moon. "Then what are you doing here?" he asked.

Jack thought a long moment before answering. The question implied he came here of his own free will; that his nightmares and hallucinations were things he had created on purpose. Was that true? He supposed that in a sense it had to be. His mind created them somehow, to force him to face something that bothered him, something that frightened him terribly. But what?

"I'm looking for some answers, I guess," he said, watching the commander carefully. For a long time the chaplain said nothing, just stared at the sky and the bright half-moon overhead.

"Maybe you're asking the wrong questions," he said simply.

Jack said nothing. But the simple statement bothered the shit out of him, though he didn't know why. What was the question he was asking? He just wanted to know he wasn't crazy, he thought. And to try and figure out what was haunting his mind so viciously that he could have created such horrible visions in his dreams. What connected him to these Marines, these young men who stretched out now in the sand, resting up to go into battle in a dusty little city, thousands of miles from their homes? Some of them would die there tomorrow, at least in his nightmare. He didn't know how to feel about that, or if he should feel anything. His mind was telling him a story, and he was just following along, trying to catch the hidden meaning. Wasn't that what Dr. Lewellyn wanted him to believe? Jack lay back in the sand beside the Navy chaplain, another creation of his troubled mind. He felt very tired now. He was done with this dream.

Time to go home.

"I'd love to stay and chat, sir," Jack said, turning to the chaplain in the sand beside him, "but I think I'm done for tonight." He yawned and closed his eyes.

"Did you find any answers here?" Commander Hoag asked softly.

"Not yet," Jack answered tiredly.

"Tomorrow I think we should talk about death, Casey. I think we should start asking the questions that will unlock your fears, okay?"

"My name is Jack," Jack answered without knowing why.

* * *

He didn't start awake. He didn't scream or tear at his throat. He actually felt kind of peaceful. He simply opened his eyes and found himself looking at the ceiling of their bedroom, the fan turning slowly in the moonlight from the window, without much surprise.

Jack let his mind wander over the conversation with Hoag, and searched for the deeper meaning that his inner voice must be trying to help him find. It no longer seemed that finding out whether Casey Stillman and his Marines had ever been real was the most important thing. There was something else. Something those nightmares represented.

Jack rolled over and wrapped his arms around Pam, hugging her tightly. He hoped tomorrow that Lewellyn would help him find the questions. Then maybe he could work on the answers.

He kissed Pam's hair, closed his eyes, and slipped into a dreamless sleep.

Finally the damn medicine was starting to work.

Chapter
17

Jack woke up feeling a lot more rested. At first he didn't remember his dream and lay in bed with a contented smirk; again the medicine had beat out his sanity. Then slowly he felt the dream rematerialize. He watched the ceiling fan turn and wondered what it meant.

Maybe you're asking the wrong questions...

Maybe. Hell, probably. He had to admit he had given up any belief that he had a clue what the hell was going on. What were the right questions?

Are you sure this isn't the dream?

Jack shuddered a bit, and then forced the thoughts from his head and swung his legs out of bed. There would be plenty of time for this horseshit when he got to Lewellyn's office. He shuffled to the bathroom slowly on stiff legs and saw a yellow Post-it note with Pam's handwriting pasted to the mirror. He squinted his tired eyes and then reached behind him to turn on the light as he pulled the note down.

Jack,

I decided to let you sleep in 'cause you looked so peaceful. I have taken Claire to her playgroup at Melissa's. I am running to the store and then I will be home. Call me after your meeting if you want and maybe we can meet somewhere for lunch.

Love you.

—Pam

Jack felt a terrible disappointment that he wouldn't see his girls before his meeting. Is that what it was, a meeting? Not her style to call it a head-shrinking session, Jack supposed. Then he realized he had no idea what time it was and dashed into the bedroom to look at the clock.

Nine fifteen? Oh, shit!

Jack took a very quick shower and then pulled on a pair of jeans and a sweat shirt. No reason to get all dressed up for Lewellyn anymore. They were way past any first impression bullshit. He dashed out the door, hoping for time to get coffee on the way. By nine thirty-five he was warming the Volvo in the driveway.

As Jack flipped through his CD case looking for a Kenny Chesney disc, he saw the newspaper he had left in the passenger seat. *Marine Corps Times* it announced in bold red script. Jack wondered why he had impulsively grabbed that paper. He started to reach for it, but then realized he was still running late. What could he hope to find in there anyway? He popped in the CD and backed out of the drive.

Twenty minutes later he was parked in the same spot he had left from the day before, feeling almost as nervous. Without much thought he grabbed the little paper off the passenger seat as he got out and tucked it under his arm as he locked the Volvo's doors with his fob, a satisfying chirp-chirp announcing his success. Maybe he would flip through the paper in the waiting room. There might be something about the 3/1 and the action in Fallujah.

Jack arrived at the glass receptionist window at nine fifty-eight, Citgo coffee in hand (black) and smiled at the receptionist, a flash of embarrassment as he recalled his last encounter with her in the waiting room.

"Good morning, Jack," she said, no hint that she remembered how crazy he had seemed just twenty-four hours earlier. "How are you this morning?"

"Feeling much better, thanks," he answered with a charming smile.

No dead guys in the waiting room today are there?

"Good." She smiled back. "Dr. Lewellyn is ready for you, so you can go right back if you like."

"Great," he said, though he felt more anxious than great. He headed for the hall, then turned and hesitated. "Could I leave my paper with you until I'm done? I'd rather not take it back," he said to the girl behind the clean glass. Why had he brought it with him? The last thing he wanted was for Lewellyn to see it. Why stir the pot?

"Sure, Jack," she answered and took the paper from him, setting it on the desk beside her.

"Thanks," Jack said with a little wave and then headed for the dark door at the end of the hall.

The psychologist greeted him warmly and offered to freshen his coffee, which Jack accepted, and then they both took their now expected seats. Jack crossed his legs and sipped his coffee, waiting for the inevitable question so he could begin recounting his day after their last session and his dream from last night. But Lewellyn had other plans.

"I want to start a bit differently today, Jack," he said, opening his little leather-bound notebook and clicking his pen. "I think today we should talk a little bit about death. I think we should start to ask the questions that may unlock your fears, okay?"

Jack felt his mouth go dry and his pulse quicken at the words. What the hell? Lewellyn couldn't possibly know about his conversation with Hoag in last night's dream. He felt a panic growing in the middle of his chest and set his coffee on the end table with a trembling hand.

"Jack?" Lewellyn sounded concerned, but maybe it was his imagination. "Jack, are you all right?"

"Yeah," Jack answered. "Just a little early for such a heady conversation. I was sound asleep less than an hour ago." His attempt at sounding casual failed miserably and he felt the psychologist's dissecting eyes on him. Jack could feel a sense of surrealism creep into his already jumbled mood. Was this the dream after all? Wouldn't that explain Lewellyn tossing back his own mind's (Hoag's) words at him?

"Are you uncomfortable talking about death, Jack?" he asked.

Jack's mind reeled and he forced himself to calm down. He was overreacting. Lewellyn was asking the inevitable question that Jack had somehow known he would ask. That was where his dream had come from.

"No," Jack lied. "No, not at all. Just a little surprised. I thought we might start with things that happened yesterday." He hoped he could intrigue the doctor to a more comfortable conversation, but Lewellyn wasn't biting.

"We'll come back to all that, Jack," he said softly. He sat motionless, and Jack felt he was studying him. "I'd like to start with this, okay? It seems to be a relevant theme for us."

"Sure," Jack said. He succeeded a little better at sounding casual this time. "Shoot."

"Well, let's start with the basics." Lewellyn scribbled in his book now. "What do you think death is, Jack?"

"Well, I don't know," he answered, "but who does, right? We all find out, I guess, but no one is talking."

At least not to everyone else.

They spent the next quarter hour talking in generalities about death. Jack was very uncomfortable talking about something he felt he knew so little about, especially now that he felt his views might be changing with all that was going on in his mind. They discussed, briefly, his beliefs about death from a religious standpoint.

"I was brought up believing that death isn't the end," he said, "that God has something else in store for us when we leave here."

"Do you still believe that?" Lewellyn asked.

"I think so," Jack answered. In fact he wasn't at all sure what he believed. His nightmares and hallucinations had him thinking a lot about the moment of death. Especially the violent and grotesque death he had seen not just in his dreams, but on the television news. He had not given much new thought to what came next.

"Are you afraid of death, Jack?" Lewellyn asked. He looked at him patiently and seemed quite comfortable with this very uncomfortable topic.

"Isn't everyone?" Jack asked, evading the question a bit.

"I don't know, Jack." Lewellyn answered. "I'm most interested in how you feel, though."

"At least during my billable session," Jack joked, vying for more time. He regretted it immediately, though the psychologist seemed unruffled.

"Right," he said easily, okay with the joke apparently.

There was a long pause during which Lewellyn watched him impassively and Jack fidgeted uncomfortably. After a few moments his doctor spoke.

"Well?" Lewellyn said.

"Well, what?" Jack asked innocently.

Lewellyn uncrossed his legs and leaned forward like he always did when Jack squirmed. His attempt at being more personal, Jack thought.

"You haven't answered the question, Jack. But I'm sure you know that."

Jack sighed heavily. He wasn't going to get out of this conversation.

"Sure," he answered. Then looked up and held Lewellyn's gaze. "Yeah, I'm scared of death. Isn't everybody, at least a little? Who knows what it really is, right? I mean, I think we all harbor fear of the unknown." There. That should do it.

"What scares you the most about dying, Jack," Lewellyn asked, not at all content to leave well enough alone.

"I'm most afraid of having to leave my girls—to be without Pam and Claire," Jack answered without a second thought. Then he leaned back against the thick leather cushion. That was true, wasn't it? Leaving his life with his family unfinished was what he feared the most.

"Okay," Lewellyn said and reassumed his cross-legged position of interrogation, scribbling again in his notebook. Then he took a moment and reviewed a few notes from farther back in his notebook. "What do you think the Navy chaplain represents in all this, Jack?" He flipped a few more pages. "Commander Hoag," he said, finding his name in his notes.

Jack thought about that a moment. Who was the chaplain to him? He was an irritating son of a bitch, that was for sure.

"He asks me questions," Jack answered simply.

"What do you mean?"

"Well," Jack thought carefully. "When I'm thinking about things, he seems to sort of show up and ask questions."

"What kind of questions?" Lewellyn asked, intrigued.

"He asks things that sort of, I don't know, get me thinking in a different way. Sort of like you do."

"Well that's interesting," Lewellyn said. "What do you make of that?"

Jack was determined to give the psychologist a good answer.

"I think that Hoag is really coming from a part of my mind that stimulates me to think and analyze things in a different way," he said. Yeah, that sounded good. "He is sort of the rational part of me.

He separates me from the emotional impact of the nightmares and stuff, and lets me think more critically, I think."

"So he's your own voice?"

"My own thoughts," Jack corrected.

Lewellyn put down his pen and seemed quite satisfied.

"That's very good, Jack." He got up and crossed over to the couch, taking up a seat next to him. "Very good." He patted Jack lightly on the leg. "So what do you make of that?"

Jack felt more relaxed. He felt like he had made some breakthrough, but was remarkably unconcerned that he had no idea what the hell it was.

"Well, I guess I'm listening to him a bit more," Jack laughed and held up a hand, "in my mind, not in a crowded restaurant, but we'll get to that. I guess listening to my own rational and unemotional side," he corrected, "will help me look at things differently and get to the answers I need."

"I think so, too, Jack." Lewellyn patted him on the leg again.

There's a good boy.

"Well, this makes a nice transition into my day yesterday after I left you," Jack said.

Lewellyn rose, crossing back over to his driver's seat and opening his little book, pen again at the ready.

"Ok, Jack," he said, "tell me about yesterday. I'll give you a break for a minute, but we have more talking about death to do, I think," he cautioned.

Jack enjoyed the moment of control and started in on his day from yesterday. Lewellyn scribbled furiously as he spoke.

Chapter 18

Jack left the office an hour later, feeling pretty good with himself. They had returned to the "death talk" as Lewellyn had promised, but had not really unraveled any great mysteries. They talked again about the idea that, to Jack, death represented separation from his family. Lewellyn seemed very interested in that for some reason. That Jack seemed not to have a great concern for what death was, where we go from here, what it all meant, also seemed to intrigue him. To Jack, the only real issue was leaving his life with his girls unfinished; not being there for them, watching Claire grow up, holding and comforting his wife. The rest seemed fairly petty and something that couldn't be answered anyway, so why worry about it? Lewellyn pointed out that this all seemed to imply a young death for Jack, and Jack had considered that only briefly. He told him that maybe that was because of his empathy for all these Marines, dying far away from home and family at such a young age, their lives so unfinished. That seemed to satisfy Lewellyn.

They agreed that Jack's dream the night before, and the control he seemed to maintain over its course and outcome, showed real progress. Lewellyn reassured him that while they didn't yet have the answers to what had precipitated all this "instability in his emotional and psychological life," that they were getting very close. He also predicted that his progress meant that things should continue to improve for him over the coming days, and that the dreams might become less disturbing.

"You may still have some setbacks, some intense emotional hallucinations or dreams," the psychologist had cautioned, "but I think you have shown real progress in your ability to deal with them both intellectually and emotionally."

Jack had felt really good about that. Again he felt filled with a sense of hope. Lewellyn's focus on finding the root cause was less important to Jack, who really just wanted the nightmares to stop and to return to his happy life with Pam and Claire. He realized he very much looked forward to going back to school on Monday, after what he hoped would be a relaxing and healing family weekend.

Before he left Lewellyn's office, he borrowed the phone to call Pam. He was now excited by the lunch they had planned. They decided to meet at an intimate little Vietnamese restaurant they both enjoyed, but rarely went to anymore, what with Claire being so young and the long drive downtown to get there. The restaurant sat just a few blocks away and Jack stopped by his Volvo to feed the meter. He decided the walk to Viet Gardens would help him relax and kill some of the time it would take for Pam to drive there to meet him. The parking meter's hunger for coins having been sated, Jack started out towards the restaurant and passed by the Military Recruiting Station without a glance or thought.

"You forgot your paper," a familiar voice said from the alley he was passing.

Jack stopped, forcing away the moment of panic at the sound of Hoag's voice. There was nothing to fear here. Hoag was just his own mind trying to help him find things that he needed to find. Jack turned to see the Navy chaplain standing just inside the alley, again dressed smartly in his dress blue uniform with white hat. He looked a bit like an airline pilot in that uniform. Jack had always preferred the crisp green Class B uniform of the Marines, which he felt looked more military. The chaplain smiled and held out a folded paper in his hand. Just a part of his own mind, Jack reminded himself again. He was unconcerned at how ridiculous it should seem that his mind had fetched his forgotten paper from the receptionist and brought it a block and a half to an alley for him to pick up.

"Thank you," Jack said and took the paper, tucking it under his arm. Then he turned to leave.

"You don't really have a choice about leaving them, you know," the commander said softly at his back. Jack stopped and turned to face his demon again.

"Who?" he asked.

"Your girls," the chaplain answered. He was cleaning his glasses again, a nervous habit, Jack thought. "Leaving our loved ones for death is not a decision any of us would make. We can only choose to love them fully while we're alive. That's what makes our lives mean something when we're gone."

Jack felt anger grow inside him, a rage almost, and he stepped towards the ghost from his mind, his fists balled up. For a moment he thought he might take a swing at the chaplain, who his mind knew wasn't really there.

"Well, that's real fucking nice, Commander," he said, his voice trembling with anger. "Especially from you. I notice you are the only one in this little passion play who isn't fucking dead or dying, so what makes you the goddamn expert?"

The commander replaced his round glasses on his face and smiled.

"And what makes you think I'm not dead?" he asked.

Then he turned and walked back into the dark alley. After a few short steps, he was swallowed by shadows. A moment later, in a flash of white light which made Jack blink and raise his hands to shield his eyes, he was gone.

Jack stared for a moment into the empty alley, his anger replaced with fear and surprise. He had lost control again, he thought. Then he shook his head.

It's just my mind fucking with me, he thought.

Then he turned abruptly, nearly knocking into a young woman dressed sharply in a grey suit, the skirt cut well above her knees.

"Are you ok?" she asked, concern and confusion in her face as she glanced past Jack into the empty alley. He noticed she clutched her purse tightly to her chest.

"Fine," he mumbled as he stepped past her. "Excuse me."

Then he headed on down the block, fuming, his paper tucked under his arm.

Chapter
19

The rest of the walk to Viet Gardens did little to settle Jack's anxiety. He felt torn between a residual sense of fear that there was much more here than just voices from his own mind, and anger at himself that he had again lost control—not only of images that were supposed to be his own creation, but of his emotional response to them. Now he sat at a small, two-top wooden table by the window in the small café-style Vietnamese restaurant and sipped on water with lemon, waiting for Pam. He watched the condensation on his glass turn to little streams that trickled down to form a darker maroon circle on the otherwise pink tablecloth, and tried for once not to sort things out. Lewellyn said he was doing very well, but would have little setbacks. Good enough for him. He gingerly fingered the *Marine Corps Times* which he had tucked under his leg in the chair. He thought about bringing it out and flipping through it while he waited, but Pam would freak out to find him reading it. So he waited and watched the maroon circle continue to grow.

Pam arrived with a big smile and a wave from the door. She looked radiant and stylish in her khaki slacks and pink shirt with a sporty blazer. Jack felt suddenly underdressed in his jeans and sweat shirt. Pam bustled over to the table and kissed him on the cheek. Jack felt better instantly.

"You look beautiful, Pam," he said and meant it.

"Thank you, Jack," she said, but blushed. It had taken him years to get her to take a compliment well. How could she not know how gorgeous she was? "So," she said, unfolding her napkin into her lap, "how did it go, sweetheart?"

"Very, very well," Jack answered, and was happy to find that he really believed that. It had gone well, and he refused to let the bullshit in the alley steal that from him.

I might have little setbacks.

"I had a dream last night that I didn't get to tell you about."

Pam's face clouded a little. "Oh, baby, I'm sorry," she said and kissed his hand again.

"No, no," Jack said and caressed her cheek. "This was different. Or, I mean, the way it affected me was different."

Jack told her about his dream. He focused on his sense that he was in control and told her of his feeling that he had gone there on purpose, like his mind was taking him on a trip to find some answers.

"What did Dr. Lewellyn say?" she asked when he was done. Her mood was still a little dampened.

"Well," Jack said, sorry that her spirits seemed a little deflated and determined to get her buoyancy back, "he said it showed remarkable progress in my ability to control my fears and emotional response to all this." Jack wasn't sure Lewellyn had actually used the word remarkable, but a little license was in order. For certain, *Jack* believed it was remarkable that he felt so much more in control after just a few meetings with the psychologist. "Suffice it to say," he said, this time kissing her hand, "that I got a gold star on my attendance calendar."

Pam laughed a genuine laugh at that, and took a sip of wine the waitress had put in front of her while Jack talked.

"Seriously, baby," Jack said, "he is really optimistic that I have turned some kind of corner. He thinks that I should be getting better and better over the next few days. And," he finished, "he thinks I'm okay to go to school on Monday."

"Well," Pam said tensing a little, "let's just see Jack. I just don't want you to lose any ground. Besides," she said, pulling her hands away from his to make room as the waitress placed their spring rolls in the center of the table and put a little plate in front of each of them, "would being at home with me and the Bear for a few more days be so horrible?"

Jack smiled at that. It sure as hell would not be bad to have a few more family days. On the other hand, he was worried about what the folks at work would start to think if he missed any more time. Stomach flu didn't last but so long, and he had sure as shit acted weird in front of a lot of people. High schools were such vicious little rumor mills.

"Being around you is never, ever anything but wonderful," he answered.

"Flirt," she said with a wave of her hand. Then they dug into the steaming spring rolls with relish.

As they enjoyed their appetizer, Jack finished telling her about the rest of the session. He also told her about seeing the image of Hoag again, but emphasized that while he had gotten upset and lost a bit of emotional control, he still did much better than only days ago. Pam had stopped eating and was listening intently. She seemed worried.

"Jack," she said taking his hand again, "when does Dr. Lewellyn think you will stop seeing these ghosts, or whatever you two are calling them."

"Images." Jack squeezed her hand tightly and tried to sound reassuring. "And I don't know, baby, but soon I think." He stopped, unsure what to say next. "Pam," he sighed and paused again. What could he say to her? What would make the hell she was going through for him okay? He thought for the thousandth time in eight years that he really didn't deserve such a wonderful woman. "Baby, I know how hard this is on you, and I am sorry. But today was progress, not a setback. I really think this is all going to resolve over the next few days."

Pam smiled a sad little smile. "Oh Jack," she said, and dabbed beneath her eye with corner of her napkin, trying not to let the tears smear her mascara. "Don't worry about any of that. I am with you forever, through whatever, for life. Okay?" She looked at him pleadingly and he nodded. She held his gaze. "It is not about me, sweetheart. I'm just so worried about you. I love you so much."

"Jack," Pam continued. "I'm your wife. I'm not going anywhere. The only suffering I have is my worry for you. I want you to be happy. I want you to be better. I need you to tell me how I can help you. Marriage is about being a team, don't you think?"

"I love you too, Pam," he said. "I wish I could tell you how to help. You already help more than you could know. I'm miserable that you need to worry about it at all." Jack thought for a minute. Was there anything more he could ask of his partner and best friend? If so he'd be damned if he could think of what it would be. He couldn't begin to tell her how much strength he gained just having her with him. "And I am doing much better. So..." He took a sip of beer and stabbed some chicken and vegetables with his fork, then reached it out to her for a bite. "Let's enjoy our lunch and have a great family weekend, okay?"

He felt great. Maybe the key was to just never be away from Pam. No goblins dared to visit him when they were together. If he could carry this feeling with him, he would be perfect. He decided that the rest of the weekend they would all stick together, and maybe by Monday it would all be over.

They enjoyed each other and their grown-up lunch. They left the serious shit for later and Jack relished in the familiar comfort of talking about mostly nothing. They sat and chatted for twenty minutes after they had paid the check and then Jack walked Pam to her SUV, holding her hand. He kissed her deeply, embarrassed her with a playful grab of her firm butt as they embraced, and then headed for his own car a few blocks away.

On his way Jack passed a small florist, and stopped for a moment.

Why not? His wife deserved more than just a bunch of flowers, but he guessed she would love the gesture. He went into the little shop and picked out a nice bouquet of mixed flowers in a pretty painted porcelain vase. He paid the smiling older woman and realized he was grinning himself.

"Must be someone pretty special from the look on your face," the lady said, handing him his change.

"My wife," Jack said, still smiling and pocketing his change. "And she is. Very special."

"Lucky girl," the woman said with a wink.

"I'm the lucky one," Jack replied.

He left the shop and continued down the block to his car, holding his flowers and grinning like a high-school senior on prom night. When he reached the car he saw a red flag on the meter, and checked his windshield for the inevitable ticket. None. This day was getting better and better. He unlocked the car and slid into the driver's seat.

Jack set down the bouquet and gingerly lifted the newspaper that sat in the front seat. He stared at in disbelief. *Marine Corps Times* it yelled back at him in bright red print. His mind raced. No, he had definitely not put it there. He had left it in the psychologist's office, he was sure of it. Hoag had given it to him in the alley, and he remembered setting it beside him in the restaurant.

Goddamnit, not again.

Jack sat there with the paper in his lap and searched his mind for an explanation. Maybe he had actually taken it with him from the office and placed it in the car when he fed the meter? That would make sense, a hell of a lot more sense than having it delivered to him by a hallucination in an alley. Maybe he had put it in the car and then forgotten somehow, and the rest was just his battered mind playing tricks on him. That had to be it.

But why the trick his mind was playing? Why the elaborate hallucination about Hoag and carrying the paper around? There must have been something there he was supposed to see. He flicked at the corner of the paper, contemplating opening it up.

No, goddamnit! Enough of this bullshit!

Jack balled the paper up viciously and angrily popped open the door to the car. He got out and scanned the street for a trash can. He saw one by the shop with the neon sign reading "Electronic Miracle." Jack strode over to the trash can and tossed the paper in. As it disappeared through the slot in the green lid, Jack's eye caught a banner tag line over a row of small composite-style pictures. "The Human Toll," it read. He was two steps into his retreat when it registered and he stopped.

The Human Toll?

Jack dashed back to the can and pulled off the slotted green lid with so much zeal he nearly tipped the can over. As he pulled the paper out, he stabilized the trash can against his leg and replaced the lid. Then he unfolded the wrinkled paper, standing next to the wobbling receptacle, oblivious to the stares of passers-by. He smoothed out the paper as he stepped back against the wall.

On the inside page was a half-page spread called "The Human Toll," under which it announced the confirmed deaths in Operation Iraqi Freedom. There was a long list with names, branch of service, age, and place of death. Above the list was a row of pictures of some, but not all, of the dead. At the end of the list of names was the total number of deaths and wounded for the week and a separate tally of the total since the war started. Jack ignored the tallies and nervously scanned the list of names. His heart pounded and beads of sweat formed on his forehead and upper lip.

Then his face turned cool and he sucked his breath in. He felt as if his heart had stopped.

Richard O. Simmons, USMC, 20
Fallujah, Iraq

Jack felt himself sway and thought he might pass out. How was this possible? Lewellyn had said it was all an elaborate creation of a confused mind. How in the fuck did his demon from a nightmare get a fucking byline in the paper? Jack looked at the row of pictures, but Simmons' face wasn't there. But another familiar face was.

The second from the last picture was of Johnny Bennet smiling in a high-school graduation cap. Jack scanned the list again and found it.

Jonathan S. Bennet, USMC, 21
Fallujah, Iraq

Bile burned in his throat and made his eyes water. Jack felt his stomach rise again and bent over, the paper clutched in his balled up fist, heaving. Somehow he kept the Vietnamese food where it belonged, but was rewarded with a second taste, much less enjoyable than the first. He fought for control and struggled upright, straightening the paper to find the final name.

The paper rattled in his hand, whipping back and forth in a sudden and violent wind. Jack tried to readjust it, but it was torn from his hands and tumbled down the sidewalk. He dashed after it, bent at the waist, his fingers grabbing frantically at the paper. His shoulder met with the dark suit-covered legs of a man who shrieked in pain as Jack crunched into his knee, dropping the man cursing to the pavement. He was on his own hands and knees now and struggled to get a hand on the paper that somehow stayed intact, but skirted away each time his fingers caressed its tearing edges. Then the paper disappeared into a huge dark hole that appeared out of nowhere in the middle of the sidewalk. Jack skidded to a halt, the skin from the heels of his hands peeling away on the rough sidewalk. He felt the knees of his jeans tear, but managed to stop just at the edge of the black hole, teetered for a moment, then steadied himself, his head and shoulders leaning out over a dark abyss.

Jack was oblivious to whatever activity might still be going on around him on the sidewalk. Instead he leaned over cautiously and peered over the ragged edge of the torn sidewalk into the black chasm. Deep in the blackness of the hole, he thought he saw little pinpoints of light. Then he felt a hot, dirty wind rush out of the hole and blow dust into his eyes, blinding him. As he fought the tears in his eyes, trying desperately to focus into the darkness, he heard another sound over the now howling wind. He strained to catch it again. He was uncertain whether it was just the wind he heard, which grew now to a nearly animallike shriek, or a haunting voice. Then he heard it again.

SAAAR'NN........SAR'N STILLLLLLMAAAAAANNNNNN!
What in the fuck!?

Then the wind mixed suddenly with blowing sand, which poured out of the hole like a giant throat vomiting up dry desert. It lifted Jack into the air and he tried to scream, but was choked by the sand which filled his lungs and eyes. His chest burned and turned tight as he struggled to get air. A familiar burning pain grew in the center of his throat and he tumbled upwards for a moment. Then he felt strong hands on his arms and legs, a pair of arms wrapped around his chest. The blowing sand reversed and he was pulled with the cyclone of an Iraqi desert down into the black pit in the sidewalk.

The last thing he heard was a coarse rattling laugh and a voice.

You belong with us Sar'n.

Then his mind went as black as the void into which he fell.

Chapter
20

Jack was unable to move, blind and paralyzed, and realized he was going to suffocate, buried under a pile of sand. His mouth was full of the foul dust, and he was unable to open his eyes. His chest bucked, his body trying desperately to find a swallow of air to pull into his lungs. He felt himself slipping again from consciousness.

Just as his mind faded, he felt strong hands grab at his shirt and arms and lift him slowly and heavily, pulling him from the sandy tomb. He felt more hands brush roughly across his face and eyes, and another set of fingers probed his mouth, scooping out handfuls of wet dust. He coughed violently and the cough caused a wracking pain through his whole body.

"We got him, Commander," a familiar voice said. Jack's body continued to convulse with uncontrollable coughing, intermixed with harsh wheezes as his lungs sucked in desperately needed air. His mind began to clear.

"Set him against the berm," another voice said. Jack recognized it immediately.

Hoag.

He felt a little strength begin to flow into his arms and legs and pushed angrily at the hands on his face. He wiped at his eyes with the backs of his own hands instead and felt the burning pain in his chest subside. His gasps slowed and he felt finally like he might live.

He opened his eyes and blinked away the tears and remaining sand that clouded his vision. There were four silhouettes in a loose circle around him, but his vision was still too cloudy to make them out. It didn't matter. He knew who they were. Jack felt a new and growing panic inside his mind. He was not, in any way, in fucking control of any of this. This was much bigger than his mind. Lewellyn was dead wrong. The names in the paper were sure to match the battered figures he would see when his vision cleared.

"Should I give him something to drink?" Simmons' voice asked. It was mushy and wet, like he remembered it being from his yard.

"Where are you gonna git him somethin', dick-cheese?" Kindrich's slow Tennessee drawl asked.

"Just give him some air and a minute," Hoag's voice commanded.

"Roger that, sir," Simmons said. Then he added, "He looks kinda funny with all of that long hair and shit."

"Yeah," Bennet said, "he done gone all civilian on us."

Jack blinked a few more times and his vision cleared somewhat. The figures were still clouded in darkness, but they were sharper now. He found that he was leaned against a sand berm, his legs stretched out in the dirt. Jack saw that he still wore his jeans and tennis shoes, which calmed him for some reason. He gave one last heroic cough and spit a mouth full of sand into the dirt beside him. Then he raised his head and stared at Hoag, venom in his gaze.

"What in the fuck is going on?" he demanded.

The chaplain sat next to him and patted his shoulder. His eyes were soft behind the round glasses, but his look did nothing to calm Jack's rage. The look incited him more, if anything.

"Sorry, Sar'n." Hoag said with sincerity. "I know that was a lousy way to get your attention." He took off his glasses and again started his irritating ritual of cleaning them on the corner of his digital cammie blouse. Jack resisted the overwhelming urge to smack the shit out of his cherubic face. "I'm afraid we're running out of time, Casey," he said.

"Time for what?" Jack demanded, and rose to his feet. The small circle of Marines behind him backed up a step. Jack resisted the urge to look at them. He knew what he would see. Simmons with his bloody half face and toothless skeleton grin. Kindrich with a quarter-sized hole over his right eye and the back of his head completely gone, yawning open over a bloody grey mush of brain and bone. And Bennet. He last saw Bennet take a round in the face behind the wall in Fallujah, but he had a fair idea what that would look like. To look would be to give up more control, which he had precious little of at the moment.

At least his anger covered up his horror and fear.

"Casey, you need to come back." Hoag said simply. "We are almost out of time and you need to come back." Jack felt a hand on his shoulder from his men behind him, but shook it off without turning.

"This is bullshit! This is all a nightmare! I created all of you," he screamed.

"How do you explain this?" Hoag asked. Jack saw that he was holding out his newspaper to him.

"This is bullshit, too!" Jack said. "And why do you all give a fuck about me dying in Fallujah anyway? Why is it any of your fucking business?" Now Jack did turn to look at his men. "Just leave me alone. I am with my family now, so leave me the fuck alone!"

"You belong with us, Sar'n," Simmons said simply. In the pale moonlight Jack saw dark blood on the boy's chin again, which Simmons wiped away with the back of his hand as if embarrassed. "We're all in this together." There was a childlike innocence in the voice and Jack felt himself drawn to the kid in a paternal way. Simmons. The boy whom he had held, forehead to forehead, when the shit hit the fan in Fallujah. Just a child.

Bennet stared off over the berm now. He put a cigarette to his mouth and took a raspy drag. With revulsion Jack saw that smoke dribbled out from a myriad of little puncture wounds in the side of his neck. Jack turned away, his stomach churning. He looked again at Hoag who watched him impassively, his glasses now back in place on his round face.

"And who the hell are you in all of this anyway?" Jack demanded. "These guys, I know. They're…" he stopped. They're what? "Well, in my nightmare anyway, they're my friends, part of my team. But just who in the fuck are you, Commander?"

Hoag looked down with what Jack sensed was a real sadness. He smoothed out the wrinkled paper in his hands and handed it over. Jack took it, his face wrinkled in confusion. What was he supposed to look at? He saw the page was again opened to "The Human Toll." He had seen this, for Christ's sake. He didn't want to look again at the names of his friends.

"What?" he asked.

"Third name from the top. Second column."

Jack looked down, straining in the poor light to see the words on the page. He found the second column of names and counted down to the third one.

Emmett G. Hoag, 41, USN
Ramadi, Iraq

Jack looked up again at the Navy chaplain, whose face was twisted in anguish. He looked older now. The commander reached both hands to the bottom of his cammie blouse and pulled up the front of the shirt and the green T-shirt underneath. Jack stared in horror at the giant gaping hole in the left side of his chest, which continued across and turned downward over the slightly pudgy belly. Through the large hole in the chest Jack saw the gnarled, fingertips of torn ribs, bits of bloody meat hanging from them. In the center was a grey pool of mush that had once been a lung. From the bottom of the gaping gash in his abdomen, a few feet of intestines protruded and hung like links of sausage over the waistband of his pants.

Hoag pulled his shirt down just as Jack tore his eyes from the horrible sight. Too late to prevent the image from being burned permanently into his mind, he was sure.

"I was on a convoy heading back to Baghdad from Ramadi when we hit an IED," Hoag said, referring to a roadside improvised explosive device that the insurgents made from electronic equipment, like cell phones and radios, linked to unexploded rockets or bombs. "Four other Marines were wounded, but I was the only one killed." He looked at Jack with sad but even eyes. "It happened the same day that you guys were hit in Fallujah. The same day you were all killed."

The words stung at Jack's overloaded mind, taking away his breath. "No..." he whispered softly. Oh, God, no! No, this was bullshit! This was a nightmare! This was some madness his mind chose to torture him with for reasons that still were far from clear. Suddenly being crazy didn't seem like such a horrible thing. Anything was better than this. What about Pam, his true love and whole life? What about Claire, their beautiful little girl? If he was crazy he could still see them (at least on visiting days), but not if he was dead. No, this was total FUCKING BULLSHIT! Jack felt himself sway, or more accurately, he felt like he was still and the whole world swayed around him. He was barely aware of Hoag's hand on his shoulder.

"Now, I don't understand it either, Sar'n. Nothing in my education or training in the clergy helps me understand any of this. But I know one thing." His hand gripped Jack's shoulder tighter, hurting him. He seemed not angry, but desperate. "None of us can go until we all go together."

"Go where?" Jack heard his own voice, far away, ask.

"Away from here. I don't know where we go next, Casey. But we are stuck here until we all go together. And," there was panic in his voice now, "we are running out of time!"

Jack's mind swam in circles. "But...but, I wasn't killed." He pleaded. "I was wounded. I was hurt bad, but I wasn't killed."

"Yes, you were." Hoag said. His voice sounded hysterical. "Yes, you were! We all were!" Jack saw a growing red stain on the front of the chaplain's uniform, and Hoag reached unconsciously to his belly with his free hand, holding his guts in while he yelled. "Goddamnit, Casey, we are running out of time!" He let go of his belly and shook him by both shoulders now, but Jack barely felt it.

"My name is Jack," Jack said in a soft and childlike voice.

"WHAT?" Hoag was now totally ape-shit, hollering and shaking him. Jack grabbed him by the wrists.

"My name is Jack." He said again, louder and evenly, with more confidence.

"NO, IT IS NOT!!" Hoag screamed. Jack heard a tearing sound and saw a loop of bowel slip out from under Hoag's shirt. The commander screamed again, and shoved Jack backwards. Jack fell, but instead of crunching to the ground on his back, he continued to fall, disappeared into the sand, and was swallowed up again by the blackness.

Chapter
21

He looked up into the sky from his position on his back. The purple hue of sunset was gone now and he saw only black night and pinpoint stars. It was incredible how many stars he could see out here in the desert, without the lights of civilization stealing away some of the darkness. Casey remembered his time aboard the LHD amphibious assault ship his unit had been assigned to—the "Gator" as the Navy sailors who crewed her called it—bobbing out in the dark night of the Indian Ocean, just a couple of years ago. He had seen stars like this then and remembered the feeling of standing up in the catwalk, the ship running with its lights out in total darkness. He had felt like he was floating in space, surrounded by only blackness and those stars. This sky was much like that.

His sense of serenity was stolen from him as a red tracer from a burst of 7.62-millimeter gunfire, likely from a Humvee-mounted machine gun, streaked over his head, accompanied by the familiar bop...bop...bop. He became aware of movement and voices around him again and tried to concentrate on the sounds—to make out words to help orient himself. He felt pain as a hand touched his tensely swollen neck.

"It's getting worse. It's getting bigger," a voice said. "We have to get him the hell out of here." He thought it sounded like Barton's voice.

"Look, Doc," a disturbingly familiar voice said, "I would like to get him on the bird as much as you, but we just can't yet. We have to get control of this street, or they'll just shoot the bird out of the fucking sky." There was a burst of gunfire, very close this time. "Do what ya' can, Doc. Maybe I can get you out of here in the next fifteen minutes, okay?"

"We're running out of time," the Battalion Surgeon's voice said. "He's bleeding to death from his neck, and I think he's bleeding into his chest, as well. We're going to lose him if we don't hurry." There was a sound in the voice that Casey definitely recognized.

Fear.

"Do what ya' can," the familiar voice he couldn't place said again. Then there was a rustling of activity as the owner of the voice moved away. "Get me mortars off the LAVs on that row of windows—that row right there. We need to end this shit." The voice faded away.

"Morphine?" HM2 White's voice, this short but wiry little corpsman from New Orleans, asked. Everyone called him Shorty or Mini-Me.

"Can't," Barton's voice said. "His blood pressure is getting too low. I think, though," more rustling as he stared again up at the night sky, "that we need to put in a chest tube on the right side. I think he's filling up with blood. I can't hear much air moving on that side."

"Okay," Shorty said, and Casey again heard activity. "I'll hang two more liters of fluid. Wish we had some fuckin' blood to give him."

"Yeah," Barton agreed. "Wish we had a fucking OR to give him. Prep his chest."

He felt a sudden burst of cold on the right side of his chest, then rough scrubbing. He was pretty numb now; he was aware of pain, but didn't really feel it. He tried to think about something else. He felt dizzy, or maybe swimmy was a better word. It was like he was floating in a warm pool. His eyes focused again on the field of stars above him. He was becoming increasingly aware that it was very difficult to get air into his lungs. Each breath brought with it the raspy, whistling noise, followed by a gurgling that he felt more than heard. He thought the gurgling might be from inside of him.

There was a sudden stab of pain in his chest and a burning, but again he was only vaguely aware of it. He thought of Pam and Claire. He wondered what they were doing. With all his might he concentrated on seeing their faces in his mind, closing his eyes to help picture them more clearly.

He felt pressure more than a pain now, deep in the right side of his chest, like someone was standing on his rib cage.

"Let me have a hemostat," Barton's voice said. "I'm nearly there. Just gotta pop in."

There was a fleeting pain, then more pressure, and he felt a sudden rush of wet warmth on his right side and arm.

"Holy fuck, that's a lot of blood." Shorty's voice now.

"Easy. Just give me the tube."

He felt another burning, this time extending all the way up into the right side of his neck. He realized that it was a lot easier to breathe, however, and his mind cleared just a little.

"Jesus, Doc," Shorty said from the darkness. "Did you expect all that friggin' blood?"

"Just give me a stitch and get a bunch of tape ready," Barton said sharply.

It was definitely easier to breathe. He let his mind drift back to the game of picturing his family, and could see them quite clearly now, Pam and Claire, sitting in the front yard. They waved to him, as if in one of those old home movies without sound. He tried to raise his arm to wave back, but couldn't. He smiled anyway.

The picture flashed suddenly to a new image. Pam looking up at him from their bed, her hair on a pillow, sheet pulled up to her bare shoulders. Her lips were moving. She was trying to tell him something. He strained to listen.

"Come home, baby," Pam's voice said. It was muffled and far away. "Please come back, Casey. Please don't leave me…"

"Daddy, Daddy…" Claire's voice sounded muted and tinny.

He had to get home. He couldn't leave them. He couldn't leave his life with them, not now, not yet.

"Please," he tried to say. But there was no sound except the wheezing gurgle and now a new, bubbling sound. But he felt his lips moving.

We are almost out of time. We have to all go together.

Hoag's voice.

Please Sar'n. You belong here with us.

Simmons' young, pleading voice.

No. No, fuck all of you. This isn't right. This isn't how it's supposed to be. I want to go home to my family.

He concentrated with all his might, his eyes closed tightly, tears hot and wet on his face.

I'm coming, Pam.

The night sky lightened, not abruptly, but gently, and was replaced little by little with a swirled stucco ceiling and a slowly turning fan. As he watched in fascination, wide-eyed, the dusty night sky was replaced by the familiar ceiling of his bedroom. As it changed, the sounds, the gunfire and rockets, the shouting voices, faded away. Like someone slowly turned down the volume on a television show, until finally it was gone, and he heard only the barely audible creak, creak of the ceiling fan.

He smiled. Pam had been asking him to balance that damn fan for weeks.

He felt himself change also. The burning pain in his chest and throat dissipated and then disappeared, and the raspy gurgling of his breathing was replaced with a soft and comfortable sighing of near sleep. He felt Pam stir beside him.

Jack's wife lay in their bed, the sheet pulled up to her bare shoulders, her hair spread out on the pillow beneath her. Jack rolled over stiffly and put his arm around his sleeping wife. He breathed deeply of her scent and hugged her gently. She squeezed his arm and sighed, then rolled over to face him, her eyes opening and a smile spreading across her sleepy, angelic face.

"Hey, you," she said.

Jack kissed her forehead gently.

"Hey, baby," he said.

Pam reached her hand up from under the sheets and caressed his face with her warm hand.

"You okay, honey?" she asked, "You look like you've been crying." Pam ran a finger lightly over his cheek then kissed her fingertip gently. "Jack, you've been crying. What's wrong?"

"Nothing, baby," he said and pulled her against him. Pam sighed and hugged him back.

"Nightmare?" she asked.

"No," he said. He closed his eyes and held her tightly. He was home. "I just love you so much, Pam." He pulled his head back from their embrace and looked her deeply in the eyes. "Do you know that, baby?"

Pam closed her eyes and smiled, then kissed him lightly on his lips.

"I know," she said. "I love you too, Casey. I'm so proud of you."

"I'm home," Jack said.

"Yes, baby," Pam said, hugging him tighter. "You're home."

Jack held her like that, feeling her breathing slow and her arms relax as she drifted off to sleep. He felt like there were so many questions he should be asking himself. So many things he needed to sort out. But he was so tired—so goddamn exhausted. He let himself slip softly and comfortably into a deep and dreamless sleep, his arms wrapped around his wife.

* * *

Jack woke feeling relaxed and content at first. The room was warm from the morning sun, and he kicked the sheet and blanket off of his legs. He stretched out his arms and back, feeling stiff, then reached for his wife, but she was gone. Her side of the bed was still warm though. Jack yawned.

Then he sat up, his mind suddenly racing. His initial thoughts were not about Fallujah, or Hoag, or falling through a black hole in the sidewalk downtown in the middle of the day. Instead, he tried desperately to remember how in the hell he got home. He remembered every detail of his afternoon, of his trip (nightmare?) to Iraq, and his conversation with Hoag. He remembered lying in the street of Fallujah again, as Casey Stillman. What he couldn't remember was anything after that. How had he ended up in their bed? His next memory was of lying in bed with Pam late last night. Where was the rest of the time? Where had he awoken from his nightmare? It had to have been downtown, so how did he get home and what happened after that?

The memories of his nightmare terrified him, but not half as much as the huge gap in his memory. He had no idea what had happened in the seventeen or eighteen hours since the horrible hallucination downtown. He also realized that he no longer believed that his trips to Fallujah or his conversations with Hoag and the others were really hallucinations. Not anymore.

Jack looked over at the clock on his nightstand. Eight thirty— still early.

He needed to talk to Pam.

Jack pulled on some sweat pants and a T-shirt and padded barefoot out of the room. Before heading down the stairs he gave into the urge to look at Claire in her crib, maybe give her a kiss. He headed down the hall and peered in, but her crib was empty.

Huh. Must be up already.

Jack realized it would be a lot more comfortable to talk to his wife about the missing time if Claire were still in bed. He wasn't sure why that was, she was only a toddler and certainly didn't understand enough to realize Dad was crazy as a shithouse wall. It didn't matter. He needed desperately to talk to his wife. Jack turned and headed downstairs.

"There's Daddy!" Pam said to the smiling little girl in her lap as Jack came down the stairs and into the living room. She sat cross-legged on the floor, her arms around their little girl as they worked together on an Elmo puzzle. "Good morning, sunshine," she said and reached out a hand to him. Jack took her hand and then Pam turned to Claire. "Daddy can help us, Claire Bear."

Jack smiled a pensive smile and squeezed her hand. He saw her face cloud a bit.

"What's wrong, Jack? Did you have a nightmare?" Her voice sounded anxious.

Jack thought a moment, unsure how to start. He looked down and picked up a puzzle piece, part of Elmo's arm holding a rubber ducky, and turned it over in his hands.

"Honey, what happened last night?" he asked.

"What do you mean, Jack? After we went to bed?"

Jack swallowed hard. Might as well jump right in.

"No," he said. "Before…I…"

I what? I don't remember a single goddamn thing after I got to my car? Except for the desert in Iraq, of course, and a street in Fallujah. My reality now.

He sighed heavily. "I had kind of a blackout, Pam," he looked up and held her troubled gaze.

"A blackout? Jack, what do you mean?"

Claire was looking at them with a pout on her face now, not at all happy about the change in mood.

He blurted it out.

"Pam, I don't remember driving home after lunch. In fact I don't remember anything until you woke up and looked at me last night." There he had said it. No going back.

"Oh my God, Jack," Pam said. She covered her mouth with her free hand. "What do you remember?"

Jack thought about telling her about Hoag and the others in Iraq. He would, he decided, but first he needed desperately to fill the gaps in his night.

"Honey, first can you tell me what we did last night?" His voice was pleading and his eyes were wet.

"You got home a little after me," she started. She handed Claire, fussy now at not being the center of attention, to Jack and loaded a DVD into the machine. Mickey and friends grabbed Claire's attention and started talking about colors. "We put Claire down for a nap, and then we lay together on the couch with the TV on. Then I, well…" She blushed. "I helped you relax."

Shame not to have that memory.

Pam sat on the couch now, her legs pulled under her, and Jack joined her. She took both of his hands in hers.

"Jack, maybe we should call Dr. Lewellyn," she said. There were tears in her eyes. Jack hugged her. "I'm sorry, Jack. I'm not trying to be an emotional mess." She pulled out of his hug, wiped the tears from her eyes and looked at him. "This is not something we can do just the two of us. You know that right?" She waited expectantly, but Jack looked down. Pam lifted his eyes back to hers gently by his chin. "We need to call Dr. Lewellyn."

"No, baby. Not right now. Not yet," he kissed her cheek. "Tell me the rest first."

Pam looked off in the distance, reconstructing the day in her mind.

"When Claire got up, we went to the playground, but it was chilly so we didn't stay long…"

Hearing his wife fill in the gaps of the day and evening gave Jack a sense of comfort. He held her hand and listened as she told him of their walk back to the house, how they played upstairs in Claire's room. She told him of their dinner (chicken and green beans with salad and au gratin potatoes) and of giving Claire a bath together. She told him how he had put her to bed while she had cleaned up, and that he had watched some TV while she talked to her mother on the phone.

"The news?" Jack asked, hoping maybe something from the news would explain what had happened to him.

"No," she answered. "I think you watched a *Frasier* rerun." Then she told him how they had opened a bottle of wine and watched a movie together, an old movie with Humphrey Bogart (she couldn't remember the name) on AMC.

"Then we took a shower together and went to bed," she said. "I must have worn you out 'relaxing' you in the afternoon because you were asleep when I got into bed." She thought hard for a moment. "I think you forgot to take your medicine," she said with hope in her voice, like maybe that explained everything.

Jack knew better. He sat quietly for a moment when she finished. She had described a wonderful evening, a typical Friday night at home (except for him falling asleep after being naked in the shower with her. That was hard to believe, his pride and libido told him). He remembered none of it. Even hearing it failed to make it real for him as he had hoped.

"What do you remember?" Pam asked. She slid closer to him and wrapped her arms around his arm. Claire bounced up and down and laughed at Mickey and Minnie as they flew around in his open-cockpit airplane, looking for more colors.

Jack told her everything he remembered. He spared her some of the gory details, but left nothing important out. He told her about the paper and seeing the names of his men from his nightmares. He told her of Hoag, and how he had become angry, nearly hysterical, and demanded that Jack, or Casey, go with them on some death journey. He relayed how he had refused, insisting that he had to get home to his family.

"They said I died in Fallujah," he said.

"Oh, Jack," she cried and hugged him tighter, her head on his chest.

Then he told her about going back to the dirty street in Fallujah, where he had lay dying, bleeding to death in the street. Jack told her about the battalion surgeon doing something to his chest that made it easier for him to breathe and how he kept just trying to picture her and Claire in his mind.

"You were talking to me," Jack said softly.

"What did I say?"

"You asked me not to leave you," Jack answered. Tears rolled down his cheeks now. "You told me to come home." He held her tightly. Pam raised her head and looked at him, a sad but loving smile on her face.

"And you did," she said, and kissed his cheek.

"Yeah," Jack replied. He didn't know what else to say.

"Jack," Pam said, her head again on his shoulder, "I really think we need to call Dr. Lewellyn. I mean, blackouts, Jack? What if something happens to you?"

"I don't think Lewellyn can help me now," Jack said.

"What do you mean?" Pam said, louder than she meant to. "You said yourself he was helping you a lot, that things were getting better." Pam's voice was higher, more desperate.

"It's different now, Pam. Can't you see that?" He spoke more harshly than he meant to and Pam looked down, her lip quivering. Jack sighed and sat beside her again, taking her free hand in his. "Pam, their names were in the goddamn paper for Christ's sake! Don't you get it? This isn't a nightmare. It's real, now. Somehow I'm connected to this Casey Stillman, or I am him, or...Shit I don't know!" He looked down at the floor and massaged his forehead in frustration.

"Where is the paper now, Jack? I never saw it." Pam demanded. She was holding Claire against her chest now.

Jack thought a minute. "I left it, I guess."

"Left it, Jack?" Pam stood up and started to pace back and forth, Claire clinging to her neck. "Left it in Iraq in some nightmare, is that what you're saying? Jesus, Jack!" She stood next to him again. Jack stared at his feet and said nothing. What in the hell could he possibly say? Everything she said made sense. Everything.

But she's wrong.

"Isn't it possible that you just imagined reading that paper? That you left it in your car or it never existed? Just because you think you remember reading names in a paper that you don't even have anymore, we're supposed to believe, that...that...Jesus, what the hell is it we're supposed to believe? That you're some kind of fucking ghost? I mean, Jack, that's just..." She stopped and Jack looked up at her sharply.

"Crazy? Is that the word you're looking for, Pam?" Jack felt a stab in his chest. He would rather endure almost anything before having this woman he loved so much think he was insane. Maybe he shouldn't have told her.

"No." She started to cry again, and she pressed her face, wet with tears against his neck. "No, baby, I didn't mean that. Something is bothering you, something deep inside you, and I want to help you." She kissed him on the lips. "I love you, Jack, and I am here for you no matter what, ok?" she cupped her hand on his cheek.

"Ok," he said. "But I don't want to call Lewellyn. Not yet. I want...I don't know. I just want to figure this out more before I call him, okay?"

Pam was with him, on his side as always, but now what? She depended on him to think of some way to sort this out, right?

What she said about the paper made sense, he supposed. But he KNEW he had gotten that paper, and that he had carried it with him more than once. Maybe it was still in the car. Jack stood up again and headed for the door. He grabbed his keys from the mirrored key hook they had mounted near the front door. "I'll be right back," he said.

"Where are you going, Jack?" Pam's voice was frightened. Jack rushed back over and kissed her.

"Baby, it's ok," he said and smiled. "I'm just going to the car to look for the paper, okay? I'll be right back."

"Ok," Pam said with a weak smile. "I'm sorry, Jack. I just don't want you to leave me."

"I'll never leave you, Pam," he said.

The Volvo was right where it should be, neatly parked in the center of the driveway. Jack clicked his fob and the door lock clicked open, the interior light coming on. He opened the door and looked inside.

No *Marine Corps Times*, although the porcelain vase full of flowers was still there. He tore the car apart looking for it but found nothing. Was Pam right? Had the paper been another hallucination? Jack gritted his teeth in frustration. He had no fucking idea anymore what was real and what was his imagination. Maybe he had been right before. Maybe he was just like the screwed up math guy in that fucking movie with the gladiator. Maybe he was schizophrenic. Wouldn't that explain all of this horseshit? And they had medicine for that now, right? I mean, that story had been in the fifties when they didn't know shit about medicine. Jack started to think that he should call Dr. Lewellyn after all.

"Bad idea, Casey."

He spun around in fear and rage and looked at Hoag with gritted teeth, fire in his eyes.

"You get the fuck out of here," he hissed. "You stay away from my family, you son of a bitch! Do you hear me?" Jack was glad that the commander didn't start cleaning his glasses, or he would have punched him in the face for sure.

"Casey," Hoag said patiently. He was the saintly chaplain again, all the hysteria and mania from the night before well hidden. "Lewellyn is just something you made up to help you escape from the reality of your death. He'll say whatever you think you want him to say."

"Bullshit!" Jack said and turned on his heel, heading for the front door. He clicked the fob, locking the Volvo over his shoulder.

"There are other ways you can check it out, Jack." Hoag hollered after him. "Go to Pendleton, Jack. You'll see. Go to Pendleton and see for yourself."

Jack watched a moment as Hoag began to shimmer, sparkling with light, and then disappeared. He looked at the flowers in his hand and stood there, his mind trying to figure out his next move while he caught his breath. Maybe Hoag, or whatever part of his mind had created that bastard, was right. He could go to Camp Pendleton, couldn't he? Go to the base and check out One MEF, especially Third Battalion and Kilo Company, for himself. That would settle it for sure. He looked again at the flowers in his hand and suddenly felt ridiculous.

Jack shrugged his shoulders and went inside.

Chapter
22

Pam had not liked the idea of a trip to the United States Marine Corps Base, Camp Pendleton, California, in the least. To her it seemed only to feed the delusion that the hallucinations, or nightmares or whatever the hell they were, could be real. She had expressed that opinion to him in no uncertain terms. It wasn't that Jack didn't appreciate where she was coming from. He knew how crazy it sounded. He worked hard to help her see his frustration that he didn't understand what he was doing, and so he most certainly couldn't help her understand what was going on. It wasn't just that the dreams seemed real. The subtle and hard to define ways that everything else—his whole life—seemed unreal and dreamlike. Everything except Pam and Claire. When it was all boiled down to shit and grease, as his granddad used to love to say (what a weird time to remember that little phrase), the only things he knew were real were his girls and his deep, almost desperate love for them. Everything else was suspect. He had admitted to Pam the fact that he wasn't sure of anything. That while it seemed plausible, in a bizarre way he knew she couldn't comprehend, that Hoag and Simmons and the others were in some way real, he also knew how fucking crazy that sounded. He told her that he needed to go to Pendleton to find out the truth. It was not to prove something he thought he knew, because he admitted he didn't know what the hell he knew and what could be dream—or insanity, he supposed.

In the end, that was what won the battle. Pam seemed able to accept that the trip could prove, once and for all, that the nightmares and hallucinations were just that. His promise that he would call Lewellyn when they returned had clinched the deal.

The only wrinkle was her insistence that she go with him. To be honest, the thought of having her by his side was a tremendous comfort. He didn't put up a tremendous struggle, as he thought he might really need the strength her presence would give him, no matter what he found in California. Perhaps more important was the realization that, as far as he knew, he had not yet had a hallucination (or whatever the hell they were) in front of her. Maybe his images, real or not, would not come to him if she was there—whether because they were unable to appear in her presence or because as products of his mind, he unconsciously protected her from them. Either way, he felt better having her along despite his guilt over the tremendous strain he believed he was putting on his wife.

The afternoon and evening had been spent putting the details together. They had first arranged for Claire to stay with her friend, Bev, and her family. He took care of the mundane—airfare, hotel, rental car. The only thing left unarranged by Sunday morning was the actual point of the trip. Jack had no idea how exactly he would go about getting them onto the Marine Corps Base, much less have the opportunity to talk to anyone. Obviously civilians were not permitted to simply drive onboard and stroll about at will, and security was even tighter since the horror of 9/11. Over breakfast, while he helped Claire get equal parts of apple and cinnamon oatmeal into her mouth and onto his lap, he told Pam that he would again try his ruse about planning his lecture for a current events class. He would be sure to pack his staff ID from school.

"I'm sure I can get in touch with the PAO and sell it to them somehow," Jack had said.

"What the hell is a PAO?" Pam had asked.

Jack explained that each base, and usually each individual unit, had a public affairs officer, or PAO. He believed his best bet was to try and gain access to Camp Pendleton through the First

MEF PAO. He knew she wondered why he would know about such a thing, but neither said anything.

As for him, he still couldn't shake the resolute belief that Simmons, Bennet, Kindrich, and Stillman were real, and that their existence would be confirmed by his visit to Camp Pendleton. What that meant for him was still a mystery way beyond his imagination. More uncertain was just what in the hell he would do if (when) his fears were confirmed. He did know that, despite Pam's yearning that he go back to Lewellyn (which he would do for her, more than himself), if he found the answers that his terrified mind suspected on this trip then Lewellyn would have very little to offer him. In fact, it might even mean that Hoag was right, and that Lewellyn was as much a fantasy of his disturbed mind as everything else in his now surrealistic life.

Jack looked out the window as he felt the airliner begin to descend. He kept his arm around his wife and watched as they turned out over the water in a circling approach to the airport. Farther south down the coast, Jack could see the line of huge grey ships at the Naval base pier. In his mind he had a flash of memory (fantasy?) of standing on that pier, a seabag over his shoulder as he hugged his new wife and prepared to walk up onto the giant LHD, a tearful goodbye before he left for five months at sea. The memory was brief but intense, like a short slide show, and it felt somehow more real than his last week at home. They turned a slow circle just inside North Island, where Jack saw one of the two huge aircraft carriers berthed there, and Coronado with its beautiful bridge connecting the islands to downtown San Diego. They headed inland towards the airport, just past downtown and at the foot of the mountains beyond. It was a beautiful city and he felt he knew it well, though he was sure that, as Jack at least, he had never been there.

"Whatcha thinking?" Pam asked and she hugged him, as if she sensed his brief departure to another reality. She wrapped her arm around his chest.

"Just thinking how pretty it is," he answered kissing her on top of the head.

"And wondering what you'll find here?" It was less of a question than her finishing his unspoken thought.

"Yeah," he said.

They watched together as the city skirted below them and they headed in for landing.

It took no time at all to get out of the airport. The traffic was heavy and as Jack maneuvered their rental car into the flow, they chatted about anything but the purpose for their trip. Neither of them mentioned how odd it was that Jack never once consulted a map. Jack had decided that maybe avoidance wasn't all that bad, at least for what was left of the afternoon and their evening. He wanted to just enjoy being with Pam, and tomorrow would be whatever fate held for him.

Even in afternoon traffic the trip downtown was a short drive. They found the Marriott easily; a short walk from the bay he noted. Maybe a nice walk after they checked in would help them find some peace. He wanted to take her out for a nice dinner. Maybe they could drive up to La Jolla and have dinner at George's at the Cove, with its beautiful bay view and wonderful food. A bit upscale, but maybe that would be a nice change. He would see how she felt.

They checked in and received the obligate brief about the various restaurants, bars, and rooftop pool, and then rode the faux marble-floored elevator up to the eighth floor and their bay view room. The room itself wasn't large, but very comfortable with a king-size bed and a little sitting area. More importantly, at least to Pam, it had a huge bathroom with a large sunken tub and separate shower. Jack had always been amused that Pam measured the adequacy of any hotel room almost exclusively by the pillows and the comfort of the bathroom. They tossed their bags on the bed and walked together onto the balcony. They held hands in silence and looked out at the late afternoon sun which reflected off the bright blue Bay. Off to the left they saw the scenic Coronado bridge stretch across the bay to North Island, the East-bound lane full with bumper to bumper traffic as the afternoon shift at the two Naval bases let out. Sailors and Department of Defense employees rushed at a snail's pace to get off the island and pretend that they might, this time, miss the traffic out of San Diego and into the various suburbs that surround it.

"Pretty," Pam said after a moment.

Jack kissed her neck. "Beautiful," he answered. They stood there quietly for a while, enjoying the peace and the view. Then she turned and faced him, her eyes beautiful, but sad.

"What do you want to do, Jack?" she asked.

Jack ignored the deeper meaning.

"Have a nice night on the town with the most gorgeous woman I have ever seen," he said and kissed her. She smiled up at him. "Let's go up to Old Town and look at the shops, and then maybe have a drink," he suggested.

"Sounds great," she said. He figured she felt just as happy as he did to put off thinking about all that had brought them to this place.

They drove to Old Town, not minding the walk but knowing that they had to cross Highway Five; "the Five" as locals referred to it. It took around twenty minutes, about twice as long as it might have at another time of day. But they passed the time as they always did, chatting about everything and nothing and holding hands, listening to a litany of hits by modern country stars on the station Jack tuned in without thinking about it. They parked at the fringe of Old Town and strolled into the quiet shopping and restaurant district.

As they walked, Jack caught sight of a sign over a restaurant called Harvey's. He smiled, the sight filling him with some type of memory of emotion, rather than a picture of an actual event. He looked at his wife.

"You want a margarita?" he asked, smiling at her.

Pam looked up ahead, obviously wondering what had prompted the offer.

"Where?" she asked.

"Just up ahead," Jack answered, pointing up the block past Harvey's. "Trust me."

They walked another half a block and came to a lively restaurant bar called Rockin' Baja, a local chain. The wait for dinner could be as much as an hour, but at this time, about six p.m. by Jack's watch, there was no real wait; though the bar area was crowded with the late afternoon revelers. They waited only about five minutes and were seated at a small table near the window, just past the bar.

"We'd like two of your special margaritas," Jack said as the waitress placed menus in front of them. "I can't remember what they're called."

"No problem, sir. I know what you want," the young girl said and smiled. "You want large or grande?"

"Grande," Pam said, before Jack could answer. "I mean, right?"

"You bet," Jack said. They could both use a grande drink about now.

"Ok, two grandes and I'll give you a minute to look at the menu," she said and then hustled off to the bar.

Pam opened the large menu and started to look through it. "Wow," she said, "a lot of choices."

"Well," Jack said without picking up his own menu, "you want to just have some chips or something and then go out to George's in La Jolla for a nice dinner later?"

"Too expensive," Pam said without much thought. Then she looked around the Rockin' Baja fondly. "Besides, there's something special about this place."

Jack agreed, though he wasn't sure why. He had the very strong feeling that this place was special to them for a reason.

"I'm having fun," she announced as she fished a bite of soft taco filled with chunky seafood and white sauce from his plate. "This is just like the night you asked me to marry you."

That was it! Jack had a sudden flash in his mind of the two of them, both younger, Pam with her hair pulled back looking tanned in her tank top and jeans. He had nervously pulled out a ring from his pocket and she had cried, and hugged him, and covered him with kisses.

"Yes, yes, yes!" she had exclaimed full of joy.

They had been sitting at this very table, he thought. He felt tears in his eyes and the memory floated away.

"What's the matter, baby?" Pam asked now, touching his face.

"Nothing," Jack said and meant it. "I am just happier than any man deserves." He kissed his wife and smiled again. "I am so glad you married me," he said.

"You should be," Pam answered. Her face relaxed and lit up again. Then she laughed and covered her mouth. "I love margaritas."

Two and a half hours later they sat outside by the poolside bar at the Marriot Hotel, stretched out in lounge chairs by the railing, looking at the city lights on the Bay and holding hands. They sipped contentedly at their complimentary drinks (they had switched to beer, knowing that the margaritas would be disappointing after Rockin' Baja's) and talked about Claire and what she was doing. Before coming to the bar they had stopped at the room and called Bev, who promised their little girl was doing fine, enjoyed being with her kids, had eaten well and was now asleep. Then they had torn each other's clothes off and made love wildly, passionately, like kids on their engagement night who had just finished off two grande margaritas. They ended up on the floor somehow, and lay together in a silent and content afterglow for a half hour before deciding to go to the pool to cash in their drink vouchers.

Jack was content and happy. He held hands with his one true love and enjoyed the cool California evening. But he also felt a quiet dread building deeper inside him, and forced the feeling away with some effort. He didn't want to think about tomorrow, and wanted less to think about what would come next. He no longer felt anxiety about what he would find at Pendleton because the evening, as perfect as it was, had only solidified his conviction that he knew damn well what he would learn there. What he didn't know was what the hell he would be able to do once his fears were confirmed. He knew for sure that he would never, ever give up on making this world right and real. He loved the woman beside him, and the little girl they had made together from their passion, more at this moment that he ever had. Whatever it took, he would make this right. Whatever it took, he would find a way to not leave his life with his girls.

"You make me so happy, Casey," Pam said dreamily from the chair beside him. Her hand was warm and soft in his. "I love you so very much."

"I love you too, Pam," he answered. He took a sip of his beer and then turned and looked at her, head back against the chaise lounge, eyes closed. "I am never going to leave you," he said.

"I know," she answered.

Chapter
23

Jack woke up in the big bed, with its perfect pillows, wrapped tightly around the warm naked body of his sleeping wife. The alarm he had set for eight a.m. had not yet gone off, so he lay there happily, legs entwined around Pam's, breathing her scent.

The alarm chirped and Jack opened his eyes, set his jaw and gritted his teeth. No matter what he found at Pendleton, he would not allow it to end here in California or in the dirty streets of Fallujah. He would find a way. He would keep his life with his girls. Pam stretched beside him and woke up, opening her eyes slowly. The realization of where they were and why enveloped her, and her face darkened. Jack rolled over, face to face with his wife, and caressed her cheek.

"Good morning, baby," he said.

"Morning," she said sadly, mourning the passing of their evening together, he thought.

"Everything is going to be ok, Pam," he said. "I promise."

"I know," she said, hugging him, but her voice did not hold much conviction.

Then they rose slowly from bed and headed together to the shower, neither wanting to be apart, not even for a moment.

As they dressed, Jack thought about Camp Pendleton, the sprawling Marine Corp Base and home to the First Marine Expeditionary Force. He knew it was a huge complex stretching over miles and miles. North of San Diego, not quite halfway to Los Angeles, he thought perhaps that the massive military base might be the only thing that prevented the two cities from eventually meeting as they grew outward like two cancers, seeking each other to become one giant tumorlike metropolis. From San Diego "the Five" connected the city and suburb commuters with the base, joining close to the base with Highway 805 to form a daily bottleneck of merging traffic.

Before joining the throngs of travelers, Jack called the information number published in the phone book for Camp Pendleton and asked to be connected to the PAO at Third Battalion, First Marines. A moment later he was speaking to First Lieutenant Sheila Rawls, the PAO for First MEF. She was very polite, and explained that there was currently no PAO for Third Battalion, but could she possibly help?

Jack rattled off the same story about a current events lesson about the Marines in Iraq. This time he added how he and his wife had spent a long weekend in San Diego, and since they were so close he thought he might be able to arrange a visit and get more information for his class. He explained that one of his students had a relative with Third Battalion and thought it might be nice to focus on that unit in particular. He also apologized for the short notice. Pam sat nervously beside him on the bed throughout the call and held his hand in silence.

Lt. Rawls proved very accommodating. She said she would arrange for someone to meet him at the gate and escort him to First MEF headquarters, where she would be happy to meet with him and answer any questions that their operational security rules would allow. Jack thanked her, gave her a rough guess of their arrival time, and then hung up.

"Well, that's it," he said to Pam with a forced smile after he got off the phone. Pam gave him a tight smile back and said nothing.

Now they sat in the slowly moving rental car, flowing with the tide of traffic. Finally north of the 805 merge they picked up speed again. They were both quiet during the drive, sipping coffee from the hotel coffee shop and munching halfheartedly on croissants, lost in their own thoughts. Neither wanted to upset the other by bringing up the obvious and myriad questions. It was enough that they were together.

After a while, Jack saw the blue sign that quietly announced that Camp Pendleton was the next exit. He felt his heart flutter and his stomach flip. This was it. Finally, he would put the biggest question to rest. What he would do next was still a frightening mystery.

Only a few minutes off the exit they approached the main gate to Camp Pendleton Marine Corps Base, and Jack felt his hands tighten on the steering wheel. He couldn't shake the sudden and overwhelming sense that he was home. He felt Pam's hand reach for his leg and squeeze it just above the knee. The feel of her was soothing. As Jack approached the gate, he snapped off the daytime running headlights, an expected courtesy to the gate guards. Then he pulled up beside the guard house, stopped, and rolled down his window. A young Marine in crisp woodland digital cammies approached the window, his rifle slung off his shoulder low, a combat configuration that allowed him to bring the weapon to bear without unslinging it.

"Hoorah, sir," he said.

"Hoorah, Corporal," Jack replied, noting the rank by his two chevrons over crossed rifles on his collar. He fumbled in his wallet for his driver's license and school staff ID, and then asked Pam for her ID, as well. He presented them to the guard. "Lt. Rawls is expecting me. She said she would send an escort to the gate."

The young Marine consulted a clipboard, searching for his name. Satisfied he pointed to a short pull-off to their right.

"Very well, sir," he said. "Just pull over into the circle there and the pick-up private will be along in just a second to escort you to MEF HQ." He handed the IDs back to Jack through the window. "Sir, you understand that access to the base implies consent to involuntary search of yourselves and the vehicle?"

"Yes, I do, Corporal," Jack replied, putting his IDs back in his wallet. He handed Pam her driver's license.

"Very well, sir," the corporal said again then motioned them to pull forward.

Jack pulled into the circle and put the vehicle in park.

"You gonna be ok, Baby?" Pam asked, the tension now clear on her face and in her eyes.

"I'm fine, sweetheart," Jack answered sounding more confident than he felt. "Thank you so much for being here with me. I don't know if I could make it without you."

"You'll never have to, Jack. I love you," she added simply as if it explained everything. For Jack it did.

Only a minute or two passed before a desert-tan painted Humvee, a Mark-19 machine gun mounted but unmanned on the roof, pulled up beside them. A very young Marine got out and walked over to them. Jack rolled down the window again.

"Morning, sir," the Marine said. "May I see some ID, please?"

Jack presented their IDs again. The Marine studied them briefly and then handed them back.

"Lt. Rawls is expecting you, sir. Just follow me and I'll take you there. I'll stop beside the spot you can park in," he said.

"Thank you," Jack said, and then rolled up the window while the Marine mounted his Humvee again. Then he followed the lightly armored jeeplike truck onto the main road. "Here we go," he said softly to no one in particular, but Pam wrapped tightly around his arm again.

First MEF headquarters was several miles from the gate at the end of the main road on which they entered the base. On the way in they passed the typical nondescript brick or grey wood buildings that made up every base he had ever been on. The traffic was fairly heavy, a mix of civilian vehicles and green or tan seven-ton trucks and Humvees. The Marines on the street were all clad in cammies, some in woodland green, others in tan and brown desert digitals, indicating those who had either just returned or were soon heading to Iraq.

Jack pulled into the parking spot which the private's Humvee stopped beside, right next to the large, brick three-story building with its towering white pillars. Over the entry was a large brown sign with yellow lettering which announced "One MEF HQ." Below it, in script, Jack read the words "Through these doors pass the finest warriors in the world." He locked the car and he and Pam followed the private through the white wood and glass doors. Jack felt a stirring inside, pride mixed with fear. He had no doubt he had passed through these doors more than once, and he knew in his heart that he was also "one of the finest warriors in the world." He unconsciously took his wife's hand.

Lt. Rawl's office was on the second floor (second deck, Jack thought to himself). The private opened the door for them and led them into a small waiting room. In it were a simple sofa and two chairs, centered around a coffee table with various military magazines and newspapers.

"Have a seat, sir," he turned to Pam, "ma'am. I'll let the lieutenant know you're here."

"Thank you," Jack said as he took a seat beside Pam, her hand still tight in his.

Jack resisted the urge to pick up one of the various and sundry military magazines on the table. His mind was a torrent of images and emotions. He had such clear pictures in his head from this place. And sitting here, with the distinctive smell and feel of the base, took him back to another time, or at least to another place. He watched a slide show of snapshots of himself and his Marines. He saw them drinking beer in the bowling alley, Pam at his side. He saw them crawling through the woods, weapons ahead of them, doing combat land navigation training and humping packs through the nearby high desert and conducting joint training with their sister Light Armored Reconnaissance unit, their heavily armed LAV-25s kicking up dust. He had a clear picture of all of them together in their gear, stretched out in the grass in front of the Headquarters and Service Platoon, waiting to debrief after a long day of training. They were laughing and joking the way young men, friends bound by a common purpose and codependence, were familiar with in unspoken ways. Jack sighed. He knew where this journey was taking him. He was still unsure how he would get back from there, but he had no doubts anymore where the journey would begin.

"Hi, folks. My name is Lieutenant Sheila Rawls," a friendly voice said behind him.

Jack rose and let go of Pam's hand long enough to shake hands with a woman about their age, dressed in woodland digital cammies with the sleeves rolled up tightly to her midupper arms. The rank insignia on her collar showed her to be a first lieutenant.

"Good, morning Lieutenant," Jack said releasing the woman's firm grip. "I'm Jack and this is my wife Pam," he said as the two women also shook hands. "Thanks so much for taking time to meet with us on such short notice."

"My pleasure, Jack," the woman said. "Why don't we go to my office and we can chat. It's always a pleasure to meet with people interested in teaching kids about our Marines and the tough job they're doing."

Lt. Rawls led them back to a small room, made smaller by a modular cubicle system that divided it into four, even smaller, office spaces. She pulled two chairs into her cramped cubicle and motioned them to sit down. Jack took in the typical space, full of Marine Corps memorabilia and pictures, and noted the scattered pictures on the desk of a handsome man holding and playing with two small boys.

"You have a lovely family," Jack said, pointing to the pictures.

"Oh, thank you," Rawls said proudly. "Steven is wonderful and our two boys are just great. They put up with a lot having a Marine for a wife and mother." Jack knew just what she meant. "What can I do for you today?" she asked.

Jack ran through a similar set of vague questions as those he had asked Staff Sergeant Perry. Rawls answered his questions with a little more spin than the recruiter had. She emphasized the tough job the Marines faced in Iraq and the fine job they were doing in a trying war with difficult rules of engagement. She focused on the role of the Iraqi people and their efforts to help them build their country. She also talked about the various humanitarian missions the First MEF Marines were engaged in to provide health and security, and "win the hearts and minds" of the Iraqis.

"What we are trying to do is give them security and safety so that they can have the confidence to build and defend a free society," she said, quoting the party line of her commander in chief. Jack had no doubt that her words were not rhetoric, and that she believed very much in the mission they had been given in the Middle East. "Stability in the Middle East begins with freedom and requires security for the people," she said. "That stability will ultimately mean safety for Americans at home and abroad," she emphasized.

As before, Jack made a show of scribbling notes in a notepad Rawls had provided. It was time to get to the tough questions.

"What about losses," he asked as casually as he could. He felt his pulse quicken, and Pam, who had been quiet throughout the conversation, put a hand on his leg and squeezed gently but nervously. "I know the action in Fallujah the last few days has been intense. Have we lost many Marines there?" Jack watched the lieutenant's face closely and saw it cloud. She shifted uncomfortably.

"Well," she began, clearly choosing her words carefully, "we're in a dangerous business, Jack. I'm sure you've seen on the news that we do lose Marines and soldiers. The action in Fallujah has cost us the lives of several brave Marines recently. I'm not at liberty to discuss many specifics, of course." She smiled, but was clearly not as at ease as she had been earlier.

"Of course," Jack said. He folded his hands on his notebook and smiled back. "Do you know many of the Marines from Third Battalion?"

"Oh, yes," Rawls answered. "We are a big, but close, family here at Pendleton. I know many of my fellow Marines, very well."

"What about Sgt. Casey Stillman?" he asked. He was nervous now and struggled not to show it. "He's the Marine who's related to one of my students," he said.

Rawl's face paled and her eyes widened, then she quickly got control of herself and smiled tightly. "I know the name, but I am not sure if I've ever met Sgt. Stillman," she said. Now she was very uncomfortable, and Jack knew exactly why she would be familiar with the name. It would have been on the list of several Marines injured or killed in Fallujah recently. By now there would have been a somber ceremony by the folks here in the rear, honoring and mourning the loss of some of their own. Jack tried to show no reaction. There was no way she would tell them, two nonmilitary strangers, the names of the dead. Did he dare ask about the others? What would she do if he suddenly rattled off a list that contained all of the names of the dead from the battle in Fallujah just over a week ago? There was no way that he could risk that, if he wanted to see anything else today. Jack quickly changed the subject and tried to cover his fear at the confirmation he felt he had just received. Casey was very real and so were the others. These were not names and faces that he had made up in his nightmares. His mind reeled and his chest tightened. He looked over at Pam who looked down at her own knees.

"What about other support services?" he asked, fighting the nausea that now churned inside him. He looked at his notepad, unable to look Rawls in the eyes again. "Medical service, ministers, that sort of thing," he said then looked up again. Her face was somber and anxious. She seemed relieved, however, by the new course their conversation was taking. "Are those sort of personnel based out of here as well?" he asked.

"Partially," Rawls answered. "We have some medical and chaplain services staff here, what we call "organic" personnel. But when we deploy, we supplement them with what we call "MAPsters," Marine Augmentation Personnel, like doctors and nurses as well as chaplains. The augmentees expand our support staff to meet our needs in theater. Most of our corpsmen, they're like medics that are assigned to each combat platoon," she said to Pam, perhaps sensing that Jack already knew this, "most of them are organic, but we do expand the corpsmen staff a great deal for deployment. They're usually put in medical companies and surgical companies that we stand up for deployment. All of the support personnel are actually Navy personnel. When they're not deployed they work at various Navy hospitals and clinics," she finished.

"I see," Jack said. He sensed that Pam was becoming more anxious and wanted desperately to know what she was thinking. He feigned scribbling another note on his pad. "Lieutenant, is there any chance of getting a little tour, maybe seeing Third Battalion's spaces and maybe the chaplain services or medical?"

Rawls made a show of looking at her watch. "I can take you on a short little tour, if you want," she said. "I don't have a lot of time, but I can show you what some of our stuff looks like. Most of our people at Third Battalion are gone, out in the field," she said with insincere apology.

"Whatever you have time for would be great," Jack said and smiled at Pam. He saw that her eyes were sad and her face terribly pale. "Is that okay with you, sweetheart?"

"Sure," Pam smiled tightly.

"Well," Rawls said, rising and grabbing a set of keys from the desk. "Why don't we ride together in my car, and I'll take you over by Third Battalion," she said, ending any other immediate conversation. "On the way back I'll drop you at your car and take you out to the main gate, okay?"

"That would be great," Jack said. He wondered why he was not more shaken by his interview with the lieutenant. Hadn't he just learned that Casey was real? Didn't that confirm his most horrifying fear? And yet he felt remarkably calm. Maybe it was because the confirmation was no real surprise to him. He wondered if all of his anxiety might be fear of how Pam was taking all this. And maybe a still undiscovered terror that he had no idea what this would really mean for him or what he could possibly do next. He was tied to a real Marine, dead or dying in Iraq. Hell, he might even be him. Was Hoag right? Was all the rest of this just an elaborate ruse of his tortured mind, a fantasy designed to protect him from his fear of death and leaving his girls? Jack shook off the thought. He would have time for this later.

Finish up and get the fuck out of here. Get Pam out of here.

He looked up and saw that Rawls was looking at him with curiosity and Pam with real concern.

"Are you okay, Jack?" Rawls asked.

"Yeah," Jack answered, screwing on another fake smile. "Just got up too fast and got a little dizzy."

"Well, let's get going," Rawls said and led them out.

They stepped into the small waiting room where Rawls left them for a moment, telling them she needed to let her office personnel know where she would be. When she stepped through the other door, leaving them alone for a moment, Pam wrapped her arms tightly around Jack.

"Oh, my God," she said, her voice trembling. "What the hell is going on, Jack? How could you possibly know these things?"

"It's okay, baby," Jack said. He hugged her again. "Everything is going to be all right."

"How?" she asked, her face against his chest. "What are you going to do? I just don't understand what's going on. I'm so scared, Jack." Jack sensed that she was no longer worried that he was crazy. Her fears were much bigger than that now.

"Shhh. It's okay, Pam," he said softly and then tilted her face up to look into her eyes. "I'll fix this Pam. I will not leave you guys, do you understand?"

Pam looked back at him with fear, but also with hope. She nodded and then dabbed her eyes on the corner of her sleeve and sniffled.

"I'm sorry," she said and took his hand, trying to straighten up and look normal for the lieutenant.

"I love you, Pam," Jack said as Rawls came back in the room.

"Ready?" the lieutenant asked brightly, like a realtor showing a house, Jack thought. She was perfect for public affairs.

"You bet," he said. They followed her down the stairwell back to the first deck and out the front door, chatting about where Rawls and her family were from, though Jack didn't really hear the answers.

Rawls drove a black Ford Explorer with Ohio plates and a yellow and orange "Semper Fi" sticker in the back window. Jack sat up front with the lieutenant, but reached his hand behind him between the seats to hold Pam's hand. He noticed that her hand was sweaty and grimaced at the pain his nightmare was causing his best friend.

They left the parking lot and turned right onto a tree-lined street that, after a mile or so, broke out into row after row of industrial-looking buildings. With each minute the base became more and more familiar.

Just behind the low brick building coming up on the left will be another one just like it — the base post office.

As they passed by, Jack saw without much surprise the United States Post Office sign. He looked out the front window without much satisfaction, knowing that they would turn right at the next stop sign. A moment later Rawls flipped on her turn signal and slowed down. Jack realized she was talking to him.

"I'm sorry, what?" he said.

"Yes," Pam answered for him from the back, "One, a little girl."

"They're great aren't they?" the lieutenant asked warmly.

"Claire is our world," Jack said and felt Pam's lightly sweating hand squeeze his.

"I know how you feel," Rawls said as they made the turn Jack knew was coming. The PAO continued on, talking about her boys, but Jack couldn't pay attention. In a minute they would come to a gym on the left, where he and his Marines spent countless hours every day. Just past it was a recreation center. Soon they would come to the building that housed the FSSG, or Fleet Services Support Group, which administratively managed supply, religious services, medical services and other support activities for the Marines. Jack had a sudden idea.

"Are the religious services people in the FSSG admin spaces?" he asked. "I would love to talk to someone from Chaplain Services about the important job they have."

"They are actually in their own offices nearby, but the admin for those folks are in FSSG," Rawls answered, looking at her watch. "We can stop for a moment and see if someone is around if you like."

"That would be great," Jack answered. What would he say? How could he find out more about Hoag? He had said he was the regimental chaplain, so his office might be over at regiment, but for sure the folks at FSSG would know who he was.

Rawls parked the truck and they all walked together over to the low brick building, entering through a side door.

"Stand by here for just a sec," the PAO said, "I'll see if there is anyone around who has a minute for you." She disappeared into the office, leaving Pam and Jack in the hallway. Pam wrapped her arms around him again.

"What are we doing, Jack?" she asked in a loud whisper.

But Jack barely heard her. Instead he stared past her where his eyes froze on the wall behind her. Next to them in the hall were several rows of pictures for the various commands that fell under the umbrella of the FSSG. The first group had yellow lettering over it that read "Medical," under which was a picture of a Naval officer in woodland cammies, labeled MEF SURGEON. Beneath the picture was his name. Then there were several rows of pictures with the various subcommanders, such as REGIMENTAL SURGEON, GROUP SURGEON, WING SURGEON, and then lower-ranking officers that ran the various medical battalions.

But it was the second cluster of pictures that froze Jack in place. It was labeled RELIGIOUS SERVICES, and under the MEF CHAPLAIN picture was another labeled REGIMENTAL CHAPLAIN. Beneath the placard was a smiling face that Jack recognized very well. The man, heavier than the man Jack knew from his nightmares, smiled out at him. The eyes behind his round glasses reflected a much happier time. Beneath the picture of the smiling face were yellow letters that read CDR EMMETT G. HOAG. Jack stared at the picture and his mind flashed to images of Hoag screaming at him hysterically in the desert, red and shiny loops of intestines falling out from beneath his desert cammie blouse.

"Jack, what is it?" His wife's trembling voice pulled him back from the moonlit desert. He turned to her, but couldn't speak. "Baby, what?" she said. He could tell she was on the verge of tears. She turned and looked behind her at the photograph and then read the name. Her face turned pale and she let go of his hand, placing it instead over her mouth. Jack heard the breath stick in his wife's throat. "Oh, my God," she said, for a moment unable to tear her eyes from the picture. Then she turned to him, her hand still over her mouth, her eyes wide with fear. "That's him, isn't it?"

Jack couldn't speak, but nodded his head. Then he took her hand and turned his back to the wall, unable to look at Hoag's face again. He wrapped his arms around his wife to comfort her, but knew he was failing miserably.

Lieutenant Rawls came back out of the office, looked at them, and then hesitated a moment. It was clear she had interrupted something. She apparently decided it was none of her business and politely ignored the emotional looks of the pleasant young couple.

"I'm sorry, Jack," she said. "There isn't really anyone around to talk to you right now."

"That's okay," Jack said, forcing a smile. He kept his arms wrapped around his wife, no longer caring about the façade or what this helpful young lieutenant might think. He suddenly, desperately needed to get them both the hell out of here. "My wife is actually not feeling very well, Lieutenant," he said. "I'm sorry to have run you around for nothing, but if you don't mind we're going to have to skip the Third Battalion tour."

Rawls smiled sympathetically. He wasn't at all surprised that she also looked relieved. They had been more than she had bargained for when she came to work this morning, he suspected.

"That's no problem, Jack," she said. "I'll take you folks back to your car." She led them towards the door. "You haven't run me around at all," Rawls said graciously. "This is exactly what they pay me for."

"Thanks," Jack said as they headed to the truck. He piled in the back with Pam this time and held her against his shoulder as they headed back to the MEF headquarters building. They rode in silence. Rawls seemed to sense that they preferred not to talk. Jack realized he had all he needed here anyway. They had confirmed that Casey and Hoag were very much real, and Jack had no doubt from the PAO's response in her office that Stillman's name appeared on a casualty report. He had confirmed in his own mind that everything he thought he knew about Camp Pendleton and his Marines was true. This had been his home, THEIR home. They had lived on base in the married enlisted housing only a few miles from here. They had been neighbors with Staff Sergeant Danny

Wilson and his wife and two little girls, both older than Claire. Jack knew that he could drive right this moment to their home in the cluster of townhouses and their house would look exactly as it did in his mind. Behind it was a green and yellow kid-sized picnic table where Danny and Beth's little girls had read books to Claire while the four of them drank beer.

He was Casey Stillman, a young sergeant of Marines. What the fuck the rest meant, other than that he was dying right now, this moment, in a dirty street in Iraq, was a total fucking mystery. What he was going to do about it was the only question that needed answering. And he realized he had no clue.

None whatsoever.

Chapter
24

Jack's mind was filled with the uncomfortable blur of images that represented the rest of their day. He tried to tuck them away, in light of the more pressing thoughts that he needed his tortured mind to address. He drove them from Pendleton to San Diego in relative quiet, Pam's head on his shoulder. He had tried to comfort her more with touch than words—touching her hand, squeezing her arm under his, leaning over and kissing her wet cheek. In any case, he had no real words to offer her. There was nothing he could say that would ease her pain since he had no clue whatsoever what this all meant, and more importantly, what he could possibly do about it. A few times he thought she was sleeping and felt his back tighten and ache as he tried not to shift positions and disturb her. Then she would begin to sob softly and squeeze his arm again.

They stopped just outside the airport at a Bennigan's. Jack insisted that they should both eat something, though neither felt the least bit hungry.

Eat when you can, sleep when you can, and shit when you have to.

The voice in his head belonged to a seasoned gunnery sergeant who had addressed the entire company just before they had left for deployment. He could see him so clearly in his mind.

They sat in a booth and picked at some appetizers and left with the food barely touched and their beer glasses still half full. They chatted a bit during lunch, but not about anything substantial. Jack had the sense that Pam had so much she wanted to say, so much she wanted to ask, but elected instead to let Jack sort things out in his mind until he was ready to talk. So they had talked about Claire, about the flight home, about whether they would be served dinner—in short, about nothing. Although he had no idea what else to tell his wife, he had no doubt that he would come up with a plan to make this all right. The alternative was simply too terrifying to even consider.

And what about Lewellyn? Would Pam still insist that he call the psychologist? Surely she could see by now that this was not all simply a hallucination. Jack wondered, in fact was desperate to know, what his wife really thought was going on. For a moment he considered that if this really was just fantasy that he was using to escape from the fear of his lingering death in Fallujah, then Pam would think whatever he wanted her to think in this dream. Too simple, he decided. Maybe he wasn't supposed to really know what was going on, but he knew with certainty that it was more than just a simple dream like Hoag had suggested. He did have control, at least some, and if that was true, then surely he could change things, fix them somehow.

He also had a fleeting thought that maybe this was all just a schizophrenic crisis like he had feared all along. Was he right now sitting and drooling in his office at home and imagining all of this? He shuddered at the thought then hugged his wife closer. He felt suddenly very tired.

Jack closed his eyes as the Delta jet flew though the late afternoon sky. As his mind continued to tear madly through his random impressions and searched for an answer, he knew sleep would be impossible. After a few minutes he heard the soft double chime and looked up to see the seat belt sign snap off. Jack unbuckled his seat belt and gently untangled himself from Pam's embrace.

"Where are you going?" his wife asked.

"Just to the bathroom. Do you want a pillow or anything?"

"Yes, please," she answered.

Jack shuffled down the narrow aisle towards the back of the plane. He squeezed past a flight attendant who maneuvered a service cart into the aisle with a mumbled apology, then slipped into the lavatory and clicked the door lock shut. The overhead light flickered and then illuminated the cramped bathroom.

Jack looked critically at himself in the small mirror, and saw that his eyes were bloodshot and his face looked haggard. He pushed the small handle with the blue dot for cold and let some water fill the stainless steel sink. Then he splashed some of the cool water onto his face and held his cupped hands to his eyes to let himself soak for a moment in the bracing feel. He repeated the maneuver several times and felt his mind clear a bit, then looked again at himself in the mirror. Not much better, just haggard and wet. Jack pulled a handful of paper towels from the dispenser and dabbed the cool water from his face. Then he stood for a moment, the paper towels pressed into his damp eyes, and stretched his back. He pushed the paper towels into the flip lid trash receptacle then looked again in the mirror. Shocked by what he saw, he grabbed the edge of the counter with both hands to steady himself.

The face in the mirror was still his, but vastly different. The hair was cropped close to the scalp in a Marine Corps "high and tight" haircut. His face was caked with dirt and dry blood and his eyes were much more bloodshot. There were red lines pressed in his forehead where his Kevlar helmet had been. Behind the face in the mirror was darkness and swirling sand. As he watched, the dust grew thicker and thicker and swirled around his reflected image, obscuring it.

Jack looked around frantically, and was relieved to find he was still safely in the airplane lavatory. No dust. No sand. He held out his arms and let his gaze pass over his own body—still in khakis and a button-down shirt. He looked again at the mirror. All he could see now was the swirling sand and dust where his reflection had been, but now he heard, softly, the sounds of voices and gunfire. It was like the mirror was now his own personal movie screen on which he watched the swirling, blowing dust settle. As it did another face came into view.

Hoag's.

The chaplain looked back at him from the mirror, a nighttime desert scene illuminated behind him by a pale moon. It was not the face from the picture at Pendleton, smiling and happy. The face was worn and older, deeply lined and thinner, the eyes full of stress and fear. The glasses were dirty, covered in a thin layer of dust. Jack expected the commander to take them off and start cleaning them, but he didn't.

"Hello, Casey," the image in the mirror said to him.

Jack started to tell the image in the mirror that he wasn't real, but then stopped. He realized that he no longer really believed that. Instead he said nothing and stared back at the sad eyes, wondering if his own eyes looked as old and sad as those that looked back at him from the mirror.

Hoag held his gaze and spoke again, the voice filled with fear and the borderline hysteria he remembered from a few nights ago.

"Now do you believe, Casey?" he asked simply.

"I don't know what I believe," Jack said loudly, then lowered his voice, not wanting the passengers and crew to hear him talking to himself in the bathroom. "I believe that you, and Casey, and the others are real. I believe that I'm tied to all of you." He stopped. He believed more than that, but was not able to say it. Or maybe he was just unwilling to let Hoag have the satisfaction of hearing it.

Hoag's eyes held an animallike fear; a dog trapped in an alley.

"We're almost out of time, Casey. It is time for all of us to go."

"I'm not going anywhere with you," Jack said. His own voice rose as fear from the real meaning of Hoag's words gripped him. The reality it carried was ugly and terrifying.

Then the chaplain let out a visceral scream that reverberated in the small bathroom, making Jack cover his ears. The blowing dust swirled again, beginning to obscure the image in the mirror.

"YOU WILL COME BACK TO US, SAR'N," Hoag's fading image screamed at him, "YOU WILL COME WITH US OR WE WILL COME FOR YOU! WE WILL TAKE YOU, AND THOSE AROUND YOU WILL SUFFER. DO YOU HEAR ME?"

The sand and dust twisted viciously in the mirror now. Jack could smell the distinctive odor of Iraqi desert, and with it, another foul smell—the smell of old blood and death. On the verge of vomiting, he tasted burning bile in his throat and mouth. Jack retched and swallowed hard.

"Leave me alone, you bastard!" he shouted at the darkening image in the mirror.

As Jack watched in fascination and horror the image, or maybe the mirror itself, began to shimmer. At first it was subtle, a waving shine like the air over hot asphalt on a brutally hot summer day. But as he watched, the shimmering itself became more distinct, like a million microscopic fireflies were fluttering on the surface of the mirror. Then as the tiny flickers of light became more distinct, it no longer appeared like it was the mirror itself that was the source. The tiny flickers of light spread out from the mirror surface and filled the room. It was then that Jack realized that the surface of the mirror was gone. It was no longer a mirror, but a glassless, open window to the world from which Hoag called him.

Jack began to choke as the sand poured out of the mirror and into the lavatory, slowly at first, then building into a howling torrent of dust and heat. As it had before, the sand started to swirl around him, building in speed until it was a whistling tornado, a dust devil like those he had seen screaming across the open desert in Iraq.

Jack held out his hands, which began to tingle, and saw that his own skin now shimmered like the mirror had. He knew where this was headed. He was being pulled—by Hoag, or the devil, or whatever fucking force controlled all of this—back to Iraq. He felt the cyclone try to spin his body around inside the cramped bathroom. He could no longer see the walls, only dust and swirling, shimmering light. He threw his arms outward in both directions, felt them impact against the flimsy plastic walls of his sanctuary. He pressed outward with all his might and riveted himself in place against the spinning cyclone of sand. All he could see in his mind was Pam, alone and frightened in her cramped airline seat. The spinning sand grew in ferocity and he felt himself lifted from the floor. Jack kicked out his legs, jammed his feet firmly against the walls, and fought the force that tried to spin him wildly in the thick and blinding cloud of sand.

"No!" he hollered over the now deafening roar of the sand tornado. "No, goddamnit! I'm not going! I won't leave her, you hear me?" He braced himself with all his might against the bathroom walls, his arms and legs pushed out, until his muscles burned with pain.

Then with a sudden flash of brilliant light, the sandstorm disappeared and Jack collapsed roughly to the floor, coughing. His stomach wretched and he covered his mouth, as if his hand would keep the vomit from spewing out of him. He struggled to his feet and looked at the mirror. It still glimmered, but only barely, and there was a faint image of Hoag's screaming, twisted face, like a light spot you see with your eyes closed after looking at the sun.

"Leave my family alone, you motherfucker!" Jack screamed. Then he lost the battle with his stomach and spun around, flipped up the lid to the silver toilet and vomited violently. He wretched several times, struggled for control, and then sat on the black rubber floor, gasping for breath. A knock on the door jarred him back to his senses.

"Sir?" a worried female voice said. "Sir, are you all right?" More knocking. Jack pulled the silver handle and his pool of sick was sucked away with a hissing vacuum of air and a swirl of blue water.

"Just a minute, please," he choked out.

"Are you sick?" the voice asked.

What the fuck do you think?

"Just a minute please." Jack flushed the toilet again. Then he struggled to his feet and braced himself weakly against the wall.

The mirror flashed back only his own pale face, the cheeks streaked with tears. Jack filled his cupped hands with cool water and splashed it on his face again. He sipped some more of the soothing liquid into his mouth and swished it around before swallowing it. He found a cup dispenser and greedily drank down two cups of water from the sink, clearing his mouth and throat.

Hoag was right. He was out of time. They were coming for him and he couldn't stop them. They would take him back to his death in Fallujah and he would be gone from his girls forever. What the hell did he mean that those around him would suffer? Could they hurt Pam and Claire? The thought almost made him throw up again, but somehow he got control of his retching stomach.

Then he stopped, frozen motionless by an idea—an epiphany, in fact. He did not have to accept this as his fate. He couldn't accept it, and he realized now that he didn't have to. There was some control here. Wasn't that what Lewellyn had tried to get him to see (or his own mind talking to him as the psychologist, or whatever the fuck this all was)? Only he could change it, and only he wanted to, apparently. And now he had a vague, but sharpening, idea of how.

Jack felt a sudden weak but growing sense that he might really be able to fix all of this. Hadn't he just prevented himself from being sucked back into the mad nightmare—prevented it with a sheer burst of will? And he had come back to Pam from that nightmare the other night on his own as well, now that he thought about it. He could fix this. He would fight it until there was no fight left.

Jack looked one last time at the face that stared back at him from the mirror, relieved to see the long hair of Jack, instead of Casey Stillman's close-cropped scalp. This time he saw eyes set with a fiery determination, jaw clenched tightly. He could do it. He had the power to change all of this. He would stop it before it started.

Jack dried his face with another towel then brushed the wrinkles from his shirt and pants. He sighed nervously and clicked open the lock to the lavatory door.

A young and agitated flight attendant stood nervously beside the door to the lavatory. Jack tried to smile and failed.

"Are you all right, sir?" she asked with real concern, and, Jack thought, a tinge of fear.

"Airsick," he said simply and squeezed past her, heading for the aisle.

The flight attendant looked past him into the bathroom, and seemed surprised that it looked normal.

"I...I, uh..." she stammered. Jack walked away up the aisle towards his seat before she could finish her thought. As he left her behind he heard her whispering to the older flight attendant beside her, "I could have sworn I heard someone else in there with him."

You have no fucking idea, sweetie.

Jack continued up the aisle to his seat. He flopped down heavily beside Pam who looked up, startled from near sleep in her seat. Her eyes got wide as she looked at her husband.

"Are you all right?" she asked. "Jesus, you look like shit."

Jack looked at her and smiled—a real and determined smile this time. Then he hugged her tightly.

"Everything is going to be all right, baby," he said. "I know I've been saying that, but now I've really got this figured out." He started to ride the wave of his own excitement at his slowly crystallizing plan. "I know how to make this right."

Pam pulled away and looked into his eyes, her own filled with hope and confusion. He could see that she wanted so much to believe him.

"How, Jack?"

"You're going to have to trust me," he said and put his arm around her in the seat. Then he pushed the call button with his free hand. Pam looked up at the illuminated call light.

"What are you doing?" she asked.

"Forgot your pillow," Jack said with a tension-relieving chuckle.

"I trust you, Jack," was all she said.

Chapter
25

The rest of the flight passed in comfortable quiet, at least it seemed to for Pam. Instead of the frightened musing and self-doubting rumination he had become accustomed to lately, Jack felt a surge of personal confidence, now that he had something to focus his mind on. No more questions, he promised himself. It was time for answers and action.

He had no idea, of course, whether his idea would work, or was even possible. He still had no clue what this was all about or, he supposed, who he really was. But he succeeded in keeping his mind away from questions he couldn't answer (Lewellyn would have a marathon session on that) and instead started to outline a plan for his night. Maybe his last night, he thought grimly.

Better to face it and go down fighting.

Hoorah.

Jack tried to remember if at any time he had touched any of his images. He didn't think so, but wasn't really sure. He knew he had felt contact when he was Casey. He had felt the corpsman's hand in his; felt the pressure in his chest when Doc Barton did whatever had made him breathe better; had felt Mac touch him.

But what about as Jack?

He had a clear memory of the feel of arms and hands on him, pulling him down into the cyclone of sand that had barfed up out of the hole in the sidewalk, but had he initiated any contact with any of the images?

Then he remembered the night in the desert, when Hoag had become hysterical and started shaking him. Hadn't he grabbed the commander by the wrists and broken his hold on him? He was sure that he had. That seemed important. He had initiated physical contact and more importantly, altered things that Hoag was doing.

Very fucking important, in fact.

The other thing that was crucial to the plan was timing. When he had gone to the nighttime desert that day, he had been with his Marines *before* the assault on Fallujah. They had been smoking and grab-assing by the berm outside the city, a moment he vaguely recalled outside of his visit to the event as Jack. And he was pretty sure that had been the night before they had gone into the Jolan neighborhood as part of the assault force, and a full day or so before his squad had been split off from the platoon and pinned behind the wall. In other words, well before any of them had been injured or killed. That was critically important, too, Jack realized. He had to be able to get to Fallujah before they were all shot up, preferably before they even got separated from the rest of his platoon. The timing was going to be everything.

Lastly, was his ability to go where he needed to go. He felt pretty good about that one. He knew he had left Hoag that night, somewhat of his own free will. And he was certain he had left the dirty street of Fallujah, had willed himself away and back to the arms of his wife, on at least two occasions. If he could leave Iraq by a sheer force of desire, shouldn't he also be able to go there as well? Jack realized that while that certainly seemed reasonable, he had no way to really know. After all, he still didn't really understand any of this. He thought he had a better understanding of what it all meant, but it was still just his own personal interpretation. Jack tried not to dwell on the things he didn't know. Hoag had said some things that implied his plan couldn't possibly work, but hadn't the Navy chaplain also admitted that he didn't understand it all either? That night in the desert, Hoag admitted he had no idea what came next, but somehow seemed to believe that they had to "all leave together." The chaplain being wrong about that was going to be incredibly important, too.

There were a lot of uncertainties in his plan, he realized, but he had no other ideas. If this didn't work, then he doubted he had any hope at all of staying with Pam and Claire. He would die in the street in Fallujah and leave Pam a widow and single mother. That was a thought he couldn't bear. He would alter his destiny, and hopefully that of his Marines. Hoag, he assumed, was on his own. He had bought it miles away in an unrelated IED attack, and Jack couldn't think of any way to incorporate the chaplain's death into his plan. He didn't let himself think about what that meant for his hope for success for him, and Bennet, and Kindrich, and Simmons—especially poor, young Simmons. He felt particularly responsible for his youngest Marine, whom he had pulled himself helmet to helmet with that day in Fallujah. He had promised the boy that they would be fine.

Maybe now he would have a chance to make good on that promise.

Jack also felt an incredible press of time on him. Would he even make it to the night, or for that matter, to the airport? Hoag's threatening promise echoed in his mind over and over, interrupting his attempts to focus on the plan.

We will come for you… We will take you and those around you will suffer…

Jack wasn't sure he could tell Pam, even if he wanted to. He was worried that her reaction to the madness of what was going on, and the insanity of what he was planning, might shake his own resolve if he were to tell it out loud. He hoped she wouldn't ask again for the details, that she would just trust him. He believed telling her would ruin his chances for some reason.

After they landed and collected their carry-on luggage, they headed out to the parking lot hand in hand. Jack felt lucky that his wife seemed content to just hold his hand and let him work things out. Lucky, but not surprised.

The Volvo was where they had left it in long-term parking, and Jack threw their two small bags into the trunk unceremoniously. They picked up Claire at Bev's and Jack felt his heart come alive at the cooing shouts of joy when their little girl saw them.

Bev assured them that Claire had been a "joy" and had done very well during her short sleepover. Having Claire in the car for the brief ride home erased some of the uncomfortable, surrealistic haze that seemed to envelop his life more and more the last several days. Jack marveled at how having the three of them together seemed the only cure, and that when the fantasylike veil was lifted by their closeness, his fears and anxieties seemed so small, almost petty. Then the weight of his plan for the night sunk back on him, and he sighed heavily. Might this be his last night with his family? He shook the thought off violently, physically shaking his head and making himself a bit dizzy. There was no point in letting his mind go there.

It is what it is.

He was trapped between his family and a world of death and ghosts no one could possibly understand.

Including him.

Chapter
26

Jack stared at the stubborn and unwavering ceiling while his wife slept beside him. Nothing was happening. His body ached with exhaustion, but his mind seemed unwilling to take the hint.

Maybe I'm trying too hard.

He tried to let his mind wander, to kind of sneak up on sleep while holding onto his destination in his mind.

Nothing.

Not a move, not a flash, not a grain of sand or dust. No sound of gunfire or helicopters.

Just a swirled stucco ceiling with a slowly turning fan.

Trying too hard.

Jack shifted his mind away from the stubborn and insistently normal bedroom ceiling and instead tried to map out some details of what he could remember about where he was going. He had no idea how the fuck this worked (or if it could) and he had a sudden fear that he would "arrive" at the wrong place, or time, or whatever the hell it was. So he tried to remember some details about the journey of Kilo Company, Third Battalion, First Marines, into the hell of Fallujah. It felt ridiculous to try and remember details of a place and time his memory swore to him he had never really seen, but it was there. He felt it. Jack forced himself to relax and settle into the memories. He just went to the memory like he was making it up, knowing that he was not.

They had moved into the city on the ninth of November, leaving behind, maybe forever, what he realized now was the relative peace and safety of the sand berm they had guarded for the days leading up to the siege on the terrorist-held city. His company, Kilo, had been assigned to move into the Jolan neighborhood in the northwest corner of the city. They had been told to expect violent resistance but had been asked, nonetheless, to retain fire control discipline. This was because, despite days of warnings, there was no way to be sure that innocent Iraqi civilians were not left behind in the city. Kilo and their sister company, Lima, would take Jolan while First Battalion, Eighth Marines worked to their east. Several army companies would be between the two Marine battalions and together they would all push south, eventually pushing the enemy ahead of them and across Highway 10, which cut across the city east to west. South of the highway they would join up with other units waiting there, establishing a kill zone bordered to the north by Highway 10, and to the south by the southern border of the city. It was a classic, time-tested, beautifully simplistic Marine Corps plan.

Jack felt himself drifting softly, nowhere near asleep, but following his mind along on its journey.

Casey had been in charge of second platoon for Kilo Company. He knew his men well and considered them more than friends. They were a family. Like most families they didn't all get along, but when the shit hit the fan, Casey had no doubt they would come together and fight like a family, taking care of each other. The first night had proven that. The initial push into Fallujah and the Jolan neighborhood was nothing any of them had imagined, despite the months—for some of them years—of training together.

Jack sighed and stared at the swirling shadow of the ceiling fan.

Maybe he wasn't supposed to make the ceiling change. Maybe it just happened, kind of crept up on you when you were distracted by other things. Jack closed his eyes with some difficulty, and he felt himself drifting deeper and farther away…

* * *

He woke up cold. There was a chill in the air that was in no way what his mind told him he should feel here, in a hammock slung between palm trees, his arms and legs wrapped around Pam's warm and wet bare skin. The hammock was the dream he found while searching for the other, dark reality in Iraq. Not the target, but he would take it for a few more minutes, he decided. Eyes closed he reached for a blanket, searching for the corner his wife must have pulled off him in her fitful slumber. His fingers dug instead into cool sand, fine to the point of being a powder. He realized that a similar grime coated his teeth and throat.

Jack's eye sprung open in realization, but he was met with darkness so complete that he momentarily thought his mind had fooled him and his eyes were still closed. He stretched his hands out behind him as he sat up in the dark, his fingers probing the now-familiar berm. He leaned his weight against it and struggled to his feet, leaning over slightly to steady himself, the blackness nauseatingly disorienting.

As his brain steadied his legs in the dark, Jack let go of the berm and stood up straight, his eyes scanning a half circle in the blackness, searching for any speck of light to focus on. As he adjusted to the dark he became aware that the sky above him, though moonless, was a field peppered with points of light so rich that he was again swept away to another place, cutting through the Pacific Ocean late at night aboard the LHD. As his eyes dropped from the sky above he made out a faint line of yellow light that marked the top of the berm.

I'm here. I made it.

He was at Checkpoint Four, an overstatement of the desolate berm that he and his men had occupied for the days before they had moved into Fallujah. He was in the right place, but Jack's stomach tightened as he realized that he was alone and that could only mean he was in no way at the right time. Was he early or late? Hours or days? There was no way to know and Jack felt a growing panic. What the fuck was he supposed to do now?

Jack scrambled up the berm, desperate for information. His fingers dug into the powdery sand and occasionally stung as they caught on bits of wood and metal, trash caught up in the berm as it had been pushed up into place by the Army bulldozers that had arrived long before he and his men had called Checkpoint Four a temporary home. Jack slowed as he neared the top of the hill of dirt and garbage and then slowly peered over the crest of the berm.

Fallujah.

There were only scattered points of light, but Jack saw burst after burst of red streaks lighting up the night—tracers from firefights spread out all over the city. Jack became aware of sporadic cracks of rifle fire, the burping bursts of machine gun fire, and occasional louder explosions of mortars and rockets. His ear was able to discern the subtle difference between the M16A of the American soldiers and Marines and the higher pitched crack of the AK-47s favored by the insurgents.

So it would seem he was late. Maybe by only minutes or hours, but definitely too fucking late.

He expected panic to start to well up, but mysteriously it didn't. Maybe he was just too damn tired to panic anymore. Instead he watched the glow and flash of his soon-to-be deathbed and struggled with what to do next. He had gotten here (he realized now he had always known he would and was surprised at that bit of insight), without really knowing how. But he knew why and that was why he knew he couldn't give up. If he could come here, could he not move about here as well? Could he not just travel again, back a few hours?

Perhaps ten blocks from the perimeter of the city, the squeal of an RPG was punctuated by a rumbling explosion and a burst of light. Jack unconsciously lowered his head, only his eyes now above the crest of the berm.

"There goes Bennet," a harsh whisper choked into his right ear. Jack rolled violently to his left in surprise, his arms raised defensively, his heart pounding at the unexpected interruption of his private viewing.

Before his eyes even focused on the shape beside him, he already knew, of course, who it was. The glow of the battle for Fallujah a few miles away reflected back at him from the filthy round glasses on the full and tired face. Hoag turned slowly towards him, his face pale and sweaty and his eyes even wilder than before.

"What did you think you would accomplish here, Casey?" the dead officer asked him. "You can't change anything, Sar'n. You see..." Hoag looked down at his stained blouse and massaged his right hand around the loops of intestines contained there, "All of this is God's will." The crooked smile barely hid a wild hysteria that frightened Jack in new way.

Another flash lit up the sky from the city below them, followed a split second later by a sharp boom, the sound catching up with the light over the few miles to the source in the Jolan neighborhood. Jack reflexively pulled his head down behind the berm again. As he did, he saw, or maybe felt, a flurry of motion beside him. He turned to face the now for sure crazy, and still dead, chaplain. Instead of the wet and wild eyes, he looked into the cycloptic black gaze of Hoag's side arm. Jack tried not to move, hands frozen still beside his head (you got me, Sheriff!), uncertain what to do. Was this possible, even? Could he be shot and killed by a ghost of a dead minister in a battlefield in a dream? With a burst of clarity Jack felt certain that he could.

"It's God's will!" Hoag said again, his voice now rising to a shaky holler. "We can't stop the will of God, Casey!" He looked out over the berm, as if scanning across a riveted congregation that only he could see. The naked black hole of the handgun never wavered in front of Jack's face, however, and he stayed still, trying to figure out what the hell to do.

"I have been washed by the blood of the Lamb, Casey," Hoag's squeaky voice spit at him in the glow of Fallujah. He peered at him now through those filthy fucking glasses, and Jack was grateful that he couldn't really see the eyes behind them. "But YOU, Sar'n..." The barrel of Hoag's gun shaking at Jack like a thick black finger in his face. "You cheated. You fucking cheated, you fucking little CHEATER!" Jack didn't like the way his voice rose, and knew what was coming. "I WON'T LET YOU CHEAT, YOU FUCK! YOU ARE COMING WITH ME! YOU WILL BE WASHED IN THE BLOOD OF THE LAMB—WASHED IN THE BLOOD OF THE LAMB— WASHED IN THE BLOOD OF THE LAMB..." Hoag gripped his gun wrist with his other hand to steady his aim. He peered down the barrel at Jack, one eye closed and the crooked grin back on his face. Spit dribbled from the corner of his mouth and his voice fell to a raspy whisper.

"You are coming with me, Sergeant Stillman." The shrill voice choked at him. "You will be washed in the blood like God meant for you to be and we will leave this shithole together. You can't cheat God you fu..."

An image of Pam, sitting in the glider chair, holding his sleeping daughter to her chest, flashed in Jack's mind and both of his hands exploded from his sides. His left hand struck the middle of the chaplain's throat and Jack felt a sickening crunch as the cartilage of Hoag's voice box collapsed under the blow. His right hand simultaneously grabbed the barrel of the gun and jerked it downward. The deafening explosion shattered the stillness of the berm and a blinding flash of light erased the dark world around him.

He felt a terrible burning in his right hand, which gripped the now-smoking pistol. Jack was sure he was dead, killed by a dead preacher.

The spray of dirt beside his face comforted him and announced that he had not taken a bullet to the head. He jerked the wrist in his grip around in a full circle, feeling bone snap as the chaplain squealed again, this time in pain. The gun was free and Jack gripped it in his hand without thinking, swinging it around in a one-handed grip like he had been born with it. His thumb confirmed the safety was off and he squeezed twice in the direction of the heavy-jowled, sweaty face, now twisted in rage and confusion.

"You must be washed in the…" And then Hoag's head exploded under the force of two nine-millimeter rounds at point-blank range. Blood, bone, and something thick and grey spattered a modern art mural on the trash and sand of the berm. Then the chubby body collapsed, arms by its sides. Two long loops of pinkish-grey intestines snaked out from beneath the blouse, seemingly alive and twisting for a moment, then lay wet and still in the dirt.

Jack took a deep whistling breath as the last echoes of the gunshot rattled off through his mind and the acrid and familiar burnt sulfur smell drifted away in the nearly imperceptible breeze. He dropped the gun beside him in the dirt without looking down, and for a moment mourned the Navy commander, dead (again) in front of him on the berm.

Was there any way around going to hell for killing a fellow soldier, especially a fucking chaplain? Did it matter if they were already dead?

Jack realized with some surprise that he couldn't possibly care less. He had no intention of going to heaven or hell just yet.

He intended to go home to his girls.

He wasn't the least bit surprised when a gentle wind started spinning around him, pushing up a growing twister of sand and trash. As it grew Jack held his arms out from his sides like a snowboarder, ready to ride. He watched with some remorse, but no real guilt, as a separate twisting cyclone spun around Hoag's lifeless body. It picked it up from the dirt and tumbled it about like a broken doll, rising higher and higher. Then there was a brilliant and blinding flash of light and Hoag's body disappeared. Or at least Jack thought it had. He was now totally blinded by his own cyclone of twisting sand. Instead of picking him up, he was again being sucked down into the twisting tornado's center. Down into the berm.

Whatever.

Jack let his head fall back and closed his eyes.

Let's ride!

He thought of Pam and Claire as his world went black.

"I'm coming, girls," he whispered and hoped to God it was true. Then he was engulfed in what was becoming an all too familiar blackness.

* * *

He was asleep in his bed. Their bed. His arms were around his wife and he could smell the sweet smell of Claire and knew she was cuddled between them without even opening his eyes.

"I'm coming, Baby," he said, squeezing Pam's waist with his arm in the dark. "I'm trying so hard."

"I know, Casey," she answered, her voice a soft and melodic whisper. "I'm so proud of you." She squeezed his arm under hers. Claire sighed a sleepy sigh between them.

Jack's mind drifted again. Back to their hammock, but this time the three of them…

"Sar'n…Sar'n…" a gentle nudge to his shoulder as the whisper probed his dream-veiled mind. Jack stretched, eyes still closed. Man, he was tired.

He opened his eyes and found only darkness, thick and black, as if his eyes had not opened at all. Jesus, it was dark. He slowly and reluctantly accepted that he was no longer in his warm dream, lying in a hammock slung between two palm trees, his arms wrapped around his sleeping girls. No, he was definitely not on his faraway beach. He was…

Here!

Jack sat abruptly upright and heard the gasp of the startled Marine beside him.

"Shit, Sar'n!" the whisper hissed harshly. "You scared the piss out of me!"

It was Simmons' voice. Jack strained to see the face through the inky darkness, but saw only a subtle silhouette, a shade of darkness different from the surrounding night. He knew from the voice, though, that it was the Simmons he wanted, the one without the bloody toothless grin, counting teeth into a bloody bandana on his patio.

"Where are we?" He whispered back in the direction of his young Marine. His hands flailed a moment before he found the young man's arm and grabbed it.

"What the fuck are you talking about, Sar'n?" The boy sounded a little bit freaked out now and pulled his arm free. "We're at Checkpoint Four, just like the last three days. You havin' a dream, man?"

Jack became aware that he was stretched out in the sand, its usually smoldering surface now cool in the night air. His legs were crossed at his desert boot-covered ankles and he felt the familiar crunchy grime covering his teeth and tongue.

Again.

Yeah, this was Iraq all right.

Jack released the boy's arm and cleared his throat, which burned in a dry and familiar way.

"Yeah, Simmons," he whispered in a cracked voice. "Dreaming I was far away from here and your goat-smellin' ass..." Jack pulled his knees up stiffly, sitting upright. "Everything all right?"

Simmons plopped down on the sand beside him and stretched his back.

"Pretty quiet," he said. He peered through the black at Casey. "You said to wake you when we changed the watch."

Jack stretched his own back then rose to his feet beside the boy as things became clearer. He was here. He was at the right time and place. It was like the most intense deja vu of your life. He was supposed to say he had to go up to company and get their game plan for morning. Simmons would try and sound tough, saying it was fucking real now, but he would sound scared instead.

"I need to walk over to company and get the final game plan for morning," Jack said, his mind reading from the invisible script.

"Fuckin' real now," Simmons answered on cue, his voice cracking.

"We'll be fine," Jack said, ad-libbing out of character. He squeezed the boy's shoulder. They were more bonded now than before.

They had died together once already.

"Sure, Sar'n," Simmons muttered, not sure what else to say.

Jack picked up his M16A and slipped his left arm through the sling, hanging the rifle across his chest in a combat carry. He checked that the safety was on and tapped his vest to ensure the extra magazines were there, both actions unconscious and reflexive. Then he headed east along the berm. He walked without hesitation, knowing exactly where he was going. He was both Jack and Casey now, he realized. He needed to hold on to Jack to save Casey's life.

Only seventy-five yards or so east of where Simmons was (no doubt stretched out in the dirt now, eyes open and staring into the blackness, sleep impossible), Jack came to a small makeshift command post of two tents. Neither had been there the last few days, since they were just guarding the barren berm perimeter around the city. Jack pushed through the flap into the first tent, the dim red light still briefly blinding after the pitch blackness of the moonless desert night.

"Hoorah, Sar'n," a young officer no older than Casey said as he entered. His eyes were grey and looked older than his face. Much older. Combat did that, Jack thought.

"Hoorah, sir," Jack replied. Then he stood quietly for a moment, arm draped over the butt of the rifle across his chest. He waited, unsure what to say next, but now comfortable that it would all happen as it should. The officer, Lieutenant Parquay, Jack remembered, finished talking to the corporal seated beside him in a metal folding chair, hands resting on the edge of a filthy, dust-covered laptop computer. Then he turned to him again.

"Second Platoon all squared away, Sar'n?" the lieutenant asked, his voice, like his eyes, much older than his dirty face.

"Good to go, sir."

"Very well, Casey," Parquay said and rubbed his tired face with the back of one dirty hand. He pulled out a can of Copenhagen snuff, took out a pinch and stuffed it behind his lower lip. Then he held the can out to Jack.

"No, thank you, sir," Jack said.

Parquay looked surprised, as if a routine had been broken. Then he shrugged and dropped the can back into the cargo pocket of his desert cammies.

"Bad luck to quit a bad habit just before going to battle, Sar'n."

"Yes, sir," Jack responded. "Not to worry, sir. This has all happened before."

The old/young lieutenant looked at him curiously, not sure what he meant. Jack realized he wasn't entirely sure either.

"Bring your guys up at oh-four-hundred for a final brief and weapons check, Casey. You guys will be left flank of the group. We are going into Jolan at oh-five-hundred, and it's going to be a shit storm." Parquay looked at him for a moment then his eyes dropped back to the laptop computer in front of the boy beside him. "Problems you need to share?" he asked without looking back up.

"No, sir. My guys are shit hot and ready to rock."

"Thanks, Sar'n."

"Hoorah, sir," Jack responded, then ducked back out of the tent.

Jack stood in the dark beside the tent and let his breath out heavily. He was here, all right. Right place at the right time. All he had to do was keep his guys away from that fucking wall. Save Bennet. Save Simmons.

Save Casey and Jack.

There should be no more Hoag to fuck things up. He didn't have shit for a plan, not yet anyway. But he did have a chance. He really believed he had a chance of getting home for good.

Chapter
27

The brief had been no surprise, especially for Jack who, theoretically, had heard it all before. The plan was Marine Corps 101, simple and tested in two hundred years of battle. They would take their respective platoons into the Jolan neighborhood, kick in doors, find and shoot bad guys, and push the enemy south towards the final kill zone at the other side of the highway. Fire control and discipline were emphasized. There might still be innocent civilians here, "so make sure what you're shooting at."

Nonetheless, the rules of engagement were much looser than they had been over the recent months. If a guy (or girl, he supposed) wasn't in a U.S. Army or U.S. Marine Corps uniform and was carrying a weapon, then they were the enemy and could be "engaged," a polite way of saying shot and killed. Innocence was given up for weapons here, and the city had been so warned for weeks. They intended to kick ass without taking any fucking names and push the insurgents into the free-fire kill zone quickly. Casey's (or Jack's or who-the-fuck-ever's) platoon would be on the left flank of the company charge into the neighborhood, but still to the right of the army unit working east of them. The point was to know who you were shooting and avoid any "blue on blue" friendly fire casualties. He had heard it all before.

Now they walked, unconsciously crouched a little low, trying to make themselves small targets, just across the outskirts of the city and into Jolan. Their weapons were up at the high port ready position and their safeties were off.

Jack knew what would happen next. He wasn't hours ahead, except for the part where they were cut to pieces at the wall, which he had seen over and over in his nightmares and planned to avoid today. Rather he was just moments ahead, a terribly disorienting bout of the world's longest, continuous deja vu. He would see a certain window or hear a certain sound and with crystal clarity, he would know what they would see next, or know that Bennet would cough…right…now.

"Caawwf."

'Shut the fuck up,' from Ballard in his tinny Boston accent.

"Shat da fuck up, Bennet!" A harsh whisper, the accent still thick.

They would come to a corner now and a scrawny dog would limp past. Simmons would jump.

The dog limped away and Simmons looked sheepishly at his sergeant who patted him firmly on the back. It was maddening, like watching a movie in one room while the sound played three seconds behind from another room. It was driving him nuts. Jack felt himself tense up and he braced against the wall. There would be a gunshot from their right. No one would see the muzzle flash and no one would be hit, but McIver and then Simmons would both burst a few rounds down the block anyway. He would have to remind them about the civilians and fire control discipline.

The shot rang out and McIver, from Northern Virginia and soon to be a survivor of a bloody battle in Fallujah, dropped to one knee and squeezed off two, three-round bursts down the block. As he sent the second burst down, Simmons leaned against the wall and sent his own burst of bullets down the street, too.

"Cease-fucking-fire, you guys," Jack barked. He slapped McIver on the back of the helmet and looked at Simmons. "You see anything?"

"No, Sar'n," Simmons admitted, looking down.

"Then what the fuck are you shooting at?" He looked down at McIver who shrugged and then stood up. "Come on, you guys. Fire discipline. Keep your shit together. We won't be the platoon that caps some little girl stuck in this shithole city, okay?"

"Sorry, Sar'n," Simmons said, the pain in his voice real. Jack didn't know if it was the thought of killing a kid or of letting down Casey that hurt him. He suspected it was a little of both.

"No sweat. Just keep it together guys," Jack peered around the corner, though he knew he would see nothing...again. "And go back to single shot. You don't need three-round bursts right now. Save the ammo."

"Roger that Sar'n," McIver said and flipped his weapon back to single shot with his thumb. Simmons did the same, but said nothing, his face embarrassed.

Trying so damn hard.

They crossed the street one at a time, Jack going first, weaving quickly but drawing no fire, which of course Jack knew beforehand would happen. They would be okay for now. They would engage a group of insurgents on a roof in a few hours, after kicking in what would seem like a billion doors, each to empty rooms. They would be just on the verge of complacency when they would take fire from a low rooftop and they would light it up in a two-minute firefight that would feel like two hours and leave five insurgents dead. In the confusion and rapid fire there would be no way to know whose bullets had killed who, and Jack remembered that he would find comfort in that.

(Ballard was certainly responsible for some, if not all. He was the best shot in the platoon.)

More importantly, they would take no injuries—except McIver would get dirt in his eye from a ricochet—and then they would move on. The boy from Northern Virginia would bitch about his eye for nearly an hour. They were still many hours from the time when they would start dying near that wall. That was good because other than avoiding the street altogether, Jack had no idea what he would do to keep Kindrich, Bennet, Simmons, and Casey Stillman alive. Not yet, at least. He worked hard to keep his mind from wandering to his sleeping wife and baby girl, thousands of miles and still only inches away across some mystic fucking threshold he didn't understand. He had to keep his mind on the game and off the prize for now, while he still had time to win.

I'm trying, baby, he allowed himself.

"I know," she echoed warmly in his mind.

Then he set his life aside and, unsure what else to do, he followed the script, hopeful that the answer to how to change things would come to him in time. They started kicking in door after door, searching the rooms, finding them empty, and moving on. Each door brought more strain to the men he led, but for Jack it was rote. He knew they would find nothing, but played the part to a tee. They could hear the occasional bursts of both friendly and higher-pitched enemy small arms fire in the distance all around them. Now and again there would be louder and deeper booms of mortar and RPG rounds reeking larger damage on both Marines and Hadjis. These would make the ground shake and cause dust to rattle off crossbeams above them, falling on their heads like thin brown snow.

They had taken a ten-minute break for water and power bars inside one low building, a shop of some sort, though Jack could understand nothing of the Arabic symbols. Whatever had been bought or sold in the now empty room had long since been moved or stolen or destroyed. He read his lines, followed the stage descriptions, and moved the story, whose ending he intended to rewrite along the way. But all the while his mind fumed, searching furiously for the answer of how to stay off the fucking street with the low wall, where the script called for him and most of his guys to get cut apart.

It was the firefight with the five insurgents on the roof that brought the answer to him as clearly as if he had been born with this plan.

Surprise. That was the key! It wasn't anything in the middle of the chaos and horror at the wall that he had to change, it was the beginning. As they returned fire from the zealots on the roof, Jack realized that he was fighting very differently. He knew that none of them would be hurt and remembered where the next muzzle flash would come from. He couldn't be certain, but he had the distinct feeling that this knowledge let him fight differently and maybe even ended the battle more quickly. The epiphany occurred when he realized that McIver had failed to deliver the line that Jack remembered vividly from the "script."

Fucking sand in my eye... He was supposed to say, and then start cursing. Jack waited.

Nope.

McIver had dropped a line.

It *was* different this time! Different because Jack knew what was going to happen and did things differently, right? He fired his rounds with more accuracy or moved through the battle more quickly, or something. Whatever small and subtle change his foreknowledge created, the ricochet round never came and McIver never got dirt (instead of a damn bullet, the big baby) in his eye. A small change that changed everything. All he had to do was make a change again, a small change, at the wall when it would matter much more.

Jack ran over in his mind what he thought he remembered from the battle at the wall. They had been driven behind the wall by the initial attack on his platoon. They had joined up with first squad just yards from that first attack which had left Kindrich dead beside that fucking wall. There they had decided to swing around opposite corners of the block and meet back in the middle, clearing the two corners and then working the opposite side of the street. As they had come around the corner they had moved along the low wall, and Kindrich had taken that horrible shot to the head. That had driven the rest of them over the wall for cover and then—well, the rest he had lived over and over in his waking nightmare.

What if they started off from that corner on the offensive? He knew roughly where they had taken fire from. What if they laid down suppressive fire from the corner before they moved into the open? And then, with the Hadjis down and defensive, what if he moved his men quickly to the far corner he had tried to get to in his mad dash, the one that left him with a smoking hole in the center of his chest and his throat torn out, bleeding to death in the dirt and choking for breath? Could it be that simple, one little change in the script at the beginning?

It could change everything.

Jack felt his excitement grow and his uncertainty wane as they searched the now dead bodies of the five insurgents, looking for additional weapons to deny to the other shitheads scattered in the city. He felt a tug on his sleeve and turned a little too quickly. Simmons jumped back.

"Y'okay, Casey?" Jack realized that the other men were looking at him as well. He scanned the young and uncertain faces. Bennet had a cigarette dangling from his dirty lips.

"I'm good," he said and wiped sweat from his face with his grimy sleeve. "Let's keep moving." Then as an afterthought, he tugged on McIver's sleeve. "How's your eye?"

McIver looked at him with confusion and fatigue, maybe even annoyance.

"My what?"

"Nothing," Jack said, certain that his shit-eating grin would confuse and annoy the Virginia boy further, but unable to contain himself.

Chapter
28

Jack leaned back against the dirty and deserted building, knees up against his chest, as he poured warm water from his canteen onto his face. Brown rivulets of mud trickled down his neck and into his blouse, feeling nothing but good. The wall behind him tipped his Kevlar helmet down into his eyes, and he tipped it back with the open mouth of his canteen. His rifle was slung awkwardly in this position, the butt up above his chin, and he cocked it over to one side with some annoyance.

They were exhausted. All of them. They were also scared, but Jack suspected that his fear was somehow different. His men, his friends, were frightened by the unknown. Meanwhile, he was terrified by his certainty of what would happen if his plan to change their fate failed. It was down to the wire now. They were waiting here for First Squad, and once they joined up, Jack's script called for them to split in two and go down opposite sides of the block in which they now sat squarely in the middle. He had no idea what awaited First Squad, but he knew goddamn well what would happen to Casey and his young team of Marines. Unless he succeeded, they would be cut to ribbons, he and some of his boys would die, and Jack would never again see his wife and daughter. He knew that there would be no goodbye if he failed. Jack closed his eyes and breathed deeply of the scent of Pam's perfume, mingled with the sweet baby smell of Claire, a smell every parent knew and loved. He knew it wasn't memory. A part of him was still lying in their bed, arms wrapped around his girls, waiting to see what would happen. And if he failed? Would he just simply evaporate from that family embrace as if he had never been there at all? Jack shuddered and opened his eyes. Focus on the plan.

Take the offensive, he reminded himself for the thousandth time in the last few hours. Pick the windows you remember, fire as a team to drive the bad guys down to the floor and then haul ass across the street to the corner that he hoped would be safe. His doorway home, he prayed to God. A part of him felt that there should somehow be a much more intricate plan, a more dramatic change to the events that haunted him, but the other part of his mind, and maybe his heart, reassured him that all he really needed was a tiny little change that could domino to a totally different outcome.

Just like McIver's eye.

Jack looked around him at the young men that he felt he loved from somewhere. He was energized by the strong sense that he was supposed to be here—that he was somehow called to make this change. It wasn't just his life he would be saving, after all. The feeling was as real as anything else (and much more real than so fucking much) and he was empowered by the sense of purpose it brought. Jack looked over at Simmons, squatted down, back against the wall. His eyes weren't closed. They were open and wide with uncertainty and fear. Jack patted him paternally on the knee.

"Hang in there, bud," he said, holding the young boy's gaze and smiling. *We're going to be fine,* he hoped his smile said. Simmons shifted uncomfortably and looked down, wanting so much to look like a man and not a boy.

"Hoorah, Sar'n," he said, but his voice cracked. He cleared his throat harshly in annoyance or embarrassment, or more likely a little of both. He turned and held his platoon sergeant's gaze again. "Good to go," he reassured Casey.

And Jack believed him.

A flurry of activity brought Jack's eyes up and his hand from his young Marine's knee. First Squad.

"Yo, man," said the wiry and short man in the lead. Chad O'Brian. A good friend, Jack remembered from somewhere. A little guy with an Irish name, an Italian face, and a very Chicago accent. "S' happenin'?"

"Glorious day in the Corps," Jack answered from the script, an old and familiar joke. O'Brian laughed through his nose.

"Fuckin'-a-right," Chad answered, dropping down beside Jack. He spit a puddle of thick brown Skoal-spit on the ground between them, and then looked up at the boys in a group around them. "Fitz, Connelly...perimeter," he said, and two of his men fanned out in the street. They dropped to one knee and pulled up their rifles, scanning the darkening and quiet street. Chad grabbed Jack's canteen and took a deep swig of the piss-warm water.

"Bag any rags?" he asked without looking at Jack.

"Five to nothing, good guys are up," Jack answered, referring to the five dead insurgents from the roof. O'Brian smiled.

"Strong work, dude," he said. "We're dry...or I think anyway. Returned some fire from the rooftops, but nothing confirmed."

Jack nodded. Then he waited. Chad had another line yet.

"Wanna clear this block together?" he asked.

"Sure," Jack read back from his playbook. "How's about you guys come around the far corner and we'll take this one. Meet you in the middle?"

"Sounds right," his friend from Pendleton answered. Chad was single and lived in the barracks, but Jack had a vivid memory flash of him and his girlfriend Kim laughing and drinking beer in their living room back home. Kim loved Claire to death, and Chad was always worried about how much she loved playing Mom to her with Pam. "We'll clear the street from the corners and then work into the middle. You guys take the far side and we'll clear our side of the block."

"Roger that," Jack answered on cue. He felt his throat tighten and his heart pounded in his chest. This was it.

Time to go home.

Jack closed his eyes tightly and for a moment he was in bed, arms around his girls. God, please don't let it be just a fantasy.

Jack pushed himself up on weak and exhausted legs. The sun was down below the low-rise brown buildings to his right and the sky was turning orange. The déjà vu was intense and nauseating. He slapped Chad on the back of the helmet and watched as he and his men hustled down the block to the far corner. He gathered his friends around him to set the plan. In his tortured mind he found himself wondering how it would work. If he reached the far side of the street intact, would he just disappear in a cyclone of sand and wake up in bed with his girls, the nightmare forever over? Would he just be

Casey again and have to finish his tour and then come home to them? And what if he failed—if he was cut down by an insurgent bullet?

He jerked his head violently, clearing his mind of the thought. He would simply not let that happen.

Jack and his friends huddled up like a high-school football team, planning the last, game-ending play.

"I want to get to the far side of the street first," he began. "We'll lay down some suppressive fire across the street and then cross, one at a time, with the rest of the team sustaining covering fire."

Bennet frowned and held Jack's eyes.

"What the hell, Sar'n?" he asked. "I thought we were supposed to maintain fire discipline. You want us to fire blindly into the buildings across the road? At what?"

Jack paused. He expected this question, but was still unsure of his answer.

"Look, guys," he said solemnly. "I can't explain it, but I have a really bad feeling about this. I think we're going to draw heavy fire from the far side of the street." He looked at the tired and now worried faces around him in his school circle. "Actually, I know we are," he finished. His proclamation was met with an awkward silence. The young Marines exchanged confused glances and then looked back at their platoon sergeant. Simmons shrugged. Jack wiped the dirty brown sweat from his face.

"Look, we'll form up at the corner, I'll fire first and then, well…" he paused. "Just engage whatever you see, OK?"

"Sure, Casey," Bennet said a little uncomfortably. "Whatever you think."

The others were quiet, but nodded their heads. Second Squad checked their weapons and ammo and moved together as a group to the corner. Jack led his team the short distance around the block and stopped at the next corner. Inches away was the kill zone set up by the bad guys hiding across the street. To his right was a low wall, the remains of a building long since gone. Jack shuddered at the images that flooded his mind at the sight—Kindrich with half his head blown off, the rest of them piling over that wall for cover, the RPG disintegrating and burying Bennet's bleeding body in rubble, his head striking the far corner of the shitty little wall as a bullet knocked him backwards, leaving a smoking hole in his flak vest…Jack squeezed his eyes shut for a moment to press the pictures out of his head and then peered around the corner, scanning desperately for movement in the doorways and windows on the far side of the street and along the low rooftops.

Nothing.

He closed his eyes again and this time he searched for images of muzzle flashes from his nightmare at the wall and tried to pick the locations from this slightly different perspective. There was a large hole in the wall of the center building, a blown out and glassless window. In his mind's eye he saw double muzzle flashes from there, twin AK-47s firing rounds at him as he had moved out from the corner of the wall in his nightmare. That was where the shots that had pounded him in the chest, knocking him from his feet and into the dirt, had come from. He was sure of it. He saw only darkness in the fading orange glow of dusk. No movement at all...but they were there. He knew his executioners, at least some of them, were huddled there. He squeezed his eyes shut tightly, forced away the sweat and tears that burned his vision. Then he checked the safety off on his rifle and raised it to his shoulder. He flicked the safety past single shot to three-shot burst and aimed into the darkness of the hole in the building.

I love you, Pam.

I know, baby... Her voice was music in his mind.

He squeezed.

Three rounds burped out of his rifle, one of them a red tracer, and he watched as the tracer clearly marked his shot, the rounds disappearing into the dark hole in the building. Jack squeezed a second burst and this time he pulled a little wide, his round tearing chunks of brown wall away in cloud of dust. Then he stared down the sights of his rifle, waiting for movement. For a brief moment he started to think maybe he had been wrong, and then he heard a shrill voice hollering in Arabic and—

Jack and his friends saw the flashes a split second before they heard the twin cracks of the rifles, bluish-white light exploding from the darkness of the room in which the Hadjis were hidden. Jack dropped his head down and pulled it back slightly, but the shots were wild. One hit the dirt ten yards in front of him in the street, the other he never saw. He heard the flurry of movement as his men raised their weapons, drawing in on the building with the hole in it.

"Suppressive fire!" Jack hollered as he sent another three-round burst into the building. It was followed immediately by a high-pitched scream from the dark recesses of the hole in the wall, which was drowned out almost immediately by the ear-shattering bursts from the M16s all around him. "McIver, Ballard, Simmons…one at a time when I tell you." He heard the men moving out sideways from the wall. "Straight to the far corner." He let his gaze stray over to the low wall where he had died once already. "And stay away from that fucking wall to your right," he added as an afterthought. Jack knew he had already changed things, maybe even enough, but his eyes scanned the rooftops and windows. He knew from the nightmare that there were a shitload more bad guys out there. Anything could happen yet. There was another wild shot from the dark room and then nothing. Jack fired at it again anyway then hollered over his shoulder "Go…go…covering fire!"

One part of Jack's mind became vaguely aware that the horribly intense and disorienting déjà vu was gone.

The times they are a changin'.

From the corner of his eye Jack saw McIver, tall and lanky and looking awkward hunched over as he was, start his sprint to the corner. His weapon was up and aimed, jerking back and forth as he scanned for targets, legs pounding in the sand and kicking up a little trail of dust. Like Wile E. Coyote in the cartoon, Jack thought for some reason. The thought made him chuckle.

McIver was halfway across the street when Jack sensed movement farther down the street and above them. He raised his rifle and scanned the rooftops through the sight like he had trained over and over at home in California… There!

Jack squeezed the trigger as the heavily bearded man came into view over his sight. The man raised an AK-47 to his shoulder, and Jack thought he hollered something, but the words were cut off as three red puffs popped up off his chest nearly simultaneously as Jack's bullets found their mark. The insurgent's arms flew up and his rifle flipped through the air. His face turned upwards as he fell behind the low wall along the edge of the roof and then disappeared from view. Jack continued his scan, looking for other targets. He heard more shots from his men, but didn't bother to search for the targets they had engaged. His own scan focused on the search for the assholes that would try and kill him and his friends, while his peripheral vision followed McIver's progress. It was only a few seconds, but it felt like forever.

McIver skidded around the corner on the far side of the street and pressed himself against the wall for a moment, his body sagging in obvious relief. It only lasted a moment. Then he shouldered his rifle again and peered around the corner from his side of the street, scanning for his own targets to cover the next sprinter. Without looking over at them he waved an arm at them.

Come on!

Jack slapped Ballard on the back of the helmet and then he immediately returned back to his scan of the doorways and rooftops. Ballard weaved across the street much like McIver had. He stopped once to aim up at something he saw on a roof and fired his rifle, and then he sprinted again. He arrived at the far corner behind McIver, grinned, and flashed Jack a thumbs-up.

Holy shit! This was going to work! Jack realized suddenly that his heart pounded now more out of excitement than fear.

Almost home!

Less than a minute or two and it would be over. He was going to save his friends and Casey Stillman. And soon he would wake up in his bed, his arms around his girls! He was really going to fucking make it!

Jack forced his mind to stay in the game and continued his scan.

"Move your ass, Simmons!" he shouted, then fired at movement he thought he saw from a doorway, but never saw his round hit anything. He continued his scan. Jack knew that this one was crucial. McIver and Ballard hadn't died the first time either, so he hadn't really proven much yet. He watched Simmons start his sprint from the corner of his eye.

Simmons ran with less self-control, his scan over the sight of his rifle a little more halfhearted. Jack knew the boy was scared. He pushed the distracting empathy out of his mind and concentrated on clearing the doorways and windows with his scan. He heard a scream of pain from down the street, piercing even over the rifles firing right beside his head. Nice shooting, someone, he thought. Bennet probably.

"Up high!" It was Kindrich's voice and it sounded panicked. "RPG! Go, Simmons, GO!"

Jack scanned along the roof edge, his own heart now pounding.

God, no! Please, no!

His scan stopped on a figure, draped in a dark robe, pulling the launcher for the rocket-propelled grenade up to his shoulder. Jack squeezed.

Dust kicked up from the lip of the roof and the man stumbled, his hip pulled awkwardly to the right as if he was trying to perfect a ridiculous dance step, then there was a blinding flash of white flame as the RPG fired.

Corporal Rich Simmons, United States Marine Corps, was just over halfway across the street when Jack's eyes were torn from the wounded Hadji and over to the boy's terrified run for cover. His rifle was no longer at his shoulder. Instead he tore across the street in a full sprint, arms pumping, rifle clutched but useless in his right hand. As Jack watched, the world slowed to half speed. In horror he saw the rocket-propelled grenade hit the ground a mere five yards from the terrified young Marine.

The street disappeared in a blinding flash and the force of the explosion knocked the three remaining Marines backwards on their asses. Jack scrambled back up to his knees and searched through the smoke and billowing cloud of sand and dust for Simmons.

"Rich!" Jack's voice was a terrified and uncontrolled scream. "Goddamnit! RICH, CAN YOU HEAR ME!" Jack had a sinking feeling, not just for the young boy he felt so bonded to and somehow so responsible for, but also for himself. If Simmons was dead he had changed nothing. Hoag was going to be right. He couldn't change shit, and he was going to die here in this shithole street, in this shithole country, seven thousand miles away from his girls. "SIMMONS!"

A weak voice billowed out from the cloud of dust and drifted through the ringing in his ears. "S...S...Sar'n?"

It was him! He was alive! Maybe there was a chance, yet.

"We're coming for you, Rich," Bennet hollered. Jack grabbed at his sleeve, but Bennet shook it off and started full speed through the cloud of dust and smoke.

"Bennet—wait, goddamnit!" But the Marine ignored him and tore across the battle-torn street, looking for his friend.

"I'm coming, Rich!" he hollered as he ran, marking himself as a target with the sound, Jack thought grimly. Next to go—different order, but same fucking ending to the nightmare. Would Casey be last, but just as dead? Jack raised his weapon to his shoulder and scanned through the smoke at the rooftops, the worst threat to his men. He saw movement through the hazy smoke and fired again. Any change could domino into a different outcome, he thought. No one was dead yet, his hopeful mind told him. Kindrich was still right beside him and he was supposed to die first, right?

"Sar'n?" Kindrich's voice was tight and high pitched. "Should we—"

Kindrich's words were cut off, and Jack would never know what his friend thought they should do. He never heard the crack of the shot that killed him, but he heard the high-pitched squeal of the round as it cut through the air beside his head. Jack turned just in time to see a high-velocity round enter his friend's head just above his right eye. It exploded out the back of his head, carrying into the street. Kindrich's helmet flipped off what was left of his head. Jack watched in horrified fascination as it spun in slow motion through the air; Kindrich fell backwards, weapon still at his shoulder and face twisted in surprise.

Just like before. Just exactly like before except along this corner instead of along that shitty little wall.

Kindrich's corpse, with its surprised face and helmetless half head, hit the ground beside him hard, raising its own cloud of dust. The arms and M16A collapsed beside the empty body. The head hit the dirt with a nauseating crunch and dark blood shot out in all directions around it in the dirt, forming a grotesque halo around the blank face. Jack turned away. No need to check. Even without the memory of his death from before Jack knew Kindrich was dead. Hard to keep tickin' without the ol' melon, he thought without appropriate emotion. Hard to get too worked up.

Seen this episode too many times before.

He fired his weapon up at the rooftops again in a detached way, not really feeling any longer like he was part of what was going on around him. He wondered what Pam was doing. What time was it there, anyway? Was Claire up?

Pop pop pop from his rifle.

Would Pam remember any of their time together? Their time as Jack and Pam? Or had that never really even happened? Maybe she was already standing at the grave of her husband, the grave of Sergeant Casey Stillman, Killed in Action, Fallujah, Iraq.

Jack's body sagged and his rifle fell to his side, his trigger finger limp. It was over, right?

Time to die.

"Sar'n! ...CASEY!!" Bennet's voice reached him through the smoke. That didn't seem right somehow. Why was that wrong? Jack felt confusion spread over him and cocked his head to the side, puppylike. "Casey, help me...Simmons' leg is tore up but he's okay..." A burst of M16 fire. Must have been from Bennet. "Sar'n, you there? I NEED HELP."

Wait a goddamn minute! Simmons was alive? How could that be? He had died before for sure, had come to him dead at school and at his house and...and he never had a fucked-up leg! His face was blown off but his skinny little legs had been fine. And anyway, he had never seen Simmons hit last time. He had already been shot himself, right? He was lying in the dirt clinging to life and fighting to breathe when they had laid his friend beside him in the dirt. And Bennet should have been dead already, his throat torn out by a bullet and the RPG burying him beside that wall.

He sure as hell sounded okay to Jack.

"Bennet, hold on!" Jack screamed through the blinding smoke, snapped back to life and heart pounding with fresh hope. He could still do it. Maybe? "I'm coming!"

"I'm coming, Bennet!" McIver's voice.

"NO!" He screamed as he pulled his weapon up and scanned over the sight. He moved into the street, hoping the smoke would give him some cover, blinding the bad guys to his position. "McIver! Ballard! Stay right where you are. Give me covering fire! I'm coming!" Jack started to run.

"Roger that, Sar'n!" Jack heard a burst of rifle fire from the far corner as McIver and Ballard tried to keep the bad guys down.

Jack tore across the street, crouched awkwardly and painfully, trying to stay small. His weapon was up, but he could see nothing through the smoke and dust. He squeezed the trigger in the general direction of the rooftops anyway, hoping to keep the insurgents' heads down. He heard almost continuous single-shot fire from his two Marines at the corner. His legs burned. In his panic he covered the distance much more quickly than he thought and tripped over the hunched figure of Bennet, up on one knee in the street, firing up at the rooftops. Losing his balance, Jack skidded through the dusty street painfully on both knees and his outstretched left hand, an awkward slide into second base. His right hand managed to keep his weapon up at his shoulder somehow, though he still could see nothing through the smoke and dust cloud that surrounded them. A low moan beside him pulled Jack's gaze away from the impenetrable cloud and down to the street.

He wasn't prepared for what he saw. Bennet had said Rich's leg was torn up, but that didn't cover it. The boy lay on his back, his eyes open and staring upward. His body shook, his arms quivered at his sides, and his hands opened and closed around nothing. Simmons' entire left side was drenched in blood, which had mixed with the fine, dusty Iraqi sand to form a brownish-grey mud. Below the knee his leg was twisted around in an impossible direction. The booted ankle faced the wrong way and the skin was shredded away with his pants, revealing reddish meat through which a stark, white finger of bone pointed at him. A small arcing spray of blood pulsed like a little fountain out of the mess that had been the boy's leg. Jack pulled a desert camouflage-printed bandana from his cargo pocket and balled it up, then pressed it firmly over the source of the little fountain. The contact made Simmons moan louder and he mumbled something that Jack didn't understand. The shredded muscles under Jack's hand began to spasm and he tasted bile in the back of his throat. He was barely aware of the gunfire around him and the acrid smoke that burned his eyes and throat. For a moment his whole world was his hand pressing ever harder into the wet flesh of his friend's leg as he tried to slow the steady dark stream of Rich's life from running out into the street.

"What the fuck are you guys doing?" McIver's voice from the corner brought Jack out of the near trance. He had to get Simmons off of this fucking street.

"I'm comin' to you with Simmons," he hollered in a raspy voice that was not his. It was tinny and foreign in his ear. He again felt detached from what was going on and struggled to hang on to the hope that he would be at home with his girls soon.

Jack let go of his pressure on the twisted flesh and bone of Simmons' leg and grabbed the boy by the straps of his load-bearing vest. He struggled to his feet under the dead weight of the wounded Marine and started a half run towards the corner. Jack could see McIver at the corner now, and realized with some panic that the smoke and dust were clearing. In a moment he would be an easy target. For a fleeting second he considered letting go of Simmons and dashing to the corner, the safety of which Jack saw as his portal out of his nightmare and back to his real life. He looked down into Simmons' face, pale and dirty and only inches from his own. His friend smiled weakly.

"Good to go, Sar'n," he wheezed.

Jack pushed on, propelling them through the dirty street. Simmons' nearly severed leg bobbed along behind them, leaving a thick bloody trail in the dirt.

"ROOFTOP!" Bennet screamed from behind them. Then the dirt around them was kicked up by rifle fire. In reply he heard the cracks of M16 fire from the corner ahead of him and the street behind him. He felt like his chest would explode at any second.

Jack fell behind the corner of the wall and quickly pulled Simmons in behind him. He allowed himself a few rasping breaths and a hacking cough, then pulled himself out from under Rich's limp body and rose to a knee at the corner beside McIver. Holy shit, he had made it! He was alive! He looked at the thin, heaving boy beside him. Simmons was alive too, at least for now.

Jack raised his rifle and peered around the corner over the sight. He doubted that Simmons would live, a horrible realization that competed with the overwhelming sense of relief that he had made it. He felt sad, and guilty, and overjoyed that he would be home any minute.

Jack fired his rifle up at the rooftops and fully expected a cyclone of sand to swirl around him and engulf him any minute, starting him on his short trip home. A part of his mind anxiously waited, fearful that he had not started his trip already. Was something wrong? Why was he still here? He had done it, hadn't he? He was safely across the street with what was left of his friends. Why the fuck was he still here?

"Come on, man! Get the fuck over here!" McIver hollered beside him.

Bennet.

Jack looked out into the clearing street, an eerie purple-orange hue from the fading sunset surrounding the running figure of Bennet as he dashed towards them. His face was set with determination and without fear. He looked like a Marine, Jack thought. He might have been a poster for a World War II movie about the fighting leathernecks.

And then it all changed. The reality of war erased any Hollywood image as Bennet's neck and upper chest exploded in a thick red cloud of blood. The high-velocity bullet spun him around. He fell to the ground, arms and legs splayed out, his momentum plowing him towards them through the dirt like a sled on his back.

Without thinking, Jack was on his feet, rifle raised, set to sprint to his friend's side.

"Bennet!" he hollered as he stepped out into the street.

Jack kicked off his sprint. Immediately the air around him came alive with whistling rounds and bright tracers. As his second boot hit the sand, a tremendous impact in the center of his chest knocked him backwards off his feet, his helmeted head smacking the corner of the wall hard enough to set off white explosions of light in his vision. Then he thumped hard on his back in the dirt. Dazed and deaf to the gunfire around him, Jack lifted his head and looked down in horror at the center of his chest where a charred hole smoked eerily in the brown canvas of his body armor. He probed the hole with a shaking left index finger and felt a hot piece of metal burn his fingertip. The round had not penetrated! Hands grabbed at him from the corner and dirt kicked up in his face as the enemy adjusted fire. With a burst of strength from some unknown source he pushed away the hands clawing at his load-bearing vest and pushed himself up to a squat, intent on starting again on his sprint to Bennet's side. When he made it to a low crouch, he felt a violent burning pain explode low in his throat and he was again driven backwards into the dirt.

Jack could hear nothing, but felt hands again on his vest and arms. He was dragged roughly back behind the corner wall, his terrified eyes staring up at a hazy purple sky. He became aware that the rough hands on his throat were his own, and that they were hot and wet. His view of the sky was suddenly blocked by a dark shape that slowly cleared into the image of his friend's face. What was his name? McIver?

"Sergeant Stillman! Sergeant Stillman!" The voice was like an old recording playing way too slow in another room. He tried to speak but instead coughed and felt warm stickiness flow down both his cheeks. Then the face was gone for a moment and a tremendously large shadow blocked out the darkening sky. A helicopter?

Jack heard gunfire again, close-by he thought, but couldn't make sense of what was going on. He heard a familiar voice hollering very nearby. He should be going home by now. Where was his dusty tornado to take him home? He wasn't sure what that meant, but it seemed right. He felt the world get dark and he closed his eyes. He saw his wife's face, and Claire, little feet kicking as she smiled up from her crib at Daddy.

My girls, he thought. I have to get to my girls.

Then everything went black.

Chapter
29

His back ached and he felt a vague heartburn like discomfort in his throat. His mouth was dry, with a hangover-type dryness that made it impossible to focus on anything but a tall glass of water. He felt himself waking but kept his eyes closed and shifted his position, with some difficulty, to ease the pain in his back. Jack heard the farting noise that had embarrassed him a few days (or was it a thousand years?) before, and realized where he was. Still he kept his eyes closed, knowing he was afraid, but unable to remember why.

"How are you feeling?"

The soft but strong voice of Dr. Lewellyn was familiar but not really comforting. Jack could almost see him, even though his eyes were closed, sitting in his comfortable chair, legs crossed at the knees with his little notebook full of Jack's mind open in his lap. Jack cleared his dry throat with more than a little pain and remembered that feeling from his childhood—the burning pain of strep throat when you were so afraid to swallow that it made you cry, which hurt even more.

"I'm good, now, I think," he answered, his voice raspy.

His eyes were still closed and he realized with some surprise that he was still afraid to open them. He couldn't remember what it was he thought he might see, but chose to trust his instincts and kept them closed anyway.

"I hope so," Lewellyn answered softly. There was a sadness in his voice. "You're a good man. I mean that. Is there any last thing you want to talk about?"

"Is this our last session?" Jack asked. His voice trembled and he thought he was starting to remember why now, why this might be more of a goodbye than a therapy session.

"I think you know it is," Lewellyn answered. His voice held that now familiar patience that Jack thought he might have come to love a little.

He sighed deeply, held his breath a moment, then let out a trembling exhale. Any last thing he wanted to talk about?

"Who the hell am I?" he asked. His voice quivered and he felt warm tears flow down over his hot cheeks. There was a long pause and he waited, crying softly.

"I think maybe we're all just whoever we choose to be," Lewellyn said softly. "It is more about what in life we use to define ourselves, I think. How do you define who you are?"

"I'm Pam's husband," Jack answered without thinking. "And Claire's daddy," he added, his voice cracking. Jack wiped away his tears with the back of one dirty hand. Then he opened his eyes.

The ceiling above was green and dirty. The light was harsh, coming from a single bulb hanging from its yellow cord above. Jack shielded his eyes with a hand that he saw, without much surprise, was filthy and caked with dry blood. He raised his head and looked down at his filthy desert cammies, out of place against the clean brown leather of the couch. With some pain, Jack turned his head on a stiff neck and the burning in his throat throbbed for attention.

Lewellyn sat in a clean leather chair, as always. The chair was the only other piece of furniture in the small tent whose flaps were rustling softly in a dusty breeze. Lewellyn had his notebook in his lap, but his hands were folded neatly on top of it. Nothing more to write, Jack realized. Lewellyn wore his own brown cammies and dirty desert boots. A brown leather shoulder holster held his Marine Corps issue nine-millimeter Beretta under his left arm. The rank insignia on his collar announced that he was a captain.

Of course. Captain Lewellyn, his company commander. Lewellyn smiled sadly back at him. Jack closed his eyes again and laid his head back down, exhausted.

"What else?" the patient voice asked.

"A Marine," Jack answered simply.

"No argument there." Jack could hear the smile in his voice. "Some would say a hero as well, Sar'n."

Jack felt his throat tighten.

"I'm sure as hell not that," he said with a cracking voice. "I had two chances at it, and still lost a lot of men." Jack's eyes squeezed tightly as he fought to control his emotions.

"Let's let the historians decide that kind of shit," Lewellyn said. Now he sounded like a Marine captain, Jack thought.

"Let's let Rich Simmons decide," he answered.

"Yes," Lewellyn agreed. "Let's do that. We'll let Simmons decide." There was an odd smile in his words. Jack realized he was too tired to care.

"So what does this all mean?" Jack asked.

"I really don't know, Casey," Lewellyn answered. "I think maybe we all deal with death in our own way. Your love for your girls bound you so tightly here." The officer sighed heavily, a deep sadness in the sound. "I know what I believe."

"What's that?"

"Well," Lewellyn shifted in his seat and Jack could picture him leaning forward, elbows on his knees, taking care of one of his men, as he always did. "I believe that death isn't an ending. I believe that for sure. I think it's just a transition for us. For you it was harder because of your fear for those you're leaving behind."

The tears ran down Jack's face in warm rivers now; his chest heaved painfully.

"You aren't losing anything, Casey," Lewellyn concluded softly. "You will live forever in the hearts of those two girls."

"Thank you," Jack said. He felt so weak, so tired.

"I hope I helped you, Sar'n."

"You did."

Jack felt a hot wind wrap around him like a dusty blanket. Slowly he felt himself rise above the couch, spinning gently this time. The wind caressed him almost soothingly and he felt, through closed eyes, that the light was fading.

* * *

Jack inhaled deeply of the scent of his girls. The bed was warm and soft, and he knew it wasn't real. He also knew he didn't care. He kept his eyes closed and explored Pam's face by feel, gently caressing her cheek lightly with his fingers. She mumbled something soft, incomprehensible, and perfect. Between them Claire stirred, and Jack felt her little hand on his chin. He dropped his face and kissed her ever so gently on her fingertips. She cooed softly beside him, still sleeping.

"I love you both so much," he said.

The exhaustion overcame him and he drifted off, arms around his whole world.

* * *

He woke from a short sleep, but long enough that his neck felt stiff again. There was a burning in his throat, and for a moment he thought maybe he was getting the flu.

Then he remembered.

There was a droning noise that irritated him. He lifted his head from where it lay atop his folded hands on the table. He felt an ache on his forehead and realized that if he had a mirror, he would see a little red crescent on his face where he had slept with his forehead on his wedding ring. The droning noise took shape in his mind and solidified into a woman's voice.

"...*for the Town of Al Fallujah. The fierce fighting continued yesterday, but not without casualties on both sides. Marines have met stiff resistance from the terrorist insurgents, but have inflicted casualties numbering perhaps as high as 50 killed and hundreds wounded or captured, according to several military sources. Coalition forces suffered yesterday as well, with three Marines reportedly killed and another seriously wounded during a brutal firefight in the city's war-ravaged streets. The names of the killed and injured Marines were not released, pending notification of families here at home. Although military authorities report that coalition forces now control nearly half of the city, they caution that the violence there is far from over."*

Jack opened his eyes. He sat at an empty table in the faculty lunch room, his tray with Sheila's cold double cheeseburger pushed to the middle. In his right hand was a balled up paper napkin.

Three Marines killed. That would be Kindrich, Bennet, and Simmons. He, of course, was the seriously wounded Marine. Soon he would be the fourth death. Jack was a little startled to realize that was not at all terrifying. He felt a deep, almost paralyzing grief over how this would devastate Pam and how Claire would grow up without her daddy. Competing with that was his remorse and guilt that he had saved none of his friends. He had gone back, had tried so hard, and nothing was different. Jack squeezed his palms into his eyes until white spots filled his mind's vision like fireworks.

"Elsewhere in Iraq, a car bomb has reportedly killed one soldier while four others were wounded in an attack near the town..." The reporter's voice announced with little emotion.

That would be Hoag, Jack supposed.

"You did a helluva a job, Casey," said a familiar voice, thick with a Chicago accent.

Jack looked over and saw Chad sitting beside him. The fact that he had appeared from nowhere didn't bother Jack in the least. He was way past any reaction to such things. Chad no longer wore his cool-teacher black T-shirt and sports coat. Instead he was in the more familiar, dirty cammies that Jack realized he also still sported. Chad still munched away on his half gone double cheeseburger, however.

Jack had the sudden thought that he was Dorothy, waking in her bed on the farm after her crazy dream in Oz.

And you were there, and you, and you were there, too!

Get off the ride, Dorothy. It ends badly.

Jack considered his friend for a moment, burger juice dribbling down his chin, then handed him the napkin he had been clutching in his hand.

"I'll ask Simmons if he agrees with you when I see him," Jack said bitterly.

Chad wiped the grease from his chin and then smiled a mysterious, knowing smile.

"You do that, Casey," he said. Then he took one last giant bite of his burger, tossed the remaining chunk on Jack's tray and rose to his feet. "Come on," he said.

Jack rose and followed him to the door.

The hall was dark, and moments after stepping through with his friend he realized it wasn't a hallway at all. The familiar smells and dusty air told him immediately where he was. Jack stopped.

"I don't think I'm ready yet," he said to Chad. He turned, but Chad was gone.

Jack stood there a moment, unsure what to do. The door he had passed through was no longer there. He could hear the sounds of gunfire and the thump-thump of an approaching Blackhawk. He felt anxious but not scared. He felt a stirring at his feet and looked down. By his right foot the tiniest little swirl of dust started circling around him. As he watched, it collected more and more dust, running circles around him that got thicker and rose rapidly to his waist and then his chest. Jack sighed.

One last ride I guess.

Things faded quickly again to blackness.

Chapter 30

It was dark as he lay there, and he felt the ground begin to tilt. In the distance Jack heard the sound of gunfire, or maybe close and the distance was an illusion. He felt nauseated, tasted the bile mixed with blood in the back of his throat. There was a burning pain there, spreading out backwards over his neck. And there was a tightness that extended into his chest. With each struggling breath, there was a high-pitched whistling and gurgling sound. He realized that the darkness was because his eyes were closed, and with great difficulty, struggled to open them. The sky above him was purplish and hazy, heavy with dust. A shadow passed over him and he heard the familiar thump, thump of a UH-60 passing overhead. A darker shadow enveloped him as someone bent over his face. He tried to force his eyes to focus on the features of the man looking down on him, but couldn't.

"Hang in there, Sergeant. You're gonna be ok!"

"How is he, Doc?"

"I don't know. He's lost a shitload of blood. The left side of his neck is swollen tight. I think he might have gotten his carotid artery." There was a pause and more light as the featureless face disappeared from view. "We got to get him the fuck out of here, Mac, or he ain't gonna make it. He needs to be in the OR, like, 5 mikes ago."

It was painfully familiar. The horrible déjà vu was back, only now, lying on his back in the dirt he had no activity to distract him from it—only the terrible radio play that he had heard before. Doc White, the young Louisiana corpsman, would tell Mac about his tracheotomy next. God, please make it stop!

"What is that in his neck? Shrapnel?"

"It's a tracheotomy, dipshit. I had to put it in so he could breathe. The bullet tore his windpipe nearly in half. He was drowning in his own blood."

There was movement around him, then another shadow, another featureless face. It had to be Ballard, or maybe someone from first platoon. Maybe even Chad. How weird. Hadn't he just had lunch with him?

Jack felt desperately short of breath and struggled to suck air into his lungs, which made the burning worse. He tried to raise an arm, to reach out for Mac, but his arms were dead weight by his sides. He felt a panic grow inside of him, and struggled to stay calm. Why the fuck couldn't he move? Was it like that before in the dream?

He forced his mind away from his burning pain, from the feeling like tight bands were wrapped around his chest, keeping him from getting air into his oxygen-starved body. He forced his mind to Pam, to thoughts of her body moving against his, of their legs entwined, her breath on his neck. The way she liked to lick his neck and earlobes. He thought of Claire, lying peaceful and calm on his bare chest, rocking in the glider beside her crib—his big girl. He tried again to let his mind wander to his girls and away from his fear of his lingering death.

He sensed more movement beside him and he blinked his eyes to clear them. He turned his head slightly to the left, forcing his eyes to focus on the dark shape beside him in the dirt. Slowly the image sharpened, like someone was fine-tuning a pair of binoculars. Jack suddenly remembered what he would see when the image cleared. He closed his eyes tightly. He had no desire to see Simmons' dead body again. He had seen that more than enough. Jack found himself wishing that, if he couldn't fade away in his chariot of swirling sand, he could just fade away all together.

Jack heard the horrible whistling and bubbling, just like in his nightmares, and then something warm and sticky poured out from the center of his neck. He felt the blood tickling down both sides of his neck and dripping off into the dirt.

Jack realized he needed desperately to know that his girls were ok. If he could just know that, he thought he might be brave enough to finish his trip. He felt a gentle breeze on his face.

* * *

Jack sat on a bench, warm in the sunshine but not hot in that oppressive, ovenlike heat of Iraq. He leaned forward, knees to elbows, and rubbed his tired face with clean and soft hands.

Then he opened his eyes.

He was in the park near their house. He could tell from the green leaves and warm breeze that it was definitely not November anymore, but rather spring or early summer. He scanned the handful of people on the playground, searching for them.

Pam stood behind Claire, pushing her in a swing. Jack saw immediately that it was not the little toddler swing, but a "big girl" swing, and the little girl seated there was much older than Claire-- at least four or five years old. She had the most beautiful blonde hair that trailed out behind her and reflected gold in the sunshine. Her blue eyes were wide and smiling. She pumped her little bare legs back and forth, her dress bunched up unceremoniously in the wind she created. The sound of her musical laughter grabbed his heart.

"Higher, Mommy, higher!" she squealed.

"High enough, Claire Bear," her mother laughed back. Jack smiled, his eyes filling with tears. "You're gonna give ol' Mommy a heart attack!"

Claire giggled and then Pam grabbed her around the waist, pulling her to a stop and then smothered her in kisses. Claire squealed again and then hopped from the swing and ran towards the jungle gym.

"Catch me, Mommy!" she shouted.

Pam started after her then stopped. She hesitated a moment, and then turned slowly towards Jack. For a moment their eyes met across the park. Pam wrapped her arms tightly around her chest, as if she had gotten a chill. Her smile tightened a bit, but Jack noted with satisfaction that she still smiled. They stared at each other like that, motionless.

Then Claire broke the moment.

"Come on, Mommy," she said with a five-year-old's fleeting irritation. "Come and catch me!"

Pam stood a moment, and then raised a hand to him in a small wave. She pressed her lips to her fingers, and waved again. Then she spun on a heel, laughed again as if the moment had never happened, and ran towards the jungle gym where her daughter climbed the wrong way up the slide.

"I'm comin' to getcha, Bear!"

Jack caught the invisible kiss in his hand and pressed his palm to his own lips.

Then the sunlight was obscured by swirling sand.

* * *

He struggled to open his eyes again, fighting the darkness and the sense of being buried alive. Thick clouds of dust and sand swirled around him, kicked up by the blades of the helicopter. The blackness continued to envelop him, although he felt quite certain that his eyes were open now. He was flat on his back, uncomfortable in his body armor. His Kevlar helmet was off, his head in the dirt, but he didn't really care. He was only vaguely aware, in a disinterested way, of the sound of gunfire, like noise on a TV in another room. He could also hear voices and was aware of activity all around him. Someone held his hand. There was a horrible burning in the center of his throat and a raspy gurgle when he sucked in a breath.

"They're coming around this side."

"Clear that space as a path."

"Hold his head! Hold his head!"

"Corporal light up that fucking window and silence that Hadji sniper!"

Jack was pretty sure it was Captain Lewellyn's voice. Not much patience in it right now. Jack wondered if Lewellyn knew what he had been to him.

A burst of gunfire.

Screams in the distance.

"Dustoff in three minutes, sir!"

"Casey! Hang in there, bud. Helo's coming! ...Casey!!"

Casey? He realized that felt truly right for the first time. All the times he had heard it now in this running nightmare, this was the first time it felt like him. A hand squeezed his own left hand and he tried to squeeze back, but couldn't be sure if he had. There were spots of light in the dark. Small, but bright, spots of light. He felt that should mean something to him. He wiggled the fingers of his left hand and felt them move.

"That's good, Sar'n. I'm here, buddy. We're gonna get you out of here."

Casey tried again to talk, but his effort brought only frustration and more pain deep in his throat. Casey thought of his wife. What would she be doing right now? What time was it there? Was it day or night at home? He wasn't sure. He only knew that he wanted desperately to be there. Where was the dusty tornado that was supposed to take him home? He concentrated on picturing them in the park, running the wrong way up the jungle gym slide.

Come and get me, Mommy!

Casey smiled.

"Bird's on the ground."

"Great," Doc's voice. HM2 White, the Navy corpsman. "Doc Barton on board?" Barton was the physician from battalion.

"He's here."

Another squeeze on his hand. He felt so fucking weak, but was able to squeeze back. His mouth was so dry. He desperately wanted a drink of water. Casey blinked his eyes as he saw red lights approaching. Flashlights. Then there was a loud explosion, close this time, and he felt Doc White lean over him to keep the blowing dust from settling on his face.

"Shit! Jesus, where did that come from?"

"No! Goddamn it, no. Check left! Check left!" he heard short bursts of M16A rifles, then the loud burp as a squad assault weapon let loose a ten- or fifteen-round burst. There was shouting as well, farther away.

"Holy shit! How long has his neck been that big? Goddamn. Got the carotid for sure. If that thing lets loose we'll sure as hell lose him."

"Doc, he's awake. He can hear you."

"Sergeant Stillman? Casey? It's Doc Barton. You're gonna be ok, buddy." He felt a squeeze on his left shoulder, but was not reassured. Casey felt a strong terror grow inside him. He didn't want to die here in this shithole. He didn't want to die at all.

"Pam...Claire." He mouthed the words but there was no sound. He was certain now that they knew how much he loved them. He pictured them again, playing and laughing in the park. Casey felt the world getting dark again, felt again like he was tumbling, falling to the left. It was nauseating and he felt a horrible sharp pain growing in his left temple. He could also feel tears, running out of his eyes and down his grimy cheeks.

I love you, Baby. I'm so sorry, but I think I've got to go.

Then he felt himself getting pulled down into a warm darkness, like the night was wrapping around him in a comfortable blanket.

Chapter
31

The young woman walked slowly up the familiar path between the identical white headstones. Around her a mix of tourists and families milled about in quiet reverence, whispering to one another as they pointed to names, or stood quietly beside a stone. The quiet ones mostly stared fixedly at the stones, eyes far away and lost in thought. Some looked off in contentment, finding comfort in easy memories of better times.

Though she walked slowly, she lost herself in thought of the man she never really knew. She walked with the steady pace of one who had walked this path many times. She pictured in her mind the strong face of her father, his easy smile, his hazel eyes which seemed to hold so much love and happiness. As she often did lately, perhaps as she grew older, she wondered whether the pictures in her mind were real memories of her father or just memories of pictures and stories, shown and told so often by her mother that they became real to her. She smiled softly. Just the kind of question her Dad might wonder. It didn't matter. Her father's memory was very real and alive for her, whether from her own very early memories or her mother's loving portrait of the man. That was what mattered.

Claire was unsure why today, this time, it seemed so important to her that she come for her visit alone. It was the first time she had ever been here without her mother, and she felt the same sense of purpose, of destiny, that had drawn her since last night. Her mother would arrive at the airport in just a few hours. Then they would come here together later this afternoon, walk this same path as they had every November for all the life her memory could share with her.

But since last night, it had felt as if she were being called here. Crazy as it sounded, she knew in her heart that she was supposed to be here alone this morning. Claire pulled up the collar of her navy blue overcoat, as much against the chill the thought gave her as against the actual cold of the crisp morning. The leaves were gone from the trees—had been for nearly a month—which was a little early for Washington D.C., but the cold had come well before Halloween this year.

Claire turned right, her pace slowing a little, both by her search for more memories of her dad and a little apprehension about standing at his grave alone. She had lived in D.C. for almost a year and a half now, since starting last year at George Washington University, and had never come here alone. She had thought about it a time or two last year, and of course had made the visit with her mother last November, but had never quite been able to make herself come alone. For some reason the thought made her feel better about this morning instead of more nervous.

Claire turned left almost without thinking. Almost there. As she approached her dad, she suddenly stopped, surprised and unsure what to do.

The man who stood at the foot of her father's grave was tall and lanky. His hair was peppered grey on top and shaved skin-close on the sides. His face looked much younger than his grey hair suggested and he had the build of an athlete, obvious even with his loose-fitting black leather jacket.

Definitely a Marine. Claire had met more than her share of Marines over the years. They had come to her birthday parties and brought their kids to the park to play with her. All of her life she had been cared for by "the rest of our family," as her Mom referred to the Corps. But she had never seen anyone else here on their visits. And she was sure she had never met this man, who stood next to her dad, his broad shoulders slumped and his head bowed. Curious, Claire approached.

"Hi," she said, unsure what else to say.

The man jumped slightly, startled from some faraway memory, and then looked around nervously.

"Um...uh, hi," he said. His voice cracked the slightest bit, as if he had been crying. Then he looked Claire in the eyes, his own wet and sad. "I'm...uh...I'm sorry. You and Pam, I mean your mom, don't usually come until the afternoon." The man shifted nervously, the emotion out of place on a Marine. "You're Claire, right?"

"Yes," she answered.

"Well, I'll come back later," the man announced and turned away from her to leave. Pam noticed the limp, slight and well adapted over sixteen years, but still easily visible.

"Wait," Pam said, catching the man by the sleeve. The Marine turned to her, pain in his eyes. "Did you know my Dad?" she asked.

"Yes," the man said simply, and he looked down at his feet. Claire saw tears running softly down his cheeks, weathered beyond his years by many deployments to harsh jungles and deserts around the world.

"You're him, aren't you?" she asked. Her heart raced with excitement. It was as if a puzzle picture of her Dad, a single piece missing for all of these years, was finally going to be finished. Without thinking, she took the Marine's hands in hers. "Are you Corporal Rich Simmons?"

The man looked up, a half smile on his face.

"It's Gunnery Sergeant Simmons now, thanks to your Dad," he said. "But Rich to you."

"Yes," Claire breathed. "Yes, I knew it!"

A pained look came over the man's face again.

"Your father died for me, Claire." He looked again at his feet. "Because of me," he whispered softly.

Claire looked away as if she hadn't heard him somehow. Her voice was still pitched with excitement.

"You used to send me presents every year," she said and squeezed the calloused hands in hers. "You sent me the beautiful necklace with Marine Corps eagle, globe, and anchor!" She let go of one of his hands and fumbled under her coat, pulling out the gold necklace for him to see. "See? I still wear it every day! You were WITH him!" her voice took on a childlike quality and she practically bounced up and down. "You were with my dad, just like Uncle Chad!"

The Marine gripped her hands firmly and looked her again in the eyes. Claire stopped bouncing and looked back at the stranger she felt she knew.

"Mom used to always invite you over, but you never came," she said. There was no judgment in her words—more of a question.

"Claire," the man swallowed and clenched his jaw. Then he started again. "Claire, your daddy is dead because of me. He died saving me." The man let go of her hands and pressed one fist to his forehead. "Casey died for me," Simmons started to sob uncontrollably and sixteen years of grief and guilt came out as it likely did every year on this day. Claire reached up, taking the Marine by his wrists so she could see his face again.

"I was raised believing that Daddy died for all of us, Gunny," she said simply. "He was a United States Marine."

The man looked at her again, smiling now, his cheeks red and wet. Claire suspected that the man knew, just as she did, that was exactly what Sar'n Stillman would have said. He hugged Claire back and then together they turned and faced his stone.

Engraved at the top was a reproduction of the Medal of Honor. Below it:

Sergeant Casey Jack Stillman, USMC
May 1978 – November 2004
Fallujah, Iraq

Beneath was inscribed an excerpt from his award citation:
...After saving the life of one member of his platoon, and while still under heavy enemy fire, Sgt. Stillman was mortally wounded while trying to rescue another...

Claire and Rich Simmons, Gunnery Sergeant, United States Marine Corps, stood hand in hand at the foot of the grave, each lost in thought about the man they loved.

CPSIA information can be obtained at www.ICGtesting.com
Printed in the USA
LVOW08s0247230616

493770LV00001BA/13/P